CRYSTAL

DARBY CUPID

STARLATTEN BOOK ONE

CHAPTER ONE

Crystal

I'm dead. That's the only possible explanation. I wince as pain flashes across my chest and neck, my blood throbbing in a steady, aching rhythm. With each pulse, my stomach clenches and I suck in my breath to keep the nausea at bay. Somewhere nearby, a slow hiss competes with a high-pitched wail. Both harmonise jarringly with the thumping rhythm in my skull as darkness pours into my nostrils, filling my lungs with every breath.

I'm dead. Definitely.

I'm also not alone. My skin prickles and my heartrate accelerates—every molecule wanting to move away from the presence I can sense looming in the darkness. A loud pop sounds in my ears and the high-pitched wailing becomes a steady beeping noise. I frown, realising that despite the dense blackness, I can feel my fingers. As I wriggle my aching digits, something cold and metallic presses against my arms.

A bark of laughter escapes my lips as I realise it's not dark. Despite the skull-crushing pulsing in my head, I force my eyes open, crying out as bright light sears my retinas. I snap my eyes shut. What in the stars? Heart pounding, I cautiously pry my eyes open once more, peeking out from under my eyelashes.

Sprawled in front of me, a control panel blinks and flashes with lights of every colour. I turn my head toward the hissing sound coming from a cracked panel and yelp at the streak of pain that shoots down my neck and along my spine. Breathing hard, I move my eyes to take in the rest of my surroundings—squinting at the pale silver metal encasing me and the large frosted window, charred grey with scorch marks. I'm in some sort of small spacecraft. I search my memory, but darkness dulls my senses.

Exhaustion floods through me and as my head rolls forward, I notice spots of blood fanning out along the shimmering white material of my robes, giving the effect of delicate crimson flowers. I peel my curls from my forehead and they crunch between my fingers. Nausea pulses in my stomach once more and any calm is replaced with panic. I need to get out of here. Now.

Scratching and clawing at the fastenings across my shoulders, hot tears streak down my cheeks as I growl and grunt in desperation. The straps retract with a hiss and I fall forwards out of the seat, landing on my knees beside the oval doorway. Concentrating on the doors, I will them to open.

Nothing happens. My heart throbs in my fingertips as I try again. Panic rising in my gut, I reach out and grasp the handle. I have to get out. I can't breathe.

Trembling, I close my eyes and concentrate on the purple amulet against my chest. It warms faintly and I stare at the handle, imagining it turning—opening.

A moment of silence, but nothing.

My body roars with heat and—with a scream that rips at my throat—I kick out at the door with all my might. The noise echoes around the small chamber, hammering back against my aching skull like a thousand fists. All my energy slips away, and I sink helplessly down to my knees. My skin, tight with dried salt, loosens with fresh tears.

I've never felt so confused. So alone. Why am I in this ship? The answer dances in the furthest corner of my mind, just out of reach, in the arms of the shadow I don't dare look at. What did my father tell me to do if I didn't know where I was?

I gasp as my chest contracts painfully—as though someone is squeezing my heart. Even though my eyes are open, the dark looming shadow is there in my peripheral vision. For a moment, I try to concentrate on it, but part of me doesn't want it to come in to focus. If I see what it is, things are going to become much worse. That, I'm sure of.

Choking back my sobs, I lick my salt covered lips, rub the tears from my eyes and draw in a deep, shuddering breath. My eyes follow tiny dancing specks of dust drifting in and out of a small stream of golden light in an otherworldly way. The light ends in a small circle on the floor nearby and I wriggle my toes within it. My breath catches in my throat. The light is streaming through a gap in the door. It's a very small gap, but it's a gap.

Reinvigorated, I heave myself up and throw my shoulder at the door once more. Concentrating on the warmth of the amulet against my chest, purple light trickles along my veins, filling my body—stronger this time. Each slam is fresh new pain, turning my shoulder from muscle to an agonising mush of flesh and bone.

The door groans open, just enough. I squeeze my body into the gap, ignoring the sharp metal edges as they shred my robes.

With a gasp, I emerge into a tangle of sharp, spiky vegetation. My forearms and hands sting as the branches clutch and claw at me and I stand, legs quivering, as I take in the vast expanse of green grass beneath a clear blue sky and bright yellow sunstar.

Wait. *Green* grass? *Blue* sky? The green, blue and yellow muddle together as the throbbing in my head mounts again and I reach out for something to lean on, but there's nothing. Panic beats steadily in my blood. Out of the corner of my eye, the dark shadow draws closer.

I put one foot in front of the other, my toes sinking into the cold grass. I need to find answers. Squinting, I try to make sense of what I'm seeing—the rows of unusual cubed dwellings. I hear a rumble somewhere, but I can't see any sign of life. Turning, I check to see whether the dark shadow has followed me.

It's not there anymore. It's in front of me with explosions and death shining in its eyes. It swallows me whole.

CHAPTER TWO

Dylan

"Are you kidding me?"

I glance up from digging a small stone from the wheel of my skateboard. Beside me, Eddie claws a hand over his face, which can mean only one thing. I turn to look in the direction of his despair and smile as his sister and her friend, Sera, cycle towards us.

"Come on, man." Jordan chuckles as he joins us, heel braking his board. "She's not that bad."

Eddie turns and glares at us in disdain. "You don't live with her."

At seventeen, Linda is only eleven months younger than Eddie. They get mistaken for twins all the time. They both have the same thick straight black hair, light brown skin and dark brown eyes inherited from their Thai mother. I've known them both since I was five and Linda honestly isn't that bad. To be honest, she's a good laugh. Then again, Eddie is usually the butt of her jokes, so I guess I can see why he feels the way he does.

"Hey dingbats!" Linda grins as she skids her bike to a halt in front of us, sending gravel flying.

Sera glides in behind her, her long blonde hair coming to rest around her shoulders like a cape.

"Dingbat yourself." Eddie frowns with no attempt to hide his annoyance. "What are you doing here?"

Linda glances around the empty skate park and shrugs. "Free country isn't it? What's up, Jordan? Dylan?"

I lift a hand and smile in response.

"Aren't you a little old for bikes?" Eddie scoffs.

Linda folds her arms and looks her brother up and down before staring pointedly at his skateboard.

"We were just getting some exercise," Sera says, diffusing the situation. "What are you guys up to?"

I bite back a smile as Sera looks at Jordan, twisting her long hair between her fingers, her cheeks flushing bright pink. To be honest, Jordan's probably a shade pinker as well, but it's harder to tell under his dark brown skin. These two have been circling around each other since spring break, but Jordan denies there's anything there.

"Not much." Jordan shrugs, then frowns. "You should be wearing a helmet you know."

Sera rolls her dark blue eyes in response, but Linda practically leaps off her bike.

"See!" Linda taps her own matte black helmet. "I keep telling her. Brain damage is for everyone."

"Well, this was fun." Eddie claps his hands together and puts a foot on his board, motioning for me to do the same. "We're off into town to get some food, so—"

"Great!" Linda grins. "We'll come with."

I fight the rising corners of my mouth, pursing my lips together at the expression on Eddie's face. Before he can respond, they've already started riding away.

"Do you guys want to stay here a bit longer?" Eddie asks, his eyes fixed on the girls as they disappear down the path.

I stand and shake my head. "Seriously, man, you need to relax. Come on. It'll be fine."

We kick off and head after them, Eddie muttering under his breath.

Rounding the corner, I frown. Standing side by side, the girls are staring out into one of the unkempt fields that line the path into town, the knee-high grass waving in the wind. I scan the area around them, failing to see any reason for them to have stopped.

Glancing across at Eddie, he doesn't even seem to have noticed. Either that or he doesn't care. Probably the latter. Jordan has already sped up, eager to be the first at Sera's side.

"What's wrong?" he asks, skidding to a halt in a shower of fine gravel.

Sera lifts an arm and points—her eyes fixed on the field in front of her. "Do you see that over there?"

I squint against the sun in the direction she's pointing and find something bright white not far from the bushes separating the field from the next.

"Probably a sheet blown off someone's washing line," Jordan suggests.

"That's what I thought," Sera murmurs, "but I can't shake the feeling we should go and investigate."

I turn to Eddie to see what he thinks but he's poking at his phone. "Eddie?"

"What?" He looks up from the screen, disinterest clear in his dark brown eyes.

I shake my head and he shrugs. Until this moment, I hadn't decided whether to humour Sera or not, but as I open my mouth, I find my brain has made the decision for me. "We're going to go and investigate."

"We are?" Linda looks up at me in surprise.

"Sure." I squint out at the white object. "Why not? Besides, if it's something important, perhaps there'll be a reward."

At the mention of a reward, Eddie's phone is in his pocket as he swings a leg over the wooden fence that separates the field from the path. "I'm not splitting it!" he calls out over his shoulder. "First one there, gets dibs!"

Sera gasps. "Hey! I spotted it first!"

"You'd better hurry then." Eddie laughs as he launches himself off the fence and into the field, ploughing through the tall grass.

After a split second, Jordan, Sera and Linda clamber over the fence in pursuit.

"You coming?" Linda asks as she jumps down on the other side.

I blink, a little disoriented by how quickly things have escalated, before propping my skateboard beside Jordan and Eddie's and swinging myself up over the fence to join the pursuit.

We're a few meters away from the object when Eddie stops dead in his tracks, his arms outstretched.

"Oh my god," he hisses. "I think it's a person."

My already accelerated heartrate increases, thudding in my ears. "What do you mean, a person?"

"A person," he repeats, glaring over his shoulder. "What else could I possibly mean?"

We stand in a line squinting at the object. It's pretty clear from here that it's not a sheet, but most of it is still obscured by the long grass.

"Why would someone be lying down in a field by themselves?" Linda asks.

Sera gives a small gasp. "Maybe they're not by themselves."

We all take a wary step back, as Sera's comment sinks in.

"No." I shake my head as I look at the object again. "Whatever it is, it's not moving."

Sera's hands fly to her mouth. "What if they're dead? Maybe this isn't such a good idea."

"Don't be so dramatic," Linda scoffs. "I'm going to take a closer look."

Before any of us can stop her, Linda stomps forwards towards the white object. I glance at Eddie, who gives a small shrug before setting off after her.

"It's a girl!"

My stomach flip-flops as the rest of us stumble after them. Linda's right. Sprawled face down in the grass, her arms are limp at her sides and long tightly curled, golden-brown hair covers her face. She's wearing something that looks like a weird shimmering white bathrobe, but it's blood-stained and torn.

"Is she alive?" Sera whispers.

Something inside me clicks and then I'm on my knees, turning the girl onto her back, careful to support her neck. Blood and dirt are streaked across her face, and blades of grass are stuck to her forehead and cheeks.

Hardly daring to breathe, I place two fingers to her neck to feel for a pulse. Everyone else stands frozen—the wind the only sound as it rustles between the grass and bushes. I resist the urge to shout at it to be quiet. An eternity seems to pass as I wait for her skin to push back against my fingers, but then it happens—I feel her heartbeat.

"She's alive."

There's an audible sigh of relief from the others around me.

I turn and look up at Linda and Sera, who are staring, mouths open. "Do either of you have any tissues?"

Linda drags her eyes from the girl's face. "Why?"

"So I can try and stop this great big cut on her head from bleeding."

Sera starts rummaging in her bag, handing me a tissue from a small pack.

"Have you seen her necklace?" Linda kneels down beside me, reaching out but stopping just short of the unusual piece of jewellery.

Peering at the long necklace in the grass beside her, I have to admit it's unlike anything I've seen before. Not that I'm an expert on women's jewellery or anything. The metal is a coppery-gold colour, twisting around a tear-shaped purple stone. As I stare at the stone, I swear the shades of indigo within it swirl and light up like a galaxy. I blink and it stops.

"Ugh." Eddie snorts. "You're such a girl."

Linda jumps to her feet and launches herself at him, punching him in the arm. "And you're so misogynistic. It's no wonder you haven't got a girlfriend."

Eddie's face reddens. "You don't even know what that word means."

Annoyance prickles on my skin. We don't have time for one of their squabbles. Not when we have someone literally bleeding and unconscious in front of us. I open my mouth to cut him off, but Jordan beats me to it.

"Stop fighting, you two." He spreads his hands out between them. "We need to decide what we're going to do."

Sera kneels beside me, handing me another tissue. "We need to call an ambulance, right?"

Jordan reaches into his pocket and pulls out his phone. "On it."

"Wait!" Linda rushes forwards, waving her hands at Jordan, her dark eyes wide. "Let's call my mum instead."

"Why would we do that?" I ask. "We need a hospital. She might have been attacked. She might be in a coma."

"Mum's a nurse," Linda persists. "She'll know what to do."

I frown. "Paramedics will also know what to do."

"Yes," Linda agrees with exaggerated patience, "but if we call an ambulance, they'll whisk her away and we'll never see her again. That will be it. The end of our adventure. Don't you want to know what happened to her?

She looks around our age. She might even be at our school after the summer."

"Adventure?" I repeat slowly. "This isn't some Netflix drama, Linda. This is real life. If we don't get her proper medical attention, she could die."

"Dylan's right," Jordan says. "We need to call an ambulance."

Linda throws her hands in the air, turning to her brother and best friend in a last-ditch plea. "We only live a couple of minutes away. Where's your sense of adventure? If Mum says we should call an ambulance, we can do it from home."

Sera watches Linda, clearly torn between logic and loyalty. "It's not the worst idea, guys," she admits. "We *are* getting her medical attention after all. If we get told off for moving her, we can always just say we didn't know."

"Absolutely not." I stand—a sudden urgency pulsing through me. "Jordan, call an ambulance. Now."

Linda starts to protest, but Jordan already has the phone to his ear. Eddie holds his hands up in mock surrender and Linda growls and stomps away. Sera rushes to comfort her, but she turns her back in a sulk.

Shaking my head, I turn my attention back to the girl lying at my feet while Jordan explains our location to the emergency services. I try to push aside the seeds of doubt as I kneel down in the grass beside her. We're definitely doing the right thing—even if I do want to know who she is and how she ended up here.

Despite being bruised and blood-splattered, she looks almost peaceful lying in amongst the tall grass. I watch her eyes flicker behind her eyelids and find myself wondering what colour they are under those dark lashes. Her skin is a gorgeous light brown colour that almost seems to glow in the sunlight and her lips are a plump, soft pink-beige.

Whoever she is, what she's been through must have been awful. My fingers reach out to touch her cheek, but Jordan's voice breaks into my consciousness, and I snatch my hand back, my own cheeks burning.

"They'll be here any minute," he says, sliding his phone back into his pocket. "They said to stay with her."

"That's good," I reply, hoping he didn't notice. What's wrong with me?

Deciding it must be exhaustion from my late night and early morning working at the bakery, I stand and brush the grass from my jeans. Sera and Linda are huddled talking— their backs to us.

"Linda?" Jordan calls out.

"What?" she snaps without turning around.

"I've had an idea," he says, glancing at me with a smile. "I agree, we all want to know who she is and how she got here. So, I was thinking. Could your mum perhaps find out which hospital she gets taken to? That way we can go and visit her tomorrow."

The spark of excitement that ignites in my chest at the idea takes me by surprise.

"Yes." Linda turns around, her frown gone. "Let's do that."

We hear the sirens long before we see the ambulance. It parks near a gate a little further down from where we climbed over the fence and Eddie waves his arms above his head as two female paramedics emerge from the fluorescent vehicle and begin wading through the long grass, medical kits in hand.

I shift from foot to foot, trying to not to bite at the skin around my nails, as they set about checking the girl's vitals, measuring her pulse and shining lights in her eyes—which I discover are dark brown.

Eventually, the short, blonde-haired paramedic stands and surveys us for the first time. "So, you just found her here, in the field? No idea where she's from? Don't recognise her from school?"

"No." Linda shakes her head. "We've never seen her before."

The red-haired paramedic squints up at us from where she's applying dressings to the head wound. "Did you move her?"

"I rolled her on to her back," I confess, "but I supported her neck. I wanted to check if she was breathing and stop the bleeding."

She nods at the blonde paramedic, who turns and jogs back down towards the ambulance. "Don't worry, kids. You did good. We'll take her in and file a report with the police. She seems okay, but she'll need a few more tests just to make sure."

We watch in silence as the red-haired paramedic returns with a stretcher and they lift her on.

"Well." Linda sighs dramatically as they carry the girl down towards the ambulance. "That was exciting, I guess."

I give a half smile. I hate to admit it, but a small piece of me regrets calling the ambulance. Would it have been the worst thing in the world if we'd taken her to Linda and

Eddie's house? You can practically see it from the sloped field we're standing on.

"You okay?"

I blink and find Eddie staring at me, his eyebrows raised. "Yeah, why?"

"You look all spaced out."

"I'm just tired."

To be honest, I'm always tired, so no surprise there. Waking up at the crack of dawn six days a week to bake bread will do that to you. I read somewhere that teenagers need nine hours of sleep a night. I'm lucky if I get six.

None of us are in the mood for going for food anymore, so we say our goodbyes and head our separate ways.

The house is quiet when I get there, but I know Katie's up in her bedroom because her shoes are strewn by the door. I pick them up and throw them in the shoe box on my way past, before climbing the stairs. Pausing outside her door, I listen for signs of life. Hearing nothing, I knock.

"I'm doing my homework!"

I open the door a crack to find Katie sitting on her bed, headphones on as she paints her nails—clearly not doing homework.

"Hey!" she shouts. "Get out!"

I cock my head, frowning at her nail polish. "Which class is this homework for?"

Katie picks up something from her bedside table and throws it at me. I quickly pull the door closed and the mystery projectile bounces off with a thud.

Daring to open the door once more, I try again. "Any messages from Mum?"

"She asked if you could go help her in the shop when you get in."

My heart sinks. Of course she did. I close the door and head to my room, collapsing on the bed. I just need a few minutes to myself, then I'll go down to the shop.

Guilt drapes over me like a lead blanket at the thought of it. I hate the bakery. It's been in our family for generations. I say *our* family. *Dad's* family. Dad left. Eight months ago, he packed his bags and disappeared, leaving nothing but wreckage behind. Mum clings to the bakery as though it will bring Dad back. We don't talk about it.

My phone buzzes in my pocket and I dig it out, swiping at the screen to find a text from Eddie.

Mum gonna find out info on that girl 4 us

visit 2moz?

As I type my reply, my mood begins to lift—that small spark flickering in my chest.

time?

I wonder if she'll be awake when we visit. Maybe Linda was right, and she'll be in our school after the summer. She did look around our age, but when you're eighteen, a couple of years makes the difference between university and way too young.

10?

I respond with a thumbs up and swing my legs off the bed, preparing to make my way down to the shop with a final stretch. As I trudge down the stairs, my mind swims with a thousand questions. What if she has brain damage?

What if she was abducted or she's an attempted murder victim?

Above everything though, I just really hope she's okay.

CHAPTER **THREE**

Jake

A door slams and I flinch, gripping the soapy sponge as if it's the only thing preventing me from slipping away between the tiles, along with the dirty water. Bubbles of bleach start to seep into the cuts on my knuckles, so I throw the sponge into the bucket and wipe my hands on my jeans. The house is quiet again. Uncle Cas must have left. Or it might have been someone else. There are always people coming and going from this place.

Grabbing the sponge from the bowl of lukewarm water, I return to my punishment. The floor is only the beginning. Uncle Cas gave me strict orders to clean the kitchen from 'top to bottom'. If I miss the smallest speck of dirt—well, there'll be no dirt.

I stretch my hands above my head and my spine cracks, my knees aching. My ribs throb from my recent 'discussion' with Uncle Cas and the bruising purpling across my torso tightens my skin. I hold my hands above my head for too long and curse as water drips on my head. Anger sparks in my gut and I scrub the floor with renewed vigour, pouring my frustration out onto the grimy tiles.

Thoughts of running away creep in at the edges of my thoughts, but I push them away in disgust. What would be the point? Cas has ears and eyes everywhere. I could run, but I'd be found and dragged back within hours. Besides, where would I go? I have no friends. No family. Uncle Cas is all I know. All I remember.

When I try to remember life before Cas, it's fuzzy—like a thick yellow smog I can't see through. Years ago, I mustered the courage to ask him about my family. A shudder runs through me at the memory. I never asked again.

Pins and needles prick my legs as I pour the dirty water down the sink and refill the bucket in preparation for the cupboards. It occurs to me that I should have done the cupboards first, but it's too late now. Hopefully he won't care.

Ignoring the aches and pains eating at my body, I climb up on to the worktop so I can start with the tops of the cupboards. He didn't tell me exactly what to clean, but he said, 'top to bottom' and I'm not going to risk not taking it literally. Uncle Cas doesn't mince his words.

Shuffling along the counter as I drag the sponge along the cupboards, I soon realise that they've never been cleaned before. Each cupboard requires a rinse of the fluff covered sponge every couple of centimetres and I wrinkle my nose as the wet fragments of grey stick to my fingers. Then, my hand knocks against something hard.

Dropping the sponge in the bucket, I reach up with both hands and ease the object towards me with my fingertips. It's a small cardboard box. I sit down on the counter and turn it carefully in my hands. It has a logo for some company I don't recognise on it and I really shouldn't open it. I know I shouldn't.

Who am I kidding? I'm going to open it.

My heart is in my mouth as I gently lift the lid and I'm not sure what I was expecting to find inside, but a necklace with a large green stone was not at the top of the list.

Frowning, I lift the necklace from the box to inspect it closer. Intricate, delicate twists of shiny copper encase the bright green stone with loops like petals. The stone seems to glow as the light from the kitchen window hits it. I don't know whether it's because I'm delirious from inhaling bleach for the past hour or so, but as I watch it spin on its chain, something about this necklace makes me calm inside. A little less ... broken.

I reach for the box to replace the necklace, but something stops me. I can't do it. I don't want to put it back in the box. Even though I know the beating of my life awaits me if Cas finds out I've taken it, I slip the necklace into my pocket.

"Are you sure?"

The sound of Uncle Cas' voice just outside the door almost makes me fall backwards off the counter. I shove the box back in place, jump down and begin scrubbing at the kitchen counter.

"How long ago did this happen?"

"We're not sure. Possibly last night."

"Last night? Why am I only finding out now?"

"Shall we send a team?"

"Yes. Anything you find, bring it to me straight away. No pictures, no souvenirs. Do you understand?"

"Yes, boss."

I force myself to continue scrubbing. I don't recognise the voice of the person Uncle Cas is talking to. One of his many cronies. The kitchen door flies open, and I hate myself for flinching as Cas strides in.

"What the hell are you doing in here?" he spits.

Unsure whether to stop scrubbing, I slow the circular motions of the sponge as I reply. "You asked me to clean the kitchen from top to bottom."

He grunts in annoyance, waving one of his shovel-sized hands in my direction. "You can finish later. Get out of my sight."

Gathering up the bucket and sponge, I waste no time in getting out of there. I risk a glance at his broad, towering figure as I move towards the door. He's seething. His neatly bearded jaw is clenched as tightly as his fists, and his unusual amber eyes are practically flaming with anger. He doesn't even look at me as I slip past him into the hallway, closing the door behind me.

Halfway to the bathroom to empty the bucket, I hear a roar followed by the sound of shattering glass. Great. I know I'll be called to clean up the aftermath of his rage, but at least I'm not at the receiving end of whatever he's thrown.

As I pour the grey, fluff-filled water down the bathroom sink, I replay the conversation in my head. What happened last night? What is the team looking for?

I finish rinsing out the bucket and sponge and return them to the cupboard under the stairs. In my pocket, the green necklace is practically burning against my thigh, so I take the stairs two at a time to my bedroom, desperate to get a proper look at it.

CHAPTER FOUR

Crystal

Darkness surrounds me again—the throbbing pain fuzzy and distant. Remembering the last time I opened my eyes, I cautiously prise one lid open a fraction. Both eyes fly open in shock. Gone is the expanse of unfamiliar green grass and bright blue sky. Instead, I appear to be in some sort of metallic bed, in a small white and grey room filled with awful yellow lights and beeping machines. I try and fail to remember the last time I woke up to a noise other than beeping.

Sitting up, I stare down at the flimsy patterned tunic I'm wearing as the throbbing in my head intensifies. Where am I? What is going on? My heart pounds in time with my head.

A movement to my left catches my attention as a tall, dark-haired woman enters the room. Her face wears a friendly smile, but her dark brown eyes show she's wary. Of what? Me? I look her up and down, noting the strange clothes. Somewhere in the corner of my eye, the shadow begins to loom once more.

"Where am I?" I demand.

The woman's smile falters and disappears. She responds, but I don't understand what she's saying. It's a language I've never heard before—all round, sloping sounds. The shadow in the corner of my mind grows darker.

"Who are you?" I try again, slower this time, my voice wobbling. "What language are you speaking?"

Glancing between me and the door and talking with the same slow, round sounds as before, she makes some sort of gesture—her palms pushing toward me, fingers to the ceiling—then leaves the room.

Fear creeps its way up from my toes as my heart pounds against my ribs. The shadow is closing in on both sides now. I try not to look at it. I don't want to look at it. I just want my mother ...

All the air is sucked from my lungs as the shadow engulfs me. My mother. My father. *Everyone*. They're all gone.

Roaring heat from the orange and white fireball that destroyed our ship tears through my memory, as it all comes screaming back to me. I cover my eyes to try and block out the image of people screaming and clawing at the escape hatch as my pod ejected—to forget the fear and panic in their wild and desperate eyes.

Leaping from the bed, I lunge toward a stand holding a bright yellow bag with a lid, open it and vomit. My shoulders heave with the effort and sobs fill the gaps between my retching.

Where in the stars am I? Which planet? Which solar system? I'm definitely not on Starlatten. How in Jetzia's name am I going to get home? I wipe my mouth with the thin gown and pause. Something's wrong. My skin flushes cold as I lift my hand to my chest, patting the cool, bare skin. My amulet is missing.

A wave of panic rolls over me as I turn a frantic circle, searching the room. There isn't much in the room at all and a transparent package sitting on a tall table beside the bed draws my attention. I recognise the bloodied material inside. With trembling fingers, I tear open the bag, digging through my ruined robes until my fingers feel—thank the stars—my amulet.

I drape the chain over my head and lean against the bed with a sigh as the stone warms against my skin. It's the first time I can ever remember not wearing it and I don't care for it one bit. My parents would be appalled.

My parents. Grief smashes into me anew at the realisation that I'll never hear Father's deep, hearty laugh or be swept up in Mother's sweet-smelling embrace ever again. Clawing at the covers, I climb back up onto the strange unfamiliar bed, curl into a ball and sob until the darkness returns.

There are two people in the room when I wake. My eyes are puffy and sore and my mouth tastes like a greyare's breath. For a blissful moment, I think I might be home, but then the cold reality creeps in, sitting heavy on my chest. This is really happening. It's not just a terrible nightmare.

"Hello again," the tall dark-haired woman from before says. "This is Nurse Kayle. She speaks several languages, so hopefully we can find a way to communicate."

Nurse Kayle gives me a big smile and says something in a language I don't recognise. It's different from before though. I stare at them in confusion. Why can I understand the tall woman now?

"Where am I?" I ask.

From the look of shock on their faces, it's clear they understand me now too. Nurse Kayle looks a little disappointed. She touches the other woman on the arm and smiles at me before leaving the room.

"So, you do speak English," the woman says, tilting her head as if appraising me. "I'm Dr. Saltzer. You're in a hospital. You hurt your head quite badly."

I'm unfamiliar with the term 'doctor' and 'hospital', but this feels similar to our healing centres back home, albeit more primitive and noisier. As I attempt to follow what she's saying about being found in a field, I try to figure out why I can understand her.

Warmth against my chest causes my eyes to widen. *My amulet*. Of course. Professor Ghudwyn often spoke of a vast range of skills and abilities but translating alien languages hadn't been one we'd discussed in lessons. I'm quietly impressed.

"Try not to worry. Your tests came back fine," Dr. Saltzer continues. I have no idea what she's just said. "Do you know your name?"

What a ridiculous question. "I am Princess Crystal Akinara," I respond, sitting up a little straighter. I can't remember ever having to introduce myself before. "Could you please tell me which planet I'm on?"

I'm unprepared for the look of shock on Dr. Saltzer's pale face. Once she gathers herself enough to close her mouth, she begins furiously scribbling on some sort of scroll she's clutching. Dread swirls in my stomach. I could tell this was a primitive planet, but if the idea of interstellar travel is as shocking a concept as this woman is making it out to be, I'm going to have to be careful. I glance at the door. How do I get out of this place?

"Miss Akinara." Dr. Saltzer steps closer, her writing implement poised above her scroll. "Can you tell me who we can call to come and get you?"

I swallow and it's like rocks descending down my throat. What can I possibly say? I need to undo the damage I've already done and convince her that I'm from this planet, but how do I do that when I have no idea where I am? My fingers clutch the itchy brown blanket at the end of the bed, and I paste a nervous smile on my face.

"What I said before," I say. "I was just teasing. The truth is, I don't remember anything other than my name and I'm scared."

The truth of the last few words causes my voice to falter and Dr. Saltzer's face melts into one of compassion. She perches on the edge of my bed and places a hand on my knee.

"It's perfectly normal to be scared," she says. "Loss of memory after a head injury is surprisingly common. There was no damage to your brain, however, so there's a very good chance your memory will return soon. Try not to worry too much."

I nod, keeping my eyes fixed on the blanket. Inside, my heart is trying to leap out of my chest. It worked.

"Dr. Saltzer?"

A small brown-skinned woman with black hair tied high up on her head and eyes a different shape to the other two women, pokes her head around the door.

"Yes, Nurse Millen?"

"Do you have a moment?"

Dr. Saltzer nods before turning back to me. "Try to relax, okay? I'm sure you'll remember everything soon, and then we can call your family to come and get you."

I sink my teeth into my bottom lip, trying to stop the tears from rolling down my cheeks. If only it was that simple. No one's coming to get me. Almost everyone important to me was on our ship—the *Galastasia*. My parents, my friends. One minute we were on our way to peace talks on a nearby planet and the next ... Nausea rises in my stomach.

"Hi! Princess? Right?"

I blink back hot tears as the small woman comes back into my room. "Excuse me?"

"You told Dr. Saltzer your name was Princess?"

A small smile pulls at my lips. "Crystal," I manage. "Call me Crystal."

"Nice to meet you Crystal," the woman says. "My name is Nurse Millen. My son and daughter are two of the kids who found you in the field."

I sit up a little straighter. "Please thank them for getting me medical attention. I owe them my life."

Nurse Millen laughs, her dark eyes bright. "I'm not sure about that, but I will. Dr. Saltzer tells me you don't remember what happened to you."

"No," I lie. "It's all very hazy."

"Don't worry. It's bound to be at first. I'm sure Dr. Saltzer told you it's quite common with head injuries. Seeing as your physical injuries are mild, the best thing to do is to get some fresh air and try and jog some memories."

My heart leaps at the thought of getting out of this room.

"How would you feel about taking a little walk around town with my daughter, Linda, and her friends to see if you can find something that brings back your memory? I've pulled some strings and Dr. Saltzer says it's okay."

I don't understand half of what she's just said, but I'm curious to see who rescued me and they might just be the people to get me out of here. "That would be wonderful." I smile. "Thank you."

"Not at all, love." She points to a small door I hadn't noticed until now. "There's a small bathroom in there. I've brought you a towel and some clothes I'm sure Linda won't mind you borrowing. Why don't you get yourself freshened up?"

I gratefully accept the strange bundle of material and slide out of bed towards whatever a 'bathroom' is.

It takes a lot of time and patience to figure out how to make water appear using the metal lever. Nothing on this planet appears to be voice or motion activated. A small rectangular mirror hangs above the water bowl and I take the opportunity to inspect my face. My hair is caked with dried blood and a bruise marks my left cheek. On my forehead, a dressing of some sort has been applied to what must be the source of the dried blood.

There's a way to speed healing using my amulet but I don't feel quite strong enough to attempt it. To be honest, I was never particularly good at it. Guilt tickles along my spine as I realise that wouldn't be the case if I hadn't skipped out on so many amulet lessons with my professor. I can practically hear my father's 'I told you so'. Swallowing the sad lump in my throat, I return to scrubbing the blood from my face.

After washing and attempting to tidy my hair as much as possible, I investigate the clothes. There are six items: a short tunic with a strange pattern on the front, some dark blue leg coverings with a rip across one of the knees, two small white objects I can only assume are supposed to cover your feet, and a pair of hard-bottomed foot coverings similar to those the first nurse was wearing.

I pull the clothes on, pleasantly surprised at how well they fit and how comfortable they are. Tucking my amulet under the patterned tunic top, I step back into my room to find two girls standing near my bed, whispering to one another. They stop, turning as I enter.

"Hi!" The one with short black hair grins at me, excitement sparkling in her dark eyes.

I decide from her features, she must be Nurse Millen's daughter. "Hello," I respond. "I believe I owe you my gratitude for saving my life?"

Her eyes almost pop out of her head. "Uh, sure. You're welcome."

"I'm Sera." The other girl smiles. "And this is Linda."

I smile back. Her eyes are a bright blue, and her blonde hair is so long and silky, I have to fight the urge to reach out and touch it. "A pleasure to meet you," I say. "My name is Crystal."

"You look a lot better than the last time we saw you," Linda says, looking me up and down.

Sera elbows her in the side. "Very tactful."

"I believe we're going to leave and see if my memory comes back?" Even as the words leave my mouth, I worry that I've misunderstood the situation.

"Yes." Linda grins and I sag with relief. "It's going to be fun. There are more of us downstairs, but Mum figured it would be better for just us girls to come in first."

I nod because I'm not sure what to say. More of them? Downstairs?

"So, you don't remember anything at all?" Sera asks gently. "Just your name?"

I push away any guilt I feel at the lie. "Yes. Hopefully I'll remember more soon."

"Are you ready girls?" Nurse Millen steps back into the room and smiles at me. "Oh, Crystal! You look great."

My cheeks grow warm at the compliment. "Thank you."

"Are you ready?"

No. "I think so."

Stepping out of the room, I follow Nurse Millen down a noisy corridor filled with pictures, messages and paintings of strange animals. My eyes are wide as I take in as much as I can. It's so loud and busy—so many people.

As we reach a pair of metallic doors, Nurse Millen reaches forward and presses a button. We stand in silence, but I'm itching to ask questions. This is all so new—so primitive. I force myself to chew the inside of my cheek instead.

After an eternity, the doors open and Nurse Millen ushers me inside. As the doors hiss shut, she presses another button and I almost squeak at the familiar downward movement. It's like a travel disc—but a box! A travel box? Sera spots the delight on my face and I attempt to arrange my features in—what I hope is—a nonplussed expression.

When the doors open again, I shrink backwards at the sudden change in atmosphere. There are people everywhere—some sitting, some standing, some shouting and some just talking. Constant repetitive noise comes at me from every direction. I've never experienced anything like it. Telepathy is clearly not something this race has mastered.

Trying not to grimace, I follow Linda and Sera out of the travel box and toward a small cluster of people.

A boy with dark brown skin and short tightly curled hair lifts his hand in a wave, his smile warm. "Hey. I'm Jordan. Hope your head doesn't hurt too much. It looked really sore."

His features remind me of my father, which makes me both comforted and sad. I push my grief aside and force a smile. "Thank you. It's not too painful, really."

A taller, male version of Linda steps forward. "Hi, I'm Eddie."

"I'm sure it's all a bit overwhelming, huh?"

I turn at the rumbling tones rippling through me and find myself staring up into the most beautiful golden-brown eyes I've ever seen. Stars save me—he's gorgeous.

"I'm Dylan," he says, his lips parting to reveal a warm, friendly smile. "We were really worried about you."

I find myself unable to speak. Maybe the head injury is more serious than they thought.

"Are you okay?"

Dylan is watching me, his beautiful face creased with concern.

"Yes, sorry." I shake my head and take a deep breath. "I'm fine. Just overwhelmed, like you said."

"Right, kids," Nurse Millen announces, eyeing everyone in turn. "Like we discussed. Don't go too far. If Crystal gets overwhelmed—or you notice anything unusual—come straight back here. *Immediately*. She's being signed temporarily out under my name, but her legal guardian will need to sign her out permanently. I'm counting on you all to be responsible. Don't do anything daft. If she remembers anything—anything at all—call me right away, so we can let the police know and they can find her family. Understand?"

"Yes, Mum," Eddie and Linda reply in unison.

Nurse Millen places her hands on her hips and surveys the rest of the group, her eyebrows raised, staring at them expectantly.

Dylan coughs and they quickly chorus, "Yes, Mrs. Millen."

Seeming satisfied, she gives a nod. "I've left some pizza money on the kitchen table. Have fun and remember to take it easy. Especially you, Crystal."

As Nurse Millen turns and disappears into the travel box, I survey the sea of unfamiliar faces hoping I don't look as terrified as I feel.

"So, we were thinking we'd head into town and see if anything looks familiar," Linda says, looking to the others for confirmation.

Dylan nods before shrugging his broad shoulders. "Bus stop then?"

Before I can even begin to imagine what a 'bus stop' is, I'm swept away through the large transparent doors and into the outside world.

CHAPTER FIVE

Dylan

To my frustration the bus is almost full, and we're forced to spread out amongst the seats. Eddie and Sera are three rows in front on the left. Jordan and I are squashed near the back behind a woman talking loudly on her phone while her two small children pull faces and gnaw the seat. I shudder with disgust and focus my attention five rows in front, where Crystal is sitting beside Linda.

Perhaps it's the amnesia, but she seems in awe of just about everything around her. When the bus pulled up at the bus stop, she jumped a foot in the air and didn't seem to ever remember using one before. She looks at everything with the same wide-eyed wonder I remember Katie having when she was a toddler. I smile at the memory. My little sister was cute before the sass and the eye rolls.

I can't tell what they're talking about, but Crystal is listening intently as Linda points at things out the window. When she laughs, her smile spreads across her face lighting her dark brown eyes.

"Come in! Earth to Dylan? Are you listening?"

I blink and find Jordan staring at me. "Sorry, what?"

He grins and nods in Crystal's direction. "Don't get too attached, mate. She most definitely has a boyfriend—or girlfriend. Even if she can't remember them."

"Don't be daft," I scoff, folding my arms. "I'm just spaced out from the early start this morning."

Jordan winces. "How're things going with the bakery?"

How do I even begin to respond to such a loaded question? I exhale. "It's okay. Sales seem to be pretty steady."

We don't really talk about this stuff. I mean, when Dad left, my friends let me shout and punch things and they did a good job of distracting me. Now, eight months later, there's not much more to say. It still sucks. It still hurts. They ask, to be polite, but I know they're not really interested in the answer anymore.

Jordan nods before looking back at the girls. "What do you reckon about this Crystal girl then?"

"Not sure, mate," I say truthfully. "Not sure."

When we arrive at the bottom of the high street and step down off the bus onto the bustling pavement, Crystal seems to shrink a few inches—cowering in our midst.

Before I can ask if she's okay, Jordan steps forward, sweeping his arms out like some sort of game show host. People in the crowd duck out of the way.

"Welcome to the high street, Crystal. Recognise anything?"

Crystal looks up at the shop fronts and the large metal statue in the middle of the square, her eyes enormous. "Nothing," she mutters.

"Nothing? At all?" Sera repeats.

"You know, she might not be from around here," Eddie says.

"Yes!" Crystal exclaims in a way that makes me think she's grateful for the suggestion. "Perhaps that's it."

"You would still have passed through," Linda presses. "I mean, how else would you have ended up in that field?"

Crystal looks between them and I watch as she folds her arms across her body, withdrawing into herself.

"Linda, we don't know what she's been through," I say, stepping to Crystal's side. "She might have been kidnapped and dumped there for all we know. She certainly doesn't need you interrogating her."

"Sorry," Linda mumbles. "It's just odd, that's all."

Crystal reaches out and touches Linda's arm. "It's okay. I'm sure I'll start remembering soon. Why don't you pretend I'm a visitor from another place and show me around?"

"Ooh! That sounds fun." Sera grins.

I stay by Crystal's side as we make our way down the street. There's something about her that makes me feel protective. Perhaps it's the way we found her. Or perhaps it's the bruises and dressing on her head making her look so vulnerable.

Jordan is in his element as tour guide—describing every little detail. Crystal seems to be loving it and it's hard to tell whether she's playing along or genuinely asking.

"So, people go into these 'shops' and use 'money' to get things they need?" she asks, eyes wide as we pass a shoe shop.

I laugh, nudging her with my shoulder. "You said to pretend you're from another town, not another planet."

She blushes and looks away.

"If you turn to your left," Jordan continues. "You'll see the train station."

I lean down and whisper in her ear. "Trains are large metal carriages linked together. They're a bit like buses, but with no wheels."

"Oh!" She looks up at me. "Do they hover?"

That's it. I stop walking and she slows to a halt half a step in front of me. "I honestly can't tell if you're joking or not, Crystal."

A steady pink rises on her cheeks, but she holds my stare before laughing and pushing my arm. "Of course, I'm joking."

I attempt a laugh in return, but it sounds hollow. Something is off. Very off. I decide to research amnesia when I get home tonight.

"Crystal? Can you please tell Jordan you've had enough of his tour guide routine? It's getting old."

I tense at Eddie's tone and turn to find him and Jordan facing each other, shoulders squared. "What's going on?" I ask.

"Nothing, mate," Jordan says, his chin raised. "Eddie can't handle not being the centre of attention."

"Crystal's just being polite," Eddie scoffs. "She's as bored as the rest of us."

Awkwardness swells around the group and I'm both embarrassed and annoyed at my friends. I turn to Crystal and give her an apologetic smile. "Sorry. These two get a bit carried away sometimes."

"Testosterone." Linda sighs.

Before I can tell Eddie and Jordan to get a grip, they lunge at each other and begin wrestling—right in the middle of the high street. My mouth falls open as I watch them scramble around on the busy pavement. Passers-by slow down to watch, frowning, pointing and sometimes laughing. At one point, someone gets out their phone.

"This is so stupid. Please stop," Sera pleads. "Stop being such ... such ... boys!"

There's no way this is going to end well, so I step forward to try and separate them. Before I can get a grip on either, however, the wrestling turns into a full-scale scuffle as someone throws a punch.

Jumping back in surprise, I glance at the girls who are watching, mouths open with shock. I catch Linda's eye and launch myself on Jordan at the same time she throws herself on Eddie's back.

It takes a lot of effort, but they finally pull apart, their breathing ragged. Jordan shrugs me off, pulling at his dishevelled t-shirt.

"What the hell is wrong with you two?" I demand, pushing my hair out of my eyes and straightening my own clothes.

"He hit me in the neck!" Eddie snarls.

Jordan snorts in response. "I did not!"

I'm about to interject when Eddie throws his hands in the air. "You know what? You guys enjoy your 'tour'. I've had enough. I'm going home."

Linda reaches for him, but he sidesteps her, raising a hand in mock salute to Crystal. "See you, Crystal. Hope you get your memory back."

What is going on? Why is he being so weird? I open my mouth to shout after him but watch, frozen, as Eddie steps backwards into the road.

The sound of screeching tyres fills my ears as a dark blue Range Rover heads swerves to avoid him, but it's too late. Someone screams and I'm not sure if it's me.

But the car doesn't hit him. Instead, Eddie lifts high up into the air as the car continues underneath him and I think for a second he's jumped, but it's way too high. The Range Rover screeches to a halt a few meters down the road and when I look back, Eddie back on the ground.

What the hell? What did I just see? Linda rushes forward and pulls Eddie out of the road. He staggers onto the pavement, his skin a deathly shade of grey and his eyes vacant. Around us, everyone's moving—excitement and wonder sparking in the air.

I look for Crystal and find her standing still as a statue, her face glazed. People begin to whisper and point, taking their phones out and pointing them towards our group. I shake my head, trying to shuffle the events into something that makes sense. Was it her? Did Crystal have something to do with what just happened? No. Impossible. She seems to sense me watching her and as our eyes meet, she snaps out of her trance. Before I can speak, she turns and runs.

For a split second, I watch her disappearing through the gawking crowd, then I start running. Pushing through the busy street, I chase after her as she weaves between the shoppers. Crystal's fast but the crowd slows her and I reach out, grabbing hold of her arm. She tries to pull away, her eyes fixed in front of her.

"Crystal, Stop! Please?"

At the sound of my voice, she slows, her arm relaxing as she turns to face me. Her face is streaked with tears and she looks terrified.

I put my hands on her shoulders, ignoring the stares people are giving us as they walk past. "You're okay," I say, trying to catch my breath. "Come on. We need to get out of here."

CHAPTER **SIX**

Crystal

Dylan leads me away from the town, toward green mounds beyond the rows of buildings. It looks similar to where I landed. Following a step behind, I watch as he strides ahead in silence. He's tall. Not as tall as a Dyja guard, but still tall. His hair is halfway between blond and brown and somewhere perfectly between tidy and too long. His shoulders are tense, and my heart sinks a little. It's my fault they're like that. We haven't spoken since the high street.

The air is cooler than when we first left the hospital and I note that the sunstar is lower in the strange blue sky. There's just so much sky here. Without three moons, it seems so vast—so solitary.

On the long walk here, I've replayed the scenario from the high street over and over in my head. It was instinct. That vehicle was going to hit Eddie. It could have killed him.

Back home on Starlatten, I never managed to lift anything heavier than a small figurine. My professors would be so impressed I managed to lift a person so high into the air. However, I have no time to relish in my success because, ultimately, I've failed. I have no idea how to even begin to explain this.

We reach a small fenced-off area filled with strange colourful apparatus and I spot Sera and Linda sitting on seats suspended from a bar by chains. Jordan and Eddie sit on opposite ends of a large circular seat made of orange bars. They seem to be purposely facing away from each other. Curiosity bubbles in my stomach and I fail to hold in the question as it bursts from my lips.

"What is this place?"

"This is a playground," Sera answers, leaving her suspended seat and folding her arms across her chest. "Now, who are you?"

"Sera," Dylan interjects. He's still standing beside me, although he's clearly keeping what he perhaps perceives is a safe distance. "Let's just slow down. We need to give Crystal a chance to explain."

As he looks down at me, I can tell he's hoping for a very normal and simple explanation. He's going to be very disappointed. I consider lying. Would they even believe the truth? After all, this planet is beyond primitive. Can they fathom the concept of life from another solar system?

"Look. Whatever happened back there," Eddie stands and offers me his hand, "you saved my life. Thank you."

I stare at his hand, then back at his face. He's smiling, but it doesn't quite reach his eyes. I wonder whether he's afraid of me. Unsure what to do, I decide it must be some sort of gesture of peace, so I hold my hand out in front of me in a similar fashion.

I very quickly realise it's a mistake.

"See!" Linda cries, leaping up from her hanging seat to join the others. She points at my hand. "What is that? Who doesn't know what a handshake is?"

Handshake. That seems quite self-explanatory. Straightening my shoulders, I take hold of Eddie's extended hand and shake it firmly up and down. "Is that better?"

Eddie stares from my hand to his and bursts out laughing, shaking his head as he flops back down on his seat.

"Okay," Dylan says, his eyes searching mine. "Let's start from the beginning. Do you really have amnesia?"

Jordan throws his hands in the air. "Eddie *literally* flies and *that*'s the first question you ask?"

"I said we were starting at the beginning," Dylan says, narrowing his eyes. "What do you think beginning means?"

Worried that things will escalate again, I take a deep breath and let the truth tumble from my lips. "No. I don't have amnesia. I just said that because I knew they wouldn't believe me. The truth is, I remember everything. I remember my ship being attacked. I remember crashing here. I remember losing ... everything."

As I choke out the last word, my eyes flood with tears and my knees buckle beneath me. Jordan and Dylan reach out, catching me by my elbows, before I hit the ground. They ease me onto the orange monstrosity as I try to breathe, but no matter how hard I try, I can't seem to inhale. Is it the atmosphere? Can I suddenly not breathe the air anymore?

My heartrate rockets into lightspeed and black spots float in the corner of my vision. This is it. This is how I die.

"Breathe, Crystal," Dylan says at my shoulder. "You're hyperventilating. You need to breathe."

I want to scream at him that I'm trying to, but I still can't get any air in my lungs. A hand starts to rub slow circles on my back, and I realise Dylan is trying to get me to look at him as he crouches beside me. I force myself to meet his gaze and he gives me a reassuring smile.

"Inhale," he says quietly. "Exhale. You can do this. Just try to relax."

There's something calming about the circles he's creating between my shoulder blades and as I relax, my chest begins to expand, allowing air into my tightened lungs.

Once my breathing evens out, I swipe the tears from my face, my body shuddering. I'm exhausted. Dylan's hand continues to rub my back and I smile gratefully at him.

"Are you okay?" he asks.

I focus on the line that's formed between his eyebrows and nod.

"So—a ship?" Sera ventures. "You've been shipwrecked?"

"Of course," Eddie exclaims, relief dripping from the words. "You're from another country."

"Are you guys out of your tiny minds?" Jordan rises to his feet again, his hands gripping at his tight curls. "That doesn't explain anything. We are literally nowhere near the sea. Where's her boat? She speaks our language but doesn't know what a bus is? How does that make sense?"

"Jordan, seriously." Dylan holds a hand up to him. "You need to calm down. Crystal, are you ready to answer more questions?"

"It's fine," I say. There's no point postponing the inevitable. "My name is Crystal Akinara. I'm the daughter of the king and queen of Starlatten. We were on our way to peace talks on the planet Ankaria when our ship was attacked by rebels. Some people managed to escape in evacuation pods. I was one of the lucky few. I crashed here and ... you found me."

I'm too scared to look at their faces as my words fade into silence. Dylan's hand leaves my back and I bite my lip. I gave them the simplest version I could, and it still might be too much.

"What is 'Starlatten'?" Eddie asks, after what feels like an eternity.

I lace my fingers together over my knees and force myself to look at him. "A planet. Quite a long way from this one."

Sera shakes her head beside me. "Okay. So, you're delusional."

"I'm going to call Mum," Linda announces, reaching for her bag.

"Wait!"

I look up to see Jordan, his arms outstretched.

"Don't you see," he says. "This is the first thing that makes sense." He crouches down in front of me, his dark brown eyes intense. "How did you do that to Eddie?"

Reaching inside my top, I pull out my amulet. "I can lift objects. My amulet amplifies and channels my mind's abilities."

"Okay then." Jordan stands and gestures to the group. "No one else have any questions?"

After a moment of silence, Linda stands and walks a short distance away. She puts the small metallic box, I think is called a 'phone', down on the floor before returning to the orange seat.

"Go on then," she says, looking at me. "Bring it over."

Bewildered, I glance at their wary faces before turning to the object on the ground. It's a lot easier to lift something so small when you've lifted a person and I barely have to concentrate as the amulet warms against my skin. I lift it off the ground and even make it spin around a couple of times before moving it to the space in front of Linda, who stands staring at it, her mouth agape.

"Aren't you going to take it?" I ask.

She reaches out and takes the phone, turning it over in her hands. "Oh. My. God. *So* many questions."

Dylan runs a hand through his dark blond hair and shakes his head. "So, you're really from another planet?"

"Yes," I say. "Which is why I didn't know what a bus was, or a train or, what in Jetzia's name this orange thing is."

Eddie points at the seat. "What? This orange thing?"

"Yes." I gesture at the other strange contraptions. "What is it? What is this place for?"

"It's called a roundabout," he explains with a chuckle. "And this place is where little kids come to play."

He motions for me to move and proceeds to show me how the roundabout spins on the spot. Dylan jumps on and the two of them go so fast, I reach a hand to my stomach as it begins to churn.

"See?" Eddie calls out. "Fun."

I'm not so sure, but they look so pleased with themselves, I can't help but smile. Linda and Sera run back to the suspended seats and start swinging backwards and forwards on them.

"These are swings!" they shout in unison.

"I guess we've got a lot to explain too."

I glance up to find Dylan standing beside me, a playful light in his eye. "It must be a lot to take in."

"I think I could say the same for you all too," I reply.

He smiles a smile that wraps warmth around my chest before turning to the others who are still running around the playground giggling. "Hey. How about we use that pizza money your mum left us?"

I reach up and tap him on the arm. "About that," I whisper. "What's 'pizza?'"

CHAPTER SEVEN

Jake

I'd give absolutely anything to be somewhere else right now, but I'm trapped. Trapped in my room, with the sounds of smashing and shouting echoing below me.

I glance at the window, considering the possibility of climbing out undetected and slipping away into the warm summer evening. Curiosity keeps my feet glued to the floor. I can't be sure, but it sounds like whatever Uncle Cas wanted retrieving has already been taken. Listening to a conversation through floorboards without context is like listening to a foreign language when you only know a few words.

A door slams and it goes quiet. Chills run up my spine and my eyes flit to the window, but I'm too slow. The sound of footsteps on the stairs barely registers before my door flies open. At six foot four, Cas fills the doorway.

His amber eyes flash with disgust at the sight of me. "Going somewhere?"

"No." I will myself not to look at the window. How could he possibly know?

His expression doesn't even flicker. "I need you to go keep watch on a house."

My mouth falls open as I realise, I mentally prepared myself for a beating not an assignment. His shoulders are tensed, his fists clenched and the deep furrows in his forehead, combined with his salt and pepper hair, make him seem older and more tired than I've noticed before. I actually have no idea how old he is, and I wouldn't dream of asking.

"Which house?" I ask.

"264 Maple Avenue." He folds his arms across his broad chest. "Any more questions?"

I know he's not really asking, but I need more information. "What am I watching for?"

"The man who lived there took something of mine." Cas' eyes bore into mine. "I think someone else will come looking for it. When they do, tell me."

Knowing this is as much information as I'm likely to get, I nod.

He stares at me for a moment before looking pointedly at the door. "What are you waiting for?"

My eyebrows shoot up in surprise. "What? Now?"

"Yes," he says as though I've asked the most ridiculous question in the world. "And don't come back without information."

Grabbing my black leather jacket from the end of my bed, I jog past him downstairs, not daring to look back. I play the conversation over in my head, repeating the address. I don't think it's particularly far away, and when I check on my phone, I find I'm right. It's only an hour's walk away.

Despite being summer, there's an evening chill creeping into the air and I'm grateful I remembered to grab a jacket. Uncle Cas' words keep coming back to me. The man who lived there. *Lived*. Past tense. I wonder when he stopped living there. Poor guy.

Sirens and flashing lights shatter the serene beginnings of a lovely sunset as I approach Maple Avenue and I know they're outside number 264 long before I reach it. It's a nice street—lots of detached and semi-detached houses with well-kept gardens and large, leafy trees dotted along the pavement. Number 264 was probably nice too, before someone blew it up.

I stop and stare from the opposite side of the road amidst the crowd of concerned neighbours. Three fire engines, four police cars and a bomb disposal unit take up a huge section of the street so it's hard to see the extent of the damage. There are black scorch marks streaked up the cream, pebble-dashed side of the house and a smouldering pile of rubble where I suspect a garage once stood.

Rolling up onto my toes, I try to see above the crowd without drawing attention to myself. Something large and silver glints amongst the remains of the garage, but a team dressed in white hazmat suits are already putting a tent up around it.

My hands clench into fists at my sides. How am I supposed to do this job without proper information? What was taken? Who is going to come looking for it? This doesn't exactly look like the kind of street where dodgy dealings happen. Am I looking for a thieving middle-aged couple?

Shrugging my jacket tighter around me, I look around for somewhere to set up watch. Behind me, narrow paths link the back gardens of the houses creating small alleyways and I choose one with a good view of number 264 and slip away into the shadows—attempting to get comfortable for what might be a painfully long wait.

CHAPTER EIGHT

Crystal

"So, what does Your Majesty think of pizza?"

Pinching at a string of something called 'cheese' stretching from my mouth to the slice I'm holding, a smile spreads across my lips at Dylan's question. "It's delicious. I've definitely never had anything quite like it before."

The past hour has been surreal. Sitting in Eddie and Linda's home—listening to them chat about their plans for the 'summer holidays'—my head hurts from trying to piece together words and phrases I don't understand. Everyone insisted that I sit on a large, soft cushioned seat, while Jordan, Sera and Linda sit on a longer version. Dylan and Eddie are sprawled on the floor leaning against the base of the soft chairs, which they insisted they didn't mind as it allowed them easier access to the pizza.

As I look around, the muscles in my shoulders start to unclench and the tightness around my lungs loosens just a little. I can't wait to tell people back home about all this.

The tightness returns with a force that makes me gasp, choking on my bite of pizza. I mask it with a cough, giving Dylan a small smile as he looks up in concern. The list of everyone I've lost starts to scroll through my head like one of my father's speeches on a holoprompter.

It takes all my might to swallow the lump in my throat and refocus on what's going on around me. I can't let myself think about it. If I do, I don't think I'll be able to stop falling. I can grieve for my family when I get home—if I get home.

"Right guys." Eddie throws a piece of crust back into the now empty box on the low table between us. "It's getting late. We need to decide what to do."

Linda frowns. "What do you mean?"

"We have to decide what to do about Crystal," Dylan explains, giving me an apologetic glance.

My stomach churns and I start to regret my last slice of pizza. "What if the doctors don't believe me?"

"Believe you?" Eddie jumps to his feet and begins pacing the room, gesticulating. "Hello Doctor. I'm an alien. Do you have a space telephone so I can call my planet?"

Dylan throws a cushion at him. "That's enough, Ed. We get it."

"I don't," Sera mutters, her eyes fixed on her slice of pizza.

"What Eddie is trying to say," Dylan explains, "is we can't tell anyone that Crystal is from another planet. Not only would they not believe us, she would probably be taken to some sort of psychiatric unit for assessment."

Eddie nods. "Exactly. Or, even worse, they might believe her."

"Why would that be worse?" Sera asks, eyes wide.

"Because they'd take her away," Eddie exclaims. "Put her in a tank. Cut her open."

My blood runs cold. Maybe I've misunderstood this planet after all. The pizza is a cold, hard rock in my stomach. How stupid of me to not ask more questions. How many visitors from other planets have suffered this fate? Are they going to cut me open to eat me? When Linda explained that 'meat' toppings available for the pizza came from animal lifeforms, I'd been disgusted. Now I find myself wondering, do Earth inhabitants eat humanoid lifeforms too?

"Crystal? Are you okay? You're practically green?"

I'm aware of Dylan perched by my side, but I can't bring myself to look at him.

"Well done, Eddie," Jordan says. "You've scared her half to death."

"Crystal?" Dylan is still at my side, trying to catch my eye. He places a hand on my knee and squeezes.

I force myself to look at him. "Are you going to eat me?"

His stares at me, open mouthed, before glancing at the rest of the group. "No, Crystal. We're not going to eat you."

As soon as the words leave his lips, he throws his head back and laughs. The others join in and my cheeks burn as I realise, I've completely misread the situation. I try to laugh, but it sounds hollow.

Jordan leans forward. "We have stories about aliens coming to this planet and in lots of them, scientists can't wait to cut them up. It's just made up, though."

"Eddie does have a point," Dylan says with a grimace. "I doubt anyone would believe you're from another planet. I still can't believe it myself."

"What do we do then?" I ask. "I really don't want to go back to the hospital."

The thought of going back to that metal bed with the papery sheets, bright lights and noisy corridors is enough to make me take my chances and run. If they want to take me back there, they'd better be prepared for a fight.

"You can stay with me."

My head snaps up to look at Sera, sitting playing with her long hair. We all stare at her for a moment before Eddie breaks the silence.

"Why is that an option, Sera? We need more words."

Flicking her hair over her shoulder, she lets out an exaggerated sigh as though the answer is obvious. "She can stay with me. My parents are at their chalet in France for the next three weeks, like they do every school holiday."

Her tone and demeanour seem all too familiar. How many times had I given my parents the cold shoulder after they'd announced yet another royal tour I wasn't allowed to join because I 'needed an education'? My heart constricts with a twinge of shame as I realise why they insisted I join them on the last journey. My pleas and guilting tactics finally paid off—and now they're gone.

"Right." Dylan claps his hands together to gain everyone's attention. "How do we explain this to Mrs. Millen? She's not going to be okay with this. No one is."

Linda claps her own hands together, excitement lighting up her face. "We fake her memories!"

I raise my eyebrows, confused as to how this is going to help me evade the hospital. "What do you mean?"

"We get one of the guys to call Mum and pretend to be Crystal's father. We could say her memory came back when we were in town. Turns out she's visiting family here for the summer holidays and got lost, fell and banged her head."

I look around at the group, who are all nodding with the same quietly impressed expression on their faces.

"It might just work," Dylan admits. "Why would she lie? There's no need to be suspicious and Crystal was cleared medically."

"Of course, it will work." Linda grins. "I'm sure they'll need someone to physically sign paperwork, but we can figure that out later. Besides, what are they going to do? They have no information on her—she's an alien. How would they find her? The real question is: who should call? It can't be Eddie, obviously. So, who's got the 'manlier' voice? Dylan or Jordan?"

She sits down and folds her arms, grinning ear to ear as she looks between the two boys, clearly anticipating some sort of argument.

"I think Jordan should do it." Dylan shrugs. "I'm pretty sure Mrs. Millen would recognise my voice too. She's known me since I was five."

"Ugh, you guys are no fun," Linda huffs. "Right, Jordan. Let's practise what you're going to say."

As the gang begins to coach Jordan on what to say and how to say it, I find my gaze resting on Sera. She joins in intermittently but seems quite content not competing with so many loud voices and personalities. I don't really know much about her yet, but I suppose that will change very soon if I'm going to be staying with her tonight.

Tomorrow, however, I'm going to figure out a way to get home.

CHAPTER NINE

Crystal

I'm running. Running so fast. My lungs burn as I follow a billowing red flame. Only it's not a flame. It's the deep red robes of a Dyja guard. We turn a corner and I'm blinded by a bright blue light. The red flame is gone, and sadness consumes me. I turn and run. I can't see. I have to get to the evacuation deck. I have to get to my parents.

I reach a maintenance access point and force it open, lowering myself into the tiny cavity. It's so dark. I push along until I reach a grating, which I kick and kick until my feet are raw. When it finally releases, I don't hear it hit the ground. Too many people drown my senses with their noise. Hundreds? No. Thousands of panicked people all fighting to get to escape pods.

More red flames find me and I'm floating towards a white flower, still amongst the chaos. The white flower wraps her arms around me. My mother. Her long blonde curls are streaked with blood and dirt. Is it her blood?

We hold each other and watch, helpless, as the crowd pushes past my father. He tries and fails to hold the heaving masses back—to keep them calm.

His words reach me, echoing in my head like the rumbles of distant thunder. There's a small single-person maintenance pod at the far end of the dock. It's my only chance.

"Crystal. Wake up."

I sit up, dragging air into my lungs, my body soaked in sweat.

"I heard you screaming," Sera says, reaching out and squeezing my knee beneath the covers. "It's just a nightmare. You're safe now."

The sweat covering my face and body is cold and I shiver—my body an empty echoing cavern. "It wasn't a nightmare, though." I draw my knees to my chest and bury my face. "It was real. Everyone's gone. Why would someone do that? We've never hurt anyone."

I'm not really asking, and I know Sera doesn't have the answers. What makes it worse is I can still remember the feeling of my mother's arms around me. It might have been a nightmare, but it was like having her back. If only for a few terrifying minutes.

"Why don't you have a shower?" Sera suggests, handing me a large fluffy sheet of green material. "It'll make you feel better, I promise."

She's right. As the warm water soothes me, I start to feel grounded again. Earth showers feel different than the water cascades at home. Here, the water plummets down on you as though you're standing in the rain or under a waterfall. On Starlatten, the water surrounds you from all angles— soft and scented.

I removed the dressing from my forehead before stepping in the shower and as I allow the water to cleanse me, I focus on my amulet, warm against my skin. Almost right away, the stinging and dull ache on the side of my face evaporate. I have no idea how good my healing skills are. It's a skill I haven't tried since I failed miserably four orbits ago.

Millions of questions fly around my mind, each fighting for a place at the forefront of my thoughts. I think back over my last day aboard the *Galastasia*. Father receiving a mysterious private telepathic message during breakfast. The Dyja running along the corridor as I walked to my lessons. There were signs. Signs I hadn't wanted to see.

Zarbilian—a small, colonised planet in our solar system—refused to sign the agreements all advanced planets in our section agreed upon, which is why they were top of the agenda at the emergency summit on Ankaria. They're the ones who killed my family.

I lift my face to the warm stream of water, pushing back my soaked curls and inhaling the sweet and spicy aromas of the cleaning products Sera has given me.

Attacking a royal ship and assassinating the royal family is a pretty big move for a tiny planet. How did they get the resources to coordinate an attack of that scale? What's their goal? My eyes fly open and I step out from under the hot spray. What's happening to Starlatten right now? Have they attacked there too? My heart hammers in my chest as panic prickles my skin.

Switching off the water, I wrap myself in the soft green sheet, filled with renewed purpose. I need to find a way to contact home. Now.

Sera has left me an assortment of clothes on the bed. I've learnt that the short tunic is called a 'top' and the leg coverings are called 'jeans'. I select the items that look the comfiest and pull them on.

As I dress, I look around the room I've been designated. Pink and gold adorn the walls in an ornate, yet simple pattern and detailed drawings of flowers hang in pretty golden frames. The bed is made of a dark wood with towering posts in each corner. It's lovely. The whole house is lovely. I have little to no knowledge of Earth dwellings, but it's clear that Sera's parents are significantly wealthier than Eddie and Linda's.

Sera appears at the door, giving me a shy smile. "How are you feeling?"

"Much better." I smile back. "You were right about the shower."

"A good hot shower makes everything clearer." She steps into the room, her delicate features creasing into a frown as she looks at me. "Your bruise and cut have gone. How did you do that? Make up?"

My fingers reach up and touch the healed skin. I must have done a better job than anticipated. I have no idea what makeup is. "I used my amulet to speed the healing," I admit.

"Wow," Sera replies, her eyes widening. "That's incredible."

"Thank you again for letting me stay." I gesture to the room in an attempt to steer the conversation back to safer ground. "You have a really beautiful home."

"It's okay I guess," she sniffs.

Without warning, Jordan comes bounding up the stairs and into the room. "Whoa! This place is huge." He stands, mouth agape, staring at the high ceilings and poking the artwork.

Sera gives me an apologetic smile. "Everyone's here by the way."

Jordan bounds out of the room and leans over the bannister, yelling for everyone to come upstairs.

"Just don't break anything, okay?" Sera pleads, shrinking into a corner as everyone leaps up the stairs and into the room.

"What? You have a four-poster bed?" Linda exclaims, throwing herself down and spreading her arms.

"Wait." I frown. "None of you have ever been here before?"

Linda sits up. "Nope. Sera's parents don't like us coming around, in case we wreck the place."

"I can see why they might be concerned," I muse, watching Jordan as he inspects a delicate golden figurine. "There are many valuable items here."

"Yeah, okay, Grandma," Linda scoffs, falling backwards on the bed again.

Dylan catches my eye from where he's leaning against the doorframe. "I guess you're not the typical rebellious teenager then?"

Blood warms my cheeks as everyone turns to look at me. "Well," I confess. "You can't really be rebellious when you're a princess. I have guards with me most of the time. Between classes and royal duties, there isn't much time left for socialising."

Eddie frowns. "That's sad."

"It must be hard," Dylan offers. "We don't really know much about you, do we?"

"That's easily fixed." Linda rubs her hands together and bounces off the bed. "We'll tell you about Earth and our lives and you can tell us about yours."

My eyes seek out Sera, who's standing in a corner inspecting the ends of her hair. After a moment, she looks up with an exaggerated eye roll.

"Fine, but let's go into one of the living rooms rather than being cramped in this tiny room."

As we file down the stairs, I lean toward Linda. "This is 'tiny'?" I whisper.

Linda grins and wiggles her eyebrows at me. "Makes you wonder how big her room is, doesn't it?"

CHAPTER TEN

Dylan

Everyone is full of energy, but I've already been up for hours and I'm starting to flag. My stomach growls and I flinch, looking to see if anyone noticed, but they're all far too preoccupied.

Sera has set us up in a room she refers to as 'her' lounge. There's a large television on one wall, three large sofas and framed posters of what look like old fashioned French adverts on the walls. Linda and Eddie are bickering over who gets to sit in the oversized revolving sofa seat, Sera is flicking through the channels on the TV and Jordan has produced a notebook and pen from somewhere, scribbling away in it.

Only one person isn't moving. Crystal is sitting in the middle of the larger sofa, watching with interest as the channels flick past on the TV, twisting her long curls around her fingers.

The disjointed sound of flicking channels, however, causes something inside my tired brain to snap. "Sera? Just put the news on or something." My voice is louder than I intend. "It's not like we're going to actually watch something, right? Do we even need it on?"

Everyone turns at my tone and I force myself to meet their curious stares. Sera shrugs and puts a news channel on, the volume low.

"Right," Jordan says. "I have a list."

"A list?" I raise my eyebrows and glance between Jordan, who looks very pleased with himself, and Crystal, who looks mildly terrified. "A list is a bit much. What if we ask one question each?"

"One question? *One*?" Jordan repeats. "We have a literal alien in the room and we only get to ask *one* question?"

"Don't call her that." The words tumble out of my mouth before I have time to think. Perhaps it's the combination of hunger and sleep deprivation, but the tidal wave of protectiveness towards Crystal catches me totally off guard. "Look, one question is enough. For now, anyway. Okay?"

Jordan holds my stare for a moment before shrugging and returning to his notepad, muttering under his breath. I'm almost afraid to look at Crystal, but I guess it's weirder if I don't, so I glance her way.

She gives me a grateful smile and a warm tingle spreads through my stomach and up my chest. I force myself to look away. What is wrong with me? She's from another planet and her entire family has just been massacred. This is not the time for a pointless crush.

Linda and Eddie are still bickering over by the round chair like five-year-olds and I'm glad of the distraction.

"Linda! Eddie!" I bark. "The chair is big enough for the both of you. Share or sit somewhere else." I swear it's my dad's voice that comes out of my mouth.

"Are you ready, Crystal?" Jordan is practically falling off his seat, he's leaning forward so far.

"Yes," Crystal says, taking a deep breath. "I'm ready. Ask away and I'll try my best to answer."

"Great." He taps the pad with his pen. "How do you know English?"

"What's 'English'?" she asks.

Jordan opens his mouth, his eyebrows raised. "English is the language we're speaking. There are hundreds of languages on our planet, but this is the one we speak in this country."

"I'm pretty sure my amulet translates for me." Crystal reaches inside the neck of her t-shirt and pulls out her purple necklace. "When I was in the hospital, I couldn't understand the doctor until I put my amulet back on. It has many abilities, and I haven't learnt about them all yet. Translation has been a very useful surprise."

Linda gasps. "So, it's translating for you right now?"

"What would happen if you took it off?" Jordan asks.

I watch as Crystal turns pale. Her hand clasps around her amulet.

"You don't have to do anything you don't want to do," I reassure her. "Keep it on."

"No," she says. "It's okay. It's just not something we do. The only time in my whole life I can remember not wearing it, is in the hospital."

As she's talking, she reaches around her neck and lifts the chain up over her head, untangling her curls as they get caught up in the delicate copper coloured metal. She places the necklace on the seat beside her and looks around at us, clearly nervous.

When she speaks, it's the most bizarre sound I've ever heard. It's fast and sharp and well—alien. As Crystal takes in our horror-stricken faces, her smile fades and colour paints her cheeks.

"Put it back on," I say, miming the action as I remember she can't understand me.

Her hands sweep up the necklace, placing it back over her head. "Is that better?"

"Yeah." Eddie shudders. "Let's not do that again."

Crystal frowns. "Was it that bad? What did I sound like?"

"It was so weird." Linda dissolves into giggles. "You sounded like an alien."

"It wasn't that bad." I try to reassure her. "You just sounded fast and squeaky. What did we sound like?"

"You sounded very odd. Round and slurry."

Jordan taps his pen against his chin before resuming his scribbling. "Interesting."

"Can I ask the next question?" Linda asks, raising her hand in the air.

Crystal nods. "Of course."

"How do you get an amulet? Does your planet make them?"

"Ooh! Yes," Sera chips in. "Do you have different coloured ones for different outfits?"

Jordan waggles his pen at them. "That's more than one question."

"So ... can I answer, or not?" Crystal asks, a small smile on her lips.

"Go ahead." He shrugs, muttering something about rules being pointless.

Crystal turns in her seat to face the girls. "We have our amulets from birth. And just the one. It's part of our history. The story of our founders is a legend passed down through generations."

"So, who gives you the amulet? Who are the founders?" Linda asks, her eyes wide.

Jordan opens his mouth and Linda silences him with a glare.

"Well." Crystal leans forward, her eyes bright. "Thousands of orbits ago, our founders, Elaini and Jetzia fled their war-torn planet of Azrala and found Starlatten—completely uninhabited—which is really rare.

"As they explored, they found a ravine so deep and wide it seemed to divide the entire planet in two. The only way to cross it was to climb down and then back up the other side. It was so deep that by the time they descended to the bottom they had used all their strength and supplies.

"Jetzia spotted a light further along the canyon floor and they discovered a cavern with a deep lake of clear, cold water. As they quenched their thirst, they discovered millions upon millions of multi-coloured stars at the bottom of the pool. They dove in and picked one each. Holding these treasures seemed to give them the hope and strength they needed to continue, so they left the cavern and began their ascent.

"Halfway up the ravine, Elaini fell down exhausted and injured herself. There was no choice but for Jetzia to continue the climb alone and try to return with provisions to save her.

"He was near the top when he fell down with exhaustion. As he lay on a ledge trying to gather the strength to continue, he heard Elaini's voice. He thought he must have been dying, as the voice was in his head and not coming from below. 'Be strong my love. I have faith in you.' As the words resounded in his head he pushed onwards and reached the top. Jetzia gathered food and supplies and returned to save Elaini.

"Ten orbits later, forty more people arrived on the planet seeking refuge from war, and a community was born. They named the planet Starlatten, which translates from Elaini and Jetzia's home language as Star Cavern.

"The Starlatten tradition evolved so that when two people have committed to each other and wish to start a family, they must undertake the journey to the Starellia cavern. They journey to the bottom together, as Elaini and Jetzia did, to retrieve an amulet stone for their unborn child.

"When a family member dies their amulet will be returned to the pool by the next member of the family to undertake the journey with their partner. There, the stone is cleansed and recharged by the waters. Everyone is united in this journey, no matter their walk of life."

"Whoa," Linda breathes. "That's amazing."

"It really is," Eddie agrees. "I mean, the beginning of your planet's history starts with space exploration. Ours starts with dinosaurs and cavemen."

Jordan groans. "Just thinking about it is making my head hurt."

As they begin discussing the story and possible follow up questions, I notice Crystal has fallen silent. I move across and sit next to her. Something's not right, and as I reach out and touch her shoulder, I realise silent tears are staining her cheeks.

"What's wrong?" I whisper. I don't think the others have noticed she's upset, and I want to try and keep it that way.

"It's fine," she croaks.

"It's clearly not fine." I wrap my arm around her shoulders, no longer caring if the others notice. "Talk to me."

Crystal looks up and I swear my heart stops. Her tears pull at my hand like a magnet and I reach out, wiping away a droplet. My breath hitches at the unexpected intimacy of the action and I hope she doesn't notice the colour rising on my cheeks.

"My mother used to tell me the legend of our founders when I was a child," she says. "I loved hearing about Elaini. When I discovered I was related to her, it was the first time I truly felt like a princess. Telling that story now—it just reminds me that I'll never hear my mother's voice again."

My heart breaks for her. She's been through so much—I can't even imagine. It makes my own problems seem so insignificant.

"I'm sorry," I murmur. Before I can change my mind or question myself, I wrap my arms around her and pull her towards me. After a moment, she relaxes against my chest and all I can think is I hope she can't hear how fast my heart is beating.

Eddie jumps up from his seat and points the remote at the television, turning the volume up so loud, Crystal jolts away from my embrace. I shudder at the sudden lack of warmth.

Eddie points at the huge screen, his eyes wide. "We're on TV."

CHAPTER ELEVEN

Crystal

Eddie's right. There on the screen, a clip of poor quality is being played on repeat. It shows Eddie stepping back into the road and almost instantly being scooped up into the air as a blue vehicle swerves beneath him. It's strange seeing it happen so fast. It felt like it was happening a lot slower at the time. I squint at the pictures. You can just about make out the backs of our heads. I focus on the voice talking over the pictures.

"… It's still unclear what happened, but the most popular theory seems to be that this was a magic stunt, inspired by illusionists. Authorities are investigating and urging people to remember that the stunts they see on television are not to be attempted at home.

"We have a witness of yesterday's events on the line. Mrs. Carol Clyde, are you there? Thank you for talking to us."

The picture on the screen splits in half—one half showing the man who has been doing the talking and the other a small picture of an older lady.

"'It was incredible. He just flew up into the air! I have no idea how they did it. I couldn't see any strings or platforms. They only seemed to be kids as well. It's not good those stunts on these magic shows. They give the youth of today all these dangerous ideas. They'll be juggling with chainsaws at the bus stops next.'

"Thank you, Mrs Clyde. Police are investigating and anyone who can provide information about the identities of the people involved are advised to contact the local police."

"Oh wow!" Linda shrieks, holding up her phone. "We're on YouTube and everything. We've had over fifty thousand views already."

I'm about to ask what that means when Dylan groans beside me, raking his hands over his face.

"That's not good, Linda. What if someone recognises us and we get arrested? What if they identify Crystal?"

I only half hear what he's saying, because my eyes are fixed once more on the screen. A new clip is being displayed. It shows a row of dwellings, but one of them is charred black with most of the side missing. People wearing strange white suits are walking around an area obscured by a yellow line that flaps in the wind. The screen swaps to a man holding a black device in front of his mouth standing beside a very elderly man.

"'He's a scientist, the man who lives there. He always seemed nice enough. Kept to himself. It's a nice quiet

neighbourhood. I almost had a heart attack when that bomb went off! Didn't have him pegged as a terrorist—'

"Thank you, Mr. McCreadie."

The reporter moves away and turns to a stern-looking man wearing a strip of material around his neck.

"Detective Inspector Reed, you're leading this investigation. What can you tell us about your findings so far?"

"'Of course, there is no evidence to suggest this was anything to do with terrorist groups. As you just heard, Dr. Erik Oakstone was a scientist. Judging from the remains and the findings of our forensics team so far, we are working on the assumption that this was a gas-based explosion—an experiment gone wrong, perhaps. We have found the remains of a large metal contraption in what appears to have been a makeshift laboratory. We are unable to identify what it was at present. There is still a lot of work to do and a lot of questions to ask before we know for sure what happened.'"

A picture of the doctor appears in the corner of the screen. He seems quite young, with floppy hair and circles of transparent material in front of his eyes.

"Excuse me, Detective Inspector Reed, you said 'was' a scientist. Have we got confirmation that Dr. Oakstone was killed in the blast?

'We have found no remains, however, to survive a blast like this would be highly unlikely.'"

The men disappear from the screen and are replaced by what looks like a map covered in symbols.

"What's going on, Crystal?" Dylan asks. "Are you okay?"

I look down at him in surprise. I hadn't even realised I'd stood up.

"Did you know that guy? That doctor?" Sera asks.

I shake my head and walk to the screen. "Did you see that metal contraption?" I point to where it had been displayed just moments before. "The one in the background?"

"What about it?" Jordan asks.

"That was my escape pod. That 'doctor' has my pod."

Everybody starts talking at once, questions spilling from everyone's lips. I let them wash over me as I consider the answers myself. I suppose he must have been alerted when my pod entered the atmosphere. Perhaps the explosion was caused by something inside the pod. If someone without the right knowledge tried to open it or take it apart, I'm sure it would be very dangerous.

I blink and try to focus on the people in front of me. Dylan is deep in conversation with Jordan, while Sera, Linda and Eddie are in the midst of an animated discussion on the other seat. I have no idea what to do. Perhaps somewhere in my head, I thought the pod would be a way for me to get home, but now I realise it was never an option. How would I even get off the ground?

"That's it then," Linda announces, her hands on her hips. "We have to go there."

"Where?" I ask as the others fall silent.

"To that Oakstone guy's house," she explains, as though it's the most obvious thing in the world.

Sera wrinkles her nose. "Why on earth would we do that? It's not like we can remove evidence from a crime scene. Especially not a great big space pod thing. I think they'd notice."

Linda sighs and holds her hands out in front of her. "We need to *investigate*. Find out who this Oakstone guy was. What kind of scientist was he? Why did he have the pod? What's left of the pod? Do the police know what the pod is?"

I nod. "Linda's right."

"How far away is this guy's house?" Eddie asks.

Jordan holds up his phone. "About an hour and a half to walk, or a twenty-minute bus ride."

"Twenty-minute bus ride it is then." Dylan gestures at the doorway. "After you, Your Majesty. Let's go find your pod."

I'm appalled at the giggle that bubbles from my lips. I try to cover it with a cough and put it down to excitement about finding the pod.

CHAPTER TWELVE

Jake

Yawning, I watch the lingering crowd from the shadowed alleyway between the houses. The number of police cars has dwindled since last night and now only the forensics team remain. I'm impressed the interest has kept up to be honest. The street, although quieter than last night, has been fairly busy all morning. Just as people grow bored and move away, new people saunter up to have a look.

If I knew what I was looking for, it would make this a whole lot easier. At some point between midnight and 3am, I considered going home—if only to ask my uncle for more information. A moment of madness brought on by lack of sleep, clearly. Cas only tells you what he wants to tell you. Do as you're told, and you get food and shelter. Ask too many questions and, well—I've seen him 'deal' with 'employees' before. I learned a long time ago that just because we're related, doesn't mean I get special treatment. Uncle Cas has made it clear on numerous occasions that he can't stand the sight of me.

Yawning again, I slap myself on the cheeks a few times, hoping it will wake me up. Something catches my eye and I press myself against the wall. A group of teenagers is meandering towards the explosion site, clearly trying to look inconspicuous and failing miserably. I shake my head with a chuckle as they nudge each other and spread out along the police line.

Leaning around the corner, I wonder what they're up to. Are they going to try to steal something? Are they just curious about the explosion? Maybe they're reporting for the school paper? A snort escapes my nose. Either way, they're most likely harmless.

A couple of them walk over to one of the policemen. One gets a notepad and pen out and I slap my thigh in satisfaction. They *are* reporting for a school paper! How *charming*.

I look around for the others and find the curly-haired girl and a tall blond guy peering at the remains of the charred garage. I can tell she's sad by the slump of her shoulders, even from here. Maybe she's related to the guy who died.

Someone starts screaming over at the far end of the site and I jolt in surprise.

"A hand! I can see a hand!"

The entire site erupts into panic. Police start to pull the screaming dark-haired lad away from the tape, but he won't shut up. This is so suspicious. I glance back at the others, finding the sad girl still standing by the tape.

As if being lifted by an invisible hand, the material of the white tent erected amongst the rubble lifts open, revealing a shiny but burned egg shaped contraption. As soon it registers what I'm seeing, the flap falls down as if it never happened and the group reconvenes under strong words from a couple of the officers.

What the hell did I just see? Alarm bells ring in my head and I know in my gut this is what Uncle Cas is looking for. I just can't draw the connection between him and a bunch of teenagers though. Who are they? What was that egg thing?

Watching the group as they saunter away from the site, consoling the curly haired girl, I'm so intrigued I step out from the alleyway. As if sensing me, the girl turns and looks right at me. I gasp and melt back into the shadows, my heart pounding.

Standing flat against the cold brick wall, I close my eyes, hoping they'll keep walking—but they don't. I hear their voices growing nearer and there's nothing else I can do but turn and run down the alley.

Skidding to a halt behind a large green, rust-covered dumpster I duck behind it and hold my breath. From the small gap between the dumpster and the wall, I catch a glimpse of the dark-haired boy and girl. They must be related—they look like twins. Are they looking for me? If they are, they're not being very quiet about it. In fact, as they draw closer, I realise they're bickering.

"Don't be so sexist," the girl sneers.

"Being protective is not sexist."

They stop just over a meter from my hiding place. It becomes clear they're arguing over who should have come to find me. Evidently, the boy doesn't think the girl should have come. If I wasn't sure they were brother and sister, I am now.

"Fine!" she shouts. "Whatever. You carry on by yourself and I'll go catch up with the others."

My heart speeds up. This could be an opportunity. I watch as the boy stomps off down the alley and out of sight, leaving his sister standing, fuming, right by me. Before I have time to second guess myself, I pounce from behind the dumpster and grab her.

My hand over her mouth, I drag her to the shadowed side of the alley, pressing her against the wall. She wriggles and kicks, but I hold fast.

Leaning forward, careful to avoid any attempts to headbutt me, I put my mouth to her ear. "Stop fighting and I won't hurt you. Scream or try to get away and I promise you—you won't get far."

My words are enough to pause her squirming and I take the opportunity to pull my knife free from my belt. As I hold it in front of her, her eyes widen with fear. Her body trembles against mine, her hot breath ragged against my hand.

"Do you understand?" I ask, trying to catch her eye. "I just want to ask you some questions. Scream or run and I'll have to kill you."

She nods ever so slightly, her dark brown eyes like saucers.

"I'm going to take my hand away now," I say, my eyes fixed on hers. "No screaming, okay?"

She nods again. I take a deep breath and pray it works.

"What are you doing here?" I ask.

She stares at me, her eyes flashing with something other than fear. "What are *you* doing here? Why were you watching us?"

My eyes widen just a fraction. Is this girl serious? I'm holding her at knifepoint and she's giving me lip? "If you're not scared of me," I press the tip of the knife against her chin. "I can certainly change that."

"Who are you?" She presses forward against the knife point and a drop of blood blooms at its tip. "Why do you care why we're here?"

"Look. I'm asking the questions here," I retort before I can stop myself, then kick myself mentally for letting her drag me in to this stupid argument.

She stares stubbornly into my eyes. "Well, I don't want to answer your questions."

I'm not sure whether I'm impressed or bewildered. I decide to take the scare tactics up a notch but voices from further down the alley echo along the brickwork. It catches me off guard and I lean away from the wall to get a better look.

Before I can react, the girl raises her hands and pushes me, knocking me off balance. The knife clatters to the ground and she runs.

She's fast, but I'm faster. After no more than a stride and a half, I reach out and grab hold of her top, pulling her to the ground. She lands with a painful sounding thud, the gravel grazing along her arm.

I crouch down, my grip on her t-shirt lost. "Are you okay?"

Her feet fly at my chest, shoving me over backwards and she scrambles to her feet, her shoes skidding on the gravel as she runs. Clenching my hands into fists, I thump the ground. What the hell just happened? I rest my elbows on my knees, tensing my fingers against my scalp. Uncle Cas needs to know about that weird object and the lifting tent, but I know it's not enough. He's not going to be happy.

With a block of concrete, heavy in my chest, I dust myself off and start the long trek home.

CHAPTER THIRTEEN

Crystal

"Linda? Are you okay?"

Sera's tone causes me to turn, and I gasp as Linda stumbles into the living room, supported on each side by Dylan and Jordan. A trickle of blood trails down her chin and she cradles a bleeding arm against her chest. The boys lower her onto the sofa and Sera grabs hold of her hand, eyes wide.

My stomach clenches with guilt. When I said I felt someone watching me from the alleyway, Eddie suggested we split up and check it out—agreeing to meet back at Sera's place to share our findings. I didn't like the idea of separating but hadn't said anything. My teeth sink into my lower lip.

"What the hell happened, Linda?" Dylan asks. "Where's Eddie?"

Everyone listens as Linda recounts her ordeal, her words punctuated by the occasional gasp or tut from her audience.

"I can't believe Eddie just left you," Jordan says.

Linda gives a nonchalant shrug. "I handled myself."

I watch her grin, shoulders high, but as my gaze travels down to her hands, I can see them trembling. The wound on her arm looks painful but not too deep. I reach over and place a hand just over the graze, focusing my concentration on the purple stone around my neck.

As it warms against my skin, I close my eyes, imagining the transfer of energy through my body, down to my hovering fingertips. I try not to think about how bad I am at this, reminding myself—not of the time I tried to heal scratches from falling into a prasalia bush while trying and failing to sneak out of the palace gardens—but of this morning, when I did a pretty okay job of healing my head wounds.

After a few moments, there's a gentle tug inside my chest and the amulet starts to cool. Acutely aware of how embarrassing it will be if this doesn't work, I open my eyes and lift my hand.

Relief and pride flood through me as I see that the graze has scabbed over and shrunk considerably. A more experienced person would have been able to heal it completely, but I'm more than happy with the results. It's only then that I realise the room has fallen silent and everyone is staring at me.

"Oh! I forgot," Sera says. "Crystal can heal."

"A little," I confess. "I'm still learning."

Linda lifts her arm and inspects it from as many angles as she can. "That is awesome. It doesn't hurt at all."

My cheeks warm. "I'm glad I could help."

Dylan stands and runs a hand through his hair, his eyes fixed on the large window behind us. "Eddie's not answering his phone. I sent him a couple of texts, but he's not reading them."

"Did you get a good look at the man?" Jordan asks. "We need to be able to make sure he hasn't followed you back here."

"He's not so much of a man, to be fair," Linda admits. "He looks our age. Maybe a year or two older? I did get a good look though. I'd be able to point him out again if I saw him."

Perhaps confident after the success of my healing, an idea sparks in my mind. "Linda," I begin, "I've only tried this once before, but I was wondering if you'd let me try and see your attacker—by accessing your memories."

Linda's face freezes and I wonder if I've gone too far. The healing was a big shock to them. Maybe accessing someone's mind is the thing that makes them realise this is all a bit too strange.

I swallow the lump of anxiety in my throat. "It's okay if you don't want me to. I know how unusual this is. Besides, it might not even work."

"Access away." Linda says, taking hold of my hands. "It's just something I've never been asked before."

I walk behind the sofa and place my hands on either side of her head. "All I have to do is hold your head and concentrate—a lot. So, don't move, okay?"

"Wait." Linda gasps. "What should I do? Close my eyes? Empty my mind?"

"You can close your eyes if you want, but you don't have to. I just need you to think about the attacker. What did he look like? Put yourself back in the alley with him and try to focus on the details."

Taking a slow, deep breath, I close my eyes and concentrate on my amulet as it grows warmer and warmer against my skin. Right away, my confidence starts to fade as doubt invades my thoughts like dark wisps of smoke. *What if I can't do this?* I visualise purple spreading down my shoulders and along my arms like veins. *What is everyone doing right now?* The purple retracts and my amulet grows cold.

Opening my eyes, I drop my hands, berating myself for getting distracted. "I'm so sorry ..."

Dylan stands and moves around the sofa to stand next to me. I watch, frozen, as he places a hand on my arm, his eyes warm and encouraging.

"You can do this," he says.

I don't know whether it's his voice, his eyes or just all of him, but Dylan is like the quiet in a storm—his presence grounding me, causing everything else to melt away.

"Okay." I exhale, placing my hands back on Linda's hair. "Let's try again."

I focus on my amulet, sending the warmth towards my fingers again and this time the warmth spreads like roots, spilling out of my fingers and into Linda's head.

It's dark. A warm, rough hand presses over my mouth— my skin damp from my breath against the fingers. I scream, but there's no sound. Pressed against a hard wall, the smell of the waste container beside me fills my nostrils as my heart pounds against the hard, lean body of my attacker.

This isn't really happening. This isn't me. Trying to stay calm, I focus my energy on my eyes and the dark retracts—a face coming into focus. Deep green eyes. Long dark lashes. Very closely cut hair. Tall. Perhaps a little taller than Dylan. He's broad and strong, but very slim. Moving my gaze downward, I see he's wearing a long-sleeved black top with a dark jacket and well-worn, dark blue jeans.

The vision starts to fade, and I look around to see if I've missed anything. I can make out a chain around his neck, but I can't see any more of it, because it's under his shirt. The perfumed scent of prasalia flowers fills my nostrils for a fleeting second and I blink in surprise. I try to catch the scent again but all I get is rotting waste and sweat. Glancing back at the intense green eyes, my heart pounds in my ears as the vision blurs—I'm falling.

I jolt, my arms flailing as I reach out for something to stop me, but I'm already caught. Dylan returns me to standing, his hand lingering on my back as I clutch the back of the chair trying to catch my breath and calm my heart.

"Are you okay?" he asks. "You just flew backwards all of a sudden."

"Did it work?" Jordan asks.

Linda turns and looks up at me with her dark eyes. "Did you see him?"

"It's like I was there," I begin. "I can still feel his hand over my mouth." Shuddering, I touch my fingers to my lips. Those eyes. The colour of Earth grass.

Linda gasps. "You saw him?".

Her squeal jolts me back to the room. "Yes," I say, rubbing my temples. "Sorry, my senses are a bit muted. I guess it takes the mind a while to readjust after being someone else. It was so strange. He wasn't what I was expecting."

"How so?" Dylan leans over the back of the sofa, his eyes fixed on mine.

"Linda was right," I explain. "He's young. There were a few things that confused me though."

Sera nudges Jordan. "I hope you're writing this down in that notebook of yours."

Jordan stands in a fluster and digs the notebook and pen from his pocket. "Go on, Crystal."

I take a breath and continue. "Well, like I said, he's about your age. He's tall—perhaps taller than Dylan. He has green eyes and very closely cut light brown hair. He was wearing dark clothes and he had a chain around his neck, but I couldn't tell what was on it."

"Oh!" Linda jumps up. "I know! I saw it. When I pushed him over to get away from him, it fell out of his shirt."

"Really? Can you describe it?" I ask. "I don't know what it is, but something is really irritating me. It's like it's just out of sight at the edge of my mind ..."

"It was a bit weird to be honest." Linda shrugs. "It was a bright green stone with really fancy designs in metal around the edges. It was pretty, but not something you'd usually see a guy wearing."

Everyone falls silent as they ponder this piece of information. Does it have any relevance? Possibly not. I stare down at my legs—the unfamiliar fabric a stark contrast from the flowing robes worn on Starlatten. My fingers reach up to stroke the smooth surface of my amulet, as I wonder whether I'll ever wear robes like that again—see home again.

"Linda?" Sera breaks the silence. "Was his necklace like that?"

I look up to see what Sera is pointing at, only to find she's pointing at me. More specifically, my amulet. My breathing halts as I turn to Linda, waiting for her response. Was it? If it was, what would that mean?

Linda's nose wrinkles as she considers the suggestion. "Yeah, I guess so," she admits. "The stone had the same weird glow, like there's something alive inside it. His was a different shape and design though."

I run my fingers over the familiar twists that encase the purple stone. "Well, the setting is different for each family," I explain. "All my family have this setting—they're passed down from generation to generation. Only the stone inside changes."

"Like a family crest?" Jordan muses. "That makes sense."

"Great," Dylan huffs.

There's something in the tone of his voice that catches my attention. He's still leaning over the back of the sofa, his head on his forearms. As I watch, he stands and runs both hands over his face and through his hair, lacing his fingers behind his head. He doesn't look happy.

Despite his clear annoyance, my eyes are drawn to the way his muscles flex as he holds his arms behind his head. Following the line of his toned torso, I notice that his shirt has lifted to expose the smallest stretch of taut, tanned, smooth skin. It's a sight you don't see back home, and my mouth is suddenly dry. I blink and swallow, refocusing on his face as he exhales and rubs his temples.

"So," he says, his eyes narrowed and his voice tight. "This guy watches us from an alley across the road from where a dead scientist has Crystal's pod. He attacks Linda, wanting to know what we were doing there and may or may not have an amulet like Crystal's? And we have no idea where Eddie is. Is that about right?"

A few people nod and shrug—his tone causing a similar wary expression on their faces. I have the urge to reach out and touch his arm, the way he did to me.

"Is no one bothered by how weird this all is?" Dylan holds out his hands in exasperation. "We have more information but zero answers. We know *nothing*. There are just more questions."

With a sigh, he turns and storms out of the room, the door swinging closed behind him. Jordan stands to follow him, but the weight of responsibility is clearly with me. I may not be one of his confidants, but this entire situation is my fault.

"Will you let me go?" I ask.

Jordan shrugs and waves his hand towards the door. "Be my guest."

I find Dylan in the kitchen leaning against the counter, his hands gripping the edge so hard, his knuckles have turned white.

"It'll be okay," I reassure him from the doorway. "We'll get more answers."

He sighs and his shoulders sag. When he lifts his head to look at me, his eyes are filled with sadness. "I'm sorry for overreacting. I'm just so tired and being so out of control just sort of, tipped me over the edge."

"It could be worse," I say.

He winces and drags a hand across his face. "I'm so sorry. I can't even begin to imagine what you're going through."

"Why are you so tired?"

Dylan's face darkens and he turns his attention to the shiny squares on the floor. "It doesn't matter."

Leaning against the opposite counter, I watch him for a moment, curious but unsure how much I can push. "If it's making you sad, it does matter," I say. "If you don't want to tell me though, I understand."

He glances at me before returning his gaze to the floor. "It's nothing, really. My dad left us last year. Just disappeared, leaving me, my mum and little sister to keep the family business going. It's been in our family for years and he just abandoned it. Abandoned us. So now, I have to get up super early to help mum and then make sure my sister gets to school and does her homework. It's fine though—I have things under control."

My heart pulls as he coughs to cover the crack in his voice. "What is the family business?"

"It's a bakery. Five generations of bakers."

I chew my lip, trying to decide how to ask what a baker is. Dylan seems to sense this and chuckles.

"Bakers bake bread," he explains, glancing around the kitchen. Opening a large container, he pulls out a pale brown object I recognise from breakfast this morning.

"Ah yes." I smile. "We have something that tastes similar on Starlatten. We call it luffta. Do you like it?"

"What, bread?" He smiles, but it doesn't reach his eyes.

"It sounds like a lot of responsibility," I offer. "It must be hard."

Dylan places the bread back in its container. "Like I said—it's fine. Sorry for offloading on you."

"Not a problem," I reassure him. "It's a nice distraction to hear about other people's problems."

He smiles and pushes the hair from his forehead. "Even so, how are you doing, honestly?"

"Honestly? I think I'm still numb from it all. I just keep moving forward. I'll have time to grieve when I get home." I say the words as though there's a good time to embrace a gaping hole you know you'll never be able to fill and will always cause you unbearable pain. My grief solidifies in my throat and my eyes burn hot with tears.

Dylan steps away from the counter towards me and as I look up to see my sadness reflected, I'm overwhelmed with guilt. It's my fault he's sad. It's my fault Linda got injured. It's my fault Eddie almost got hit by that vehicle.

I drop my head and stare at the cold white and grey floor, willing my tears not to fall. "I'm so sorry I've brought this upon you all."

"Don't be," he says. I watch his shoes as he steps closer, our toes almost touching. "I'm glad we found you."

He reaches out, lifting my chin with the tips of his fingers and all I can hear is my heart pounding. Our eyes meet and the intensity of his stare causes my breath to catch in my throat. He's so close, I can see the different shades of brown and gold beneath his dark lashes. I feel it again—the calming warmth that wraps itself around me when I'm near him. Why is that? I mean, he's beautiful, but it's more than that. I've been trying not to think about it too much, as there's really no point. There are things of much more importance happening around us but … those eyes … those lips.

Realising my breathing has slowed to almost nothing, I try to take a breath that isn't a gasp. His thumb strokes across my cheek, burning the skin in its wake and I stare mutely as his gaze moves down my face, lingering on my lips. My chest aches and my head spins as the space between us closes.

"Dylan! Crystal! Get in here—now!"

CHAPTER FOURTEEN

Dylan

I step back. It takes a second to get my bearings before I realise what almost happened. I am the world's biggest idiot. My cheeks flame and I drop my hand, trying to grasp for something to say, but I can't find the words.

Crystal blinks and steps away towards the door. "Come on. Let's see what's going on."

What was that? I need to apologise to her the second I get a chance. What kind of jerk makes a move on someone when they're grieving? Fighting the urge to pound my fists against my skull, I push the shame to the pit of my stomach and follow Crystal out of the kitchen towards the commotion in the living room. I almost crash into the back of her, realising too late she's come to a halt at the entrance to the room.

Sera and Linda are crouching beside a vaguely familiar man slumped on a chair—his face streaked with blood and his hair matted. Eddie stands beside him, blood staining one side of his shirt.

"What the hell?" I slip past Crystal and sprint over to Eddie, trying to find the cause of the bleeding.

Eddie waves me off. "I'm okay, mate. It's Oakstone that needs our attention."

"Oakstone?" I turn my attention to the man in the chair. His wire-rimmed glasses are cracked and his face is a mess. As my brain finds the connection, I realise it's the scientist from the news.

"What the hell, Eddie?" Jordan demands as he enters the room carrying a wet towel and a glass of water. He hands the towel to Sera, who starts to dab at Oakstone's head.

"Well," Eddie says, rolling his neck, "I was trying to find the guy who was watching us, but I found Dr. O hiding down an alley. He was really hurt, so I brought him back here. It took us a while because we had to take the side streets. I figured all this blood would look a bit conspicuous."

"Why didn't you just call an ambulance?" My mind spins as I look between Eddie and the man bleeding on the chair. "What makes you think he'd be better here?"

"Someone tried to kill me," Oakstone says, speaking for the first time. "If they think they succeeded, I'd like to keep it that way. At least for now."

I glance over my shoulder at Crystal, who's still standing frozen in the doorway, one hand clasped around her amulet. Things are getting more bizarre by the second—it's time to get some answers.

"Why would someone try to kill you?" I ask, standing in front of Dr. Oakstone and folding my arms.

He glances at Eddie, pushing his glasses up his nose. "Eddie has assured me I can trust you. However, I'm sure you can understand that this is very unusual."

"Look," I say firmly. "We're just as wary of you, but here's the deal. We know what you had in your lab, and we know a lot more about it than you do. If you want to find out what we know, you're going to have to tell us everything. Now."

Oakstone holds my stare and tension fills the space between us. As the silence stretches out, I realise I'm not sure what I'll do if he refuses the ultimatum. I'm banking on the fact he'll be too curious about the pod.

Finally, Oakstone sighs and takes off his broken glasses, rubbing the bloodied bridge of his nose. "Fine. I work in the field of astrophysics and astrology. The other night, I was completing standard atmospheric checks when I noticed something strange. It was heading straight for Earth, but it didn't follow the usual parameters for an asteroid or space debris. It was going unusually fast and didn't burn up when it entered our atmosphere.

"Of course, I reported it to my head of department, who told me I was more or less delusional. He suggested I look into it independently." He pauses for breath and shifts amongst the cushions, wincing. "So, I followed the coordinates I'd pinpointed and found an unusual metal contraption. I arranged to have it moved to my lab so I could investigate further."

Jordan pauses in his pacing up and down the length of the lounge. "Then what?"

The tension in the room is high and my heart pounds with nervous energy. Out the corner of my eye, I glimpse Crystal, still silent by the door.

"Well," Oakstone continues, "I was running tests on the object when someone broke into my lab. They knocked me out and left me for dead. When I woke, I managed to crawl out, just before the explosion."

The room spins a little and my stomach clenches. We're in too deep. Linda has already been assaulted and now it's pretty clear we're dealing with murderers. I open my mouth to suggest we call the police.

"Did you see who attacked you?" Linda asks from where she's sitting huddled with Sera.

"He had a balaclava on, so I couldn't see most of his face, but he had extremely unusual eyes." He shudders. "They were an orange-yellow colour—like flames."

Linda blows out her breath and relaxes back in her chair. "That's not the guy who attacked me. His eyes were green."

"What?" Eddie roars. "You were attacked?"

I step toward him, but Jordan reaches him first, placing a hand firmly on his shoulders. "Focus, mate," he says. "She's fine. We'll fill you in later."

Eddie huffs, staring between us all for a moment, before throwing his hands up in resignation.

I turn my attention back to the scientist. "Is there anything else you can tell us about the man who attacked you?"

"There is one thing," Oakstone begins, his brows knitting together as he recalls the incident. "You honestly won't believe me if I tell you."

I think about everything we've seen over the last forty-eight hours. "Try us."

"There was a crowbar," he says, staring at a cut on his forearm. "It lifted up into the air, like a bizarre magic trick. The guy was nowhere near me when he knocked me out—I could see him on the other side of the room. It's impossible, I know. Perhaps there was another attacker behind me."

My breath sticks in my throat and I turn to Crystal. I realise everyone else has made the same connection and we all watch as Crystal walks towards the bloodied scientist.

"I have answers for you," she says, "but I need to know for sure you're telling the truth. Will you let me access your memories so I can see what happened for myself?"

Oakstone's eyes widen as he looks at each of us. He opens his mouth to ask a question, but Crystal cuts him off.

"Head first. Answers second."

He stares at her, his eyes narrowed before giving a small nod of acceptance.

The room is silent as Crystal reaches forward and places her hands on either side of his head.

"You've got to think about last night, Doc," Jordan hisses.

Every muscle in me is tensed as I watch—her eyes closed and her fingers lightly touching Oakstone's blood-stained hair. If she flies backwards again like last time, I'll be ready to catch her.

She doesn't. After a moment, Crystal lifts her hands from Dr. Oakstone's head and flops down on the nearest sofa. Relief floods through me and I perch on the arm of the chair Linda and Sera are huddled in, waiting for her to centre herself. Oakstone's face is the picture of confusion. If this whole situation wasn't so damn serious, it would be pretty funny.

Crystal takes a deep breath and turns to the doctor. "My name is Crystal Akinara. I am the daughter of the king and queen of Starlatten. My ship was attacked, but I was fortunate enough to escape in one of the maintenance pods. That is what you found."

I watch Oakstone's face as he processes this information. Instead of asking the intense scientific questions I'm expecting, his mouth twitches and a burst of laughter escapes his lips. He claps a hand over his mouth, and I frown. This is all too much for him. He's snapped.

Crystal seems unfazed by his hysteria. Instead, she slips down off the sofa and kneels at his side. Reaching up, she places her hand above the dark red wound on the back of his head. Oakstone takes a second to acknowledge her, but when he does, the laughter stops. A calmness seems to come over him and he closes his eyes, relaxing back against the chair.

After a few minutes, Crystal sits back. "Your head is not completely healed, as I'm not well practised at large wounds. The bleeding has stopped though and it should feel a lot less painful."

Oakstone hesitates before reaching a hand to the back of his head. As his fingers find the healed wound, his mouth drops open.

"Cool, isn't it?" Linda grins.

"So," Oakstone ventures. "You're an alien."

Crystal gives him a tight smile. "It depends which way you look at it."

"I guess that's true." He laughs. "This must be a very confusing experience for you."

"It's not been easy."

Oakstone sits forward, resting his forearms on his legs. "I'm afraid there's not a great deal left of your 'pod', as you put it. Do you have any idea why someone would want to destroy it?"

Crystal shakes her head. "What concerns me more, is that you were attacked by someone with an amulet like mine. It's the only explanation for the floating weapon."

"It must mean you're not the only one who made it off the ship, Crystal," Jordan interjects. "Right?"

"If they escaped, why would they want to destroy the pod?" I look at Crystal for confirmation. "Surely it would be their only way of getting home?"

"No," Crystal says, her face falling. "I'm fairly certain the pod can only be launched from another spacecraft. It wouldn't be able to take off from Earth by itself."

As this information sinks in, I realise with dismay I thought the pod was the answer to her problems. From the moment we found out the scientist had it, I was sure we had an end goal—a solution. If the pod is useless, how will she get home? I'm such an idiot. I really want to help, but I can't even begin to fathom a way for her to leave Earth. I don't even know what solar system she's from. Or is it galaxy? Universe? Jeez. I'm not even sure I know which is bigger.

"Maybe they were covering their tracks," Eddie suggests, breaking the silence, "because they don't want people knowing they exist."

Oakstone scratches his chin. "That's a possibility. They might not want the entire planet looking for them—but why try and destroy the pod? Some of it is still there. Surely you'd steal it instead?"

"What if the pod isn't what they were looking for?" The words form on my lips at the same time as the thought and my stomach flips. "Perhaps they wanted to know who arrived in the pod."

Crystal looks at me, her brown eyes filled with fear as we try to arrange the information we have into something that makes sense. There are just too many unanswered questions.

"Where does Linda's attacker fit into this then?" Sera asks.

Linda nods. "We need to find him."

"Like hell you do!" Eddie booms.

"Calm down." I shoot him a warning glance and motion to Jordan who's chewing the end of his pen. "Let's put everything we know together to see if we're missing anything. Jordan? Do you want to give us a summary?"

Jordan clears his throat and flicks back a couple of pages in his notebook. "Crystal landed on Earth and we found her. She has an amulet that gives her powers." He glances at Crystal for confirmation.

She smiles. "More or less."

"Dr. Oakstone finds the pod and takes it to his house. Someone with an amulet breaks in, attacks him and destroys the pod," he continues. "A guy watching Dr. Oakstone's house—also possibly with an amulet—attacks Linda, but he's not the same guy. Does that sum it up?"

Disappointment swells in my gut. I had hoped a summary would make things clearer. In reality, all it's done is make it abundantly clear, we know absolutely nothing.

I turn to Eddie, who's still standing, arms folded. "Sorry mate, but Sera's right. We need to find the alley guy."

CHAPTER FIFTEEN

Jake

Perched on the edge of my bed, I rub my fingers over the deep, swirling green stone—soothed and entranced by the way it seems lit from within. I should be sleeping. After being up all night, the smart choice would be to take advantage of however long Uncle Cas is out of the house, but I can't sleep. My brain is wired.

Leaning back against the wall, I tuck the amulet under my shirt and take a deep breath—trying to block out the thoughts pinging around my head like lightning bolts. What were those kids doing? How did that tent flap lift up by itself? What will Cas do when he finds out I've got no real information?

My bedroom door flies open, tearing me from my thoughts. Uncle Cas stands there, tall and tense, his amber eyes burning with an almost red gleam as he glares at me.

"Get up."

I jump to my feet trying not to wince as his bark echoes around my barren room. "Sorry, Uncle."

"Anything to tell me?"

My heart thuds like an all-consuming baseline inside my body. "Some teenagers came to the house. They were snooping around. One caused a distraction and," I pause, weighing up which is the worst option—explaining the weird tent lifting or leaving it out, "this girl seemed to make the tent around that metal thing lift up, even though she was nowhere near it. Of course, it might have been wind or ..." My words trail off as something strange happens to Cas' face. I stare at him, unable to read his expression.

He advances toward me, his eyes like two coals as they burn into mine. "Did I not make it clear to you?"

I edge backwards until my back slams against the wall. He's so close, his angry breath hot on my face. Even though he's not touching me, his presence presses against my chest, crushing me against the wall.

It takes me a moment to realise my feet have left the floor and another to realise that the all too familiar sensation of his hands around my throat is missing. How am I off the ground? I start to struggle against the invisible force holding me up against the wall, but I can only flail like a fish without something to grab hold of.

"I want those kids found and I want answers," he hisses.

Gravity claims me and I fall to the ground—my legs buckling as I collapse in a heap at my uncle's feet.

"You lost them," he says, standing over me like a boulder waiting to crush me. "You find them."

My head spins as I scramble to my feet. Cas doesn't move, and I force myself, trembling, to meet his burning gaze. It seems like an eternity that we stand, almost nose to nose, as his flaming eyes sear into my soul.

Then he's gone—the sound of the door slamming echoing around my room. Ignoring the exhaustion clawing at my eyes, adrenaline pushes me forward as I grab my jacket from the chair and head downstairs.

My mind is in pieces as I break into a run. I don't stop until I'm at least three streets away, but I know no matter how far I run, I'll feel those eyes boring into me. It's like he can always see me. I shudder and slow to a walk, head down, my hands in my pockets.

What does he think these kids know? Or have? I don't think I've ever seen him so worked up about something. My feet slow to a stop as my mind finally processes what I've been trying to push away. He lifted me up off the ground without touching me. A cold shiver runs down my spine. What on earth is going on? My mind is screaming, but I will myself to keep moving forward.

I try for the millionth time to remember life before Uncle Cas—to remember my parents—but it's like a brick wall in my mind. I spoke to one of Cas' 'associates' about it once, years ago. He was a scarred and gnarled older man called Dave. He'd looked out for me, and for a while he was the closest thing to family I could ever remember having. Dave said it happened sometimes when people survive severe trauma. Repressed memories, he'd called it. Self-preservation. I miss Dave. He was a terrifying beast of a man, but he always had time for me. One day he went on a job and didn't come back. No one told me anything. He was just gone. I swallow the lump in my throat and keep walking.

I have no idea where to start, so I go back to the alley. Perhaps there's a clue there. I consider asking the police if they took any details from the teenagers, but I really don't want anyone to know that I've been here. Instead, I return to the place where I caught that girl, hoping against hope that there's something there. Maybe something fell out of her pocket. Something. Anything.

I'm almost on the verge of crawling along the floor to look for clues when I hear a noise. I flatten myself against the wall, pressing myself into the frame of a side door. Voices. I close my eyes and focus on them.

"Is this where he attacked you?"

"I'm pretty sure it is."

"What the heck are you taking photos of?"

I can't breathe. I'm almost certain that two of the voices are the brother and sister from before. I'll have to find some sort of god to thank later, because this is beyond luck.

"I'm looking for clues," the new voice says.

"I just want to find this guy and get some answers," the brother says. "Come on."

"Relax, Eddie," the girl says. "We can take a minute to look for clues."

"Whatever," Eddie grunts.

After a tense pause, the girl says, "Why do you have to be so angry all the time? It's not like you were the one who got attacked."

"Guys, guys," the other voice soothes. "Let's just take a breath."

"There's no time," Eddie says. "We need answers and if we mess around here, we might lose the only chance we have of finding him. Our best option is to keep looking."

"Okay, okay." The girl sighs. "Let's go looking."

Footsteps head my way and I squeeze myself as flat against the door as I can. If I'd known they were going to come this close, I'd have tried to hide somewhere else—or perhaps made a run for it—but it's too late now. I cross my fingers and hold my breath as they trudge past within a meter of me. The boys disappear around the corner, the girl a fraction of a second behind them and I slip a foot forward, ready to follow.

The girl stops and I freeze. I'm pretty sure I made no sound. She takes out her phone and starts tapping away. Maybe she didn't hear me. Maybe she's just using her phone. The silence of the alley seems deafening as I try to breathe as quietly as possible. If she turns around, she'll be looking right at me. I decide I have two options: run and try to lose them or confront her and attempt to get the answers I didn't before. I have no idea which option to choose.

The girl puts the phone to her ear and I swear I can hear the ringing, she's so close. I wonder if I can swap my hiding place. I close my eyes for a second to calm myself.

"Worst camouflage ever."

My eyes fly open and I find the girl staring right at me. Every instinct screams at me to run, but I'm frozen to the spot.

She tucks her dark hair behind an ear and shoots me a nervous grin. "We've been looking for you, Green Eyes."

I raise my eyebrows, my surprise quelling. "Green Eyes?"

"Well, you didn't exactly introduce yourself last time."

Pushing myself off the door, I step down from the stoop towards her, my right hand poised ready to grab my knife. Her eyes take in my stance, but she doesn't flinch. Why isn't she scared?

"So now you've found me," I take another step, darting a glance down the alley to check it's clear for my escape, "what are you going to do?"

"We need answers," she replies, backing away from me as though she might run too.

I sneer, taking a final glance at my escape route. "Why would I give you answers?"

"Because we know about your amulet."

My body freezes, one foot already outstretched. I turn to face the girl once more. "Amulet?"

"The one you're wearing right now. The one with the green stone."

My hand flies to my neck, my fingers touching the copper chain. "What are you talking about?"

What on earth is an amulet? The light is fading and as I step closer to the girl, I can see she's not quite as calm as she seems. Her breathing fast, she's scared—she's just very good at hiding it.

"I have a friend with one very similar," she explains.

I know it's highly unlikely they could tell me anything about a weird necklace I found hidden in my uncle's house, but curiosity eats away at my better judgement. I need answers and playing nice with these guys might be the best way forward.

"My name's Linda, by the way."

"Jake."

She grins. "Not Green Eyes then?"

My laugh surprises me. "No."

"So, *Jake*." Linda sighs. "Let's cut the chit chat. We know you're from another planet and my friend needs answers. Will you help us?"

Laughter rises in my throat again but comes out as a strangled sort of cough. Another planet? This Linda has a twisted sense of humour, but she's not laughing. Her face is a picture of absolute seriousness. In fact, she's looking at me like *I'm* the strange one.

"Look, Linda." I hold my hands up. "I know there's some weird stuff going on right now, but I can assure you, I'm definitely not from another planet."

"Oh, really?" Linda screws up her nose and looks me up and down. "Well, your amulet certainly is."

Exhaustion smacks into me and I sink down on the stoop like a bag of cement. What do I do? This Linda girl is talking absolute nonsense, but Cas wants answers. This friend she keeps talking about might have more information. If I go back with only half a story, Cas will be furious and that's something I want to avoid at all costs.

"Okay." I slap my hands on my thighs decisively. "Let me meet this friend of yours."

Linda laughs and holds up her hands. "Whoa there, cowboy. You attack me in an alley, and you think I'm going to just march you through town to meet my friends?"

I open my mouth to argue, but I get the feeling there's no point. "So, what then?"

Before she can answer, the sound of shouting echoes down the alley and I flinch, my hand reaching for my knife.

"It's my brother," Linda whispers. "He's looking for me."

I raise my eyebrows. "He likes leaving you alone in alleyways, doesn't he?"

"They can't find you," she says, ignoring my comment. Stepping forward, she reaches out and touches my arm. "He's still super pissed that you attacked me."

I stare at her arm on my sleeve. "Yeah, I can imagine."

She seems to realise what she's doing and snatches her hand back. "Look, how about you come meet us tomorrow at a neutral place? Just you though. No one else."

I try to wipe the disappointment from my face. If we meet tomorrow, it means another night on the street. I can't go home without answers and a possible meeting is not enough. The frantic shouting grows closer and I realise she's staring up at me, her big dark brown eyes pleading. "Sure." I shrug. "When and where?"

"Crestfield Park. Midday. The benches near the playground." She starts to head in the direction of the voices and away from me. "I'll lead them away. Stay hidden."

I nod and give a half wave, half salute. I'm not sure why, but words seem to have failed me.

"Later, Green Eyes," she calls over her shoulder as she jogs around the corner and out of sight.

CHAPTER SIXTEEN

Crystal

My heart is in my stomach. It's been ten minutes since Eddie called, asking if we'd seen Linda. I can't believe this is happening again. What if Green Eyes has hurt her? I swallow, wincing at the effort.

As we hurry to meet Eddie and Jordan, I clutch my amulet—even though I know it can't help. Beside me, Sera puts her phone to her ear for the tenth time, trying to ring Linda.

If I was back home, I'd be able to speak to her telepathically and we'd know instantly if anything was wrong. The thought gives me pause. Usually, messages and conversations happen in my mind throughout the day. Here, it's silent. I think back, trying to remember the last time I heard a voice in my head. It was my mother, telling me to be brave—that she loved me.

"Over here!" Jordan waves from further down the alley. Eddie stands beside him, his phone to his ear.

"How could you lose her again?" Dylan growls as we reach him. "This is ridiculous."

"Jordan lost track of her a few meters further down there," Eddie seethes, nodding towards his friend.

Jordan holds his hands up in front of him. "Hey! If you hadn't stormed off, maybe she wouldn't have had trouble keeping up."

"Guys." Dylan stands between them and puts a hand on Eddie's shoulder. "We'll find her. Okay?"

"Find who?"

I spin around to see Linda walking towards us from the far end of the alley. Eddie runs forward and grabs her shoulders, inspecting her for new injuries as the rest of us gather around.

"I'm fine," she insists, shoving Eddie off. "I was just checking out the alley. He's not down there. Did you guys find him?"

"We've been too busy looking for you." Jordan groans.

"I think we need to go home and regroup," Dylan says, his voice tired. "It's getting late and it's been a really long day."

Our disappointment is palpable, and everyone murmurs in agreement as we head back toward the road and into the dwindling summer sunshine. Just before we emerge onto the quiet street, I flinch as my amulet grows warm against my chest—so warm it causes me to gasp and take it into my hands.

"What's wrong?" Dylan asks, stopping at my side.

"I'm not sure," I reply. "My amulet felt really hot for a second, but it's gone now."

"Does it do that often?"

"No," I say, frowning at the purple stone. "That's the first time it's ever happened. Maybe it was my imagination." The amulet is back to its normal temperature between my thumb and forefinger and I start to wonder if it happened.

"My head is a mess." Dylan chuckles. "I can't imagine the state of yours."

I smile as his comforting tones envelop me like a warm embrace. Despite all the unanswered questions and seemingly insurmountable problems ahead, I know I'm incredibly lucky that this group of brave and caring people were the ones to find me. Things could have been so very, very different.

"What now then?" Sera asks as we reach the end of the road. "Back to mine to check on Oakstone?"

"He's fine," Jordan says with a cough.

I stare at him in confusion, along with the rest of the group, awaiting further explanation.

"I've been keeping him in the loop by sending messages to the laptop he's using," Jordan shrugs nonchalantly. "I thought it might be useful to have an open line of communication."

Dylan breaks the astonished silence with a laugh and claps Jordan on the back. "You were right—that's a great idea. I think we forget you're the clever one sometimes, mate."

"Hey!" Eddie and Linda cry out.

Sera laughs. "He's right though."

The look on Linda and Eddie's faces is too much and I start laughing too.

"Okay, okay," Linda says, rolling her eyes. "Jordan is a genius, but I have a brilliant idea too—if I don't say so myself."

"Go on," Dylan prompts, trepidation clear in his voice.

Linda grins wider, almost unable to contain her glee. "Bowling."

Everyone looks at each other, a quiet rumble of discussion beginning on the pros and cons of the idea, but I'm completely in the dark.

"Excuse me? What's 'bowling'?"

Linda throws an arm around my shoulder. "Something fun. Things have got way too tense and I think a bit of down time will help freshen up our brains."

"Why not?" Eddie smiles, visibly relaxing for the first time today. "Beats sitting around Sera's place watching Dr. O tapping away on his laptop."

Looking at the relaxed and happy faces around me, I decide with a smile that whatever this 'bowling' is, it might be just what we need.

I flinch at the cacophony of noise as we walk into the bowling alley. My eyes must appear the size of planets as I stare at the many see-through contraptions with dangling claws and the large black boxes with flashing lights. People laugh, talking loudly on every side—some clustered around the machines and others leaning on tall tables, eating and drinking. My mind swims with questions and I long to go and explore the strange boxes, but the group sweeps me toward the back of the enormous high-ceilinged room.

My mouth falls open as I take in the long row of shiny aisles and I watch with fascination as a girl picks up a large sphere and rolls it towards some white ornaments at the end of one of the aisles. When the sphere knocks down the majority of the ornaments, the noise is tremendous and everyone around her cheers. The girl seems quite pleased with the destruction and I watch in awe as a machine sweeps away the mess and replaces the ones she missed.

I turn to Dylan with a dozen questions on my lips, only to find him watching me, clearly amused, his mouth twitching.

"Kind of weird, I guess?" He smiles.

I smile back. "Just a little."

"It's quite simple," Jordan explains. "You pick up the ball using these holes and roll it towards the pins—"

"The white things," Dylan whispers in my ear and I try to hide the shiver it sends down my spine.

"—and you try and knock down as many as you can in two tries."

"Well, that does sound quite straightforward," I agree.

"I'm starving," Sera announces, twirling her blonde tresses up into a pile on the top of her head. "I'll go order us some food and drinks."

"Amazing." Eddie rubs his hands together. "I can't remember the last time I ate."

Dylan and the others begin pulling strips of paper and small pieces of metal from their pockets. *Money,* I remember. They'd shown me when they ordered pizza that first night.

"Are you kidding me?" Sera rolls her eyes. "This place is hardly Michelin star. They're on me."

Everyone starts to protest but she's already started to walk towards the counter adorned with pictures of food.

Eddie shrugs in defeat. "I guess I don't feel that bad now we've seen her house."

"I'll give her a hand," Jordan declares, jogging off in her direction.

I smile to myself, fairly certain there's something more than friendship between Jordan and Sera. I wonder how things work on Earth when it comes to relationships. Although, I'm not sure I know much about how they work on Starlatten. It's not as if I ever had someone special and I'm not sure how my parents would have dealt with it if I had.

I watch Dylan as he picks up different balls, testing their weights. With his strong arms and broad shoulders and the way his hair falls forward onto his forehead, I decide he's possibly the most gorgeous person I've ever seen.

As much as he's physically beautiful, there's something more—something that radiates from him when I look in his eyes. When I'm around him, I feel strong and safe and in the kitchen at Sera's house, it was like he could see right into my heart and understand.

The memory of his warm breath on my lips sends a tingle through my body and I blink several times and look away. Yes, he's handsome, kind and smells like bliss, but I can't develop any sort of feelings for him. What would be the point? I'm going home. After today, I can't help but wonder how and my stomach lurches at the thought.

My laughter catches me by surprise as Eddie bowls another 'gutter ball'. Linda was right—it's wonderful to have some relief after the events of the last couple of days. Everyone is sprawled on the benches alongside our 'lane'—our chatting and laughter interrupted only by cheers when someone bowls a 'strike'.

Although everyone has been kind and supportive, it turns out that bowling is not one of my strongest skills. The same kindness and support, however, is not provided when someone else in the group fails.

"Crystal, you're up." Jordan grins at me. "You've got it this time, for sure."

"We'll see." I smile as I select the shiny purple ball I've decided to use—purple and shiny like my amulet. *My amulet.* I glance over my shoulder at the group. Dylan's gone to get some more drinks, Sera and Linda are sitting chatting intensely about something and Eddie is scowling at the scoreboard. Only Jordan is watching, sticking his thumbs towards the ceiling in what I can only assume is an encouraging gesture.

Carefully, I focus on the centre pin, swing my arm back and roll the ball forward. Almost instantly, it starts to roll to the left, but keeping my back to the group, I concentrate on the ball and as the amulet warms against my skin, the ball swerves away from the gutter towards the middle pin. All the pins promptly topple over, and cheers erupt behind me.

"Wow!" Jordan and Eddie exclaim simultaneously.

Linda jumps up and hugs me. "Your first strike! Well done!"

I hug her back, hoping my burning cheeks don't give me away. I'll confess later, but for now I bathe in the congratulations. Taking a seat beside Jordan as Linda takes her turn, I scan the bowling alley for Dylan, but I can't see him anywhere.

"Looking for Dylan?" Jordan closes one eye briefly as he looks at me. "He had a missed call from his mum. He went outside to call her back."

I open my mouth to deny the truth, but Jordan's huge grin and wiggling eyebrows make me blush and look away.

"He's totally into you, you know."

"Excuse me?" I ask, equally puzzled and bemused.

Jordan laughs and whispers loudly, "He. Likes. You."

My stomach flips upside down. "He's spoken with you about it?"

"No," he admits, "but he doesn't need to."

Turning my gaze to the scoreboard, I wonder if it's true. Dylan has been so kind and caring towards me, but haven't they all? Of course, my heartrate doesn't go into lightspeed when any of the others brush against me.

I frown and try to push the rising excitement into a dark corner. It doesn't matter if he has feelings for me. With everything that's going on right now, I should concentrate on finding Green Eyes and getting home.

Should. I hate that word. It reeks of duty and responsibility and the absence of free will. You should never smile with your teeth unless it's close family and friends. You should always lift your glass after your father at government meals. You should try harder in class. You should try to use your amulet more. You should be proud to be the heir to the throne.

Perhaps here—stranded on a planet a trillion miles from my royal responsibilities—I could do something I *shouldn't* do. A spark runs along my spine at the thought and I turn back to Jordan, but he's not looking at me anymore. He's staring at Sera.

"She's 'into' you too," I say, hoping I've used the phrase correctly.

He chokes on his mouthful of drink and turns—his dark eyes wide. "What did you say?"

"She likes you."

Jordan's mouth opens and closes a few times, reminding me of a water-based animal on my planet called a zorgat.

"You should tell her how you feel," I continue. "You never know what's around the corner."

He shakes his head as his gaze returns to Sera. "I wouldn't know where to start."

"Jordan." I reach out and place a hand on his arm. "What do you do on this planet if you like someone?"

"Um. You ask them out?" he says. "It's called a date."

I give his back an encouraging rub. "Then go ask her on a date."

"You're right," he exclaims, his eyes bright. "Life's too short."

Before I can respond, Jordan folds me into an embrace and kisses me on the cheek. I giggle, watching with excitement as he saunters over to sit next to Sera and for a second, I allow myself to imagine myself in her shoes—with Dylan asking me on one of these 'dates'. I smile and shake it off, dismissing it as the reckless notion it is and try to focus on the game.

CHAPTER SEVENTEEN

Dylan

My vision blurs at the edges as I watch Jordan hug Crystal and kiss her on the cheek. Shoving the drinks down on the nearest table, I turn and stomp off into the arcade. I can't shake the sight of them giggling and whispering, her hand rubbing his back. When did that happen? I thought we ... okay ... I don't know what I thought, but it wasn't this.

I'm breathing hard, my blood red-hot in my veins as I come to a stop near the 2p machines. Squeezing my eyes shut, I attempt to suppress the heavy wall of throbbing emotion pounding in my skull. What is wrong with me? How can I possibly be jealous? My cheeks flare with embarrassment. If things were different, then sure, I would be interested, but she's a literal alien princess for crying out loud.

I picture her face earlier this morning as we stood in the kitchen—her deep brown eyes so all-consuming. I'd come so close to losing control and kissing her. Now, as I replay the image of Jordan kissing her on the cheek, I'm glad I didn't. Maybe if I had though, I wouldn't have lost my chance. *Gah*! There is no chance. The whole reason she's with us, is so we can get her home—home to another solar system. I press the heels of my hands into my eyes in frustration. There's enough on my plate at the moment, without adding girl problems to it.

It's becoming all too familiar, this spiralling sensation of being out of control, and I'm sick of it. For the past eighteen months, I've been under so much pressure, not just from my mum but my teachers too. How are you supposed to know how you want to spend the rest of your life, when you haven't even lived two decades of it?

Mum would never admit it, but I know she's terrified I'll go off to university. If I did, she'd have to sell the bakery. She wouldn't be able to run it by herself and I know we can't afford to hire someone. I don't want that on me.

Maybe it's because Dad left, but the bakery isn't where I see my future. I'm not sure if it ever was. I want to do something that means something—but what? The pounding in my head intensifies as I picture the stack of university brochures on my desk at home. Do I even want to go to university? I groan and screw my eyes tighter as my emotions threaten to manifest in liquid form.

A loud giggle takes me by surprise.

"Dylan? I thought that was you."

Taking a deep breath, I turn to face the source of the saccharine voice. "Hi, Chloe."

Chloe is in my year at school and now she's standing—as always—just a little too close as she twirls a strand of long dark brown hair around her finger.

"Fancy bumping into you here," she purrs, fluttering her lashes in my direction. "Enjoying the summer holidays?"

I lean back against the machine. "It's been ... interesting. How about you?"

"Oh, you know. The usual." She turns and leans against the machine beside me, reaching out a finger and running it down my arm. "Looks like you've caught a bit of sun. I hope you're using sunscreen."

I watch her finger trail down towards my wrist as if it's someone else's arm. She's a very pretty girl and the message that she's interested in me has been passed to me several times—sometimes quite bluntly—through various members of her entourage over the past month or so. I look up from her hand to her face and find her dark eyes studying me intensely. Her lips shine with some sort of gloss I'm pretty sure would taste like strawberry.

Tearing my eyes away, I turn to the 2p machine, feeling in my pockets for change—desperate for a distraction. As I feed a couple of lint covered coins into the machine, I feel her eyes boring into me. I imagine this is how a gazelle must feel when it knows it's being stalked by a lioness.

She pushes up onto her tiptoes and kisses me on the cheek. "For luck," she murmurs.

I'm lost for words. The spot where her lips touched my skin burns like acid. This is not how I envisioned today going—not that anything that's happened recently is anything I could have foreseen. But why not? Why shouldn't I be happy that she's kissed me? We're both single and she's hot. I mean, I know exactly why I shouldn't and why it doesn't quite feel right, but I push those thoughts aside before they can fully form.

Chloe seems to sense my acceptance and leans into me, resting her head against my arm as we watch the coins make their way onto the retracting shelf of copper discs. Her hair smells of fruit and perfume and it floods my senses.

"So, who's the new girl?"

I blink several times as her question jolts me back to the present. *Crystal.* "She's, umm, Sera's cousin from Europe," I lie.

She nudges me and grins. "I was worried she might be your new girlfriend."

My jaw tenses and I focus on the shelf of coins as it moves backwards and forwards. "No. Definitely not. Besides, she's got something going on with Jordan."

Chloe laughs and strokes her fingers down my back. "Maybe you should talk to your friends more often."

"What do you mean?"

"Well, it seems pretty clear to me that Jordan's with Sera," she says, stepping back a little at my tone. "They were all over each other a few minutes ago."

My heart plummets and my mouth runs dry. The noisy arcade seems silent as I turn and look back across the room at the group. Blood pounds in my ears as I watch Jordan and Sera cuddled up together in the booth, looking extremely happy.

As I turn back to face Chloe, however, something else catches my eye. *Crystal.* Standing near the grabber machines a couple of meters away, her face is unreadable.

I open my mouth to call out to her, but she turns and disappears into the crowd.

CHAPTER EIGHTEEN

Crystal

Pushing my way towards the entrance, I shove open the doors and the cool night air makes me gasp. I make my way to a low wall and sit down, my face burning even as my body shivers with ice cold humiliation. I really thought that Dylan and I had a connection—that he cared about me.

Anger bubbles inside me, but I'm not angry at Dylan. I'm angry at myself—angry for letting myself think it was acceptable to get distracted. A boy? My parents would be so disappointed. Seeing Jordan and Sera so happy made me forget and for a fleeting moment, happiness seemed like such a simple thing. In reality, it was a fleeting moment of recklessness in which I forgot where I was—who I am. As future queen of Starlatten, I have far more important things to concern myself with than happiness. Just like my grief, I can deal with happiness when I get home.

The familiar wave of nausea swells in my gut as I think about getting home. This is why I can't afford to lose focus: getting home is all that matters. Why am I here, laughing like everything is okay—like everything is 'normal'?

I draw a sharp intake of breath at the sudden clarity. I need to be back at Sera's house with Dr. Oakstone. What is he working on? Has he found a way to get me home?

"Crystal?"

I look up to find Dylan standing a few steps away. He opens his mouth to speak but then—with an almost imperceptible shake of his head—shuts it again.

"We need to go." I stand with renewed determination. "I have to get back to Dr. Oakstone."

Dylan takes a step toward me.

I turn towards the entrance. "I'll go tell the others."

He takes another step towards me, his eyes shining with something I don't want to see—something I don't have time for.

"What?" Annoyance nips at my edges as I force myself to maintain eye contact. "Why aren't you saying anything?"

As Dylan closes the gap between us, my heart thuds so fiercely it makes my body tremble. He hasn't taken his eyes off mine for a second and I watch with a slight frown as we stand there, staring in silence. Finally, I'm unable to bear it and I open my mouth to speak.

He speaks first.

"I'm sorry."

"Sorry?" I echo. "For what?"

"For being an idiot." Breaking eye contact, he studies the ground between us for a moment and when he lifts his head again, his cheeks are pinker than before. "I saw you and Jordan together and I jumped to conclusions. Before you say anything, I know he and Sera seem to have got together and, well ... that's why I'm an idiot."

"You don't owe me an explanation," I say. "Besides, your pretty friend doesn't seem to think you're an idiot."

The spiteful words escape my lips before I even really know I'm thinking them. It seems the pang of jealousy I felt when I saw Dylan and that girl together has reached the surface, erupting without warning. I force myself to meet Dylan's eyes again, half expecting to see the disgust I feel for myself mirrored there. Instead, I only see sadness.

"Crystal." He shakes his head. "It's been, what ... three days since we found you? My entire perception of the universe has shifted, and I've seen things I couldn't have dreamed of. It sometimes still feels like a dream."

I stare at the ground, my head pounding in time with my heart. Has it really only been three days since I crashed onto this planet?

"Crystal?" Dylan says, his voice soft but edged with urgency. "I need you to listen to this, because I don't know if I'll have the courage to say it again."

I drag my gaze from the ground, forcing myself to look at him, and pushing down the urge to move the strand of hair falling across his forehead.

"I've never met anyone like you," he breathes.

"That's because I'm from another planet."

"That's not what I mean," he continues with a slight shake of his head. "I feel like I've known you for a lot longer than three days. I honestly can't explain it, but when I'm around you, I feel different—calmer, centred."

My eyes widen and I take a small step back at hearing my own thoughts—feelings—recited. How is it possible?

Dylan pauses for a second, his eyes narrowing as though worried I might run. "With everything that's going on at the moment, it seems ridiculous to even consider ..."

Panic flutters in my chest and I take another step back. I need to focus—I *should* focus. "I need to get back to Oakstone. I have to get home."

Dylan's face falls, and he nods in understanding, but neither of us move. Staring up at him, feeling that pull between us, I find myself taking a step towards him instead. I tell myself it's because I want to tell him that it's okay— that I feel it too—but it's reckless and stupid and ...

He reaches out and traces the side of my face, causing the muscles in my legs turn to liquid ... causing me to lean forward, closing what little gap between us there was.

Dylan reaches for me, placing his mouth on mine. All thought and reason evaporate as I melt into him—my heart exploding at the softness of his lips.

We pull apart and I swallow—my entire body shaking with each thunderous pulse of my heart. Dylan watches me, concern etched on his face.

"This ..." he breathes. "We shouldn't ..."

Something settles in me at his words—overriding all logic and common sense. My life is in tatters and amidst all the 'what ifs' and 'maybes', I know one thing for certain: Dylan makes me feel happy and safe. I reach up and brush the hair from his forehead.

"I've never really done something I shouldn't," I say. "So maybe that's a good enough reason why we should."

Dylan watches me for a moment, and I see the same back and forth playing out in his golden-brown eyes. I begin to wonder whether logic and common sense will win, but then he reaches for me.

Pulling me to him, he moves his hands up my back into my curls and kisses me again. I smile against his mouth and as the kiss deepens, I wonder how I ever contemplated not choosing this.

When we finally pull apart, flushed and breathless, Dylan holds me close and I lay my head on his chest.

"Let's get the others and go see what Oakstone's up to," he murmurs into my hair. "I want to get answers for you."

I sigh into his chest. "Thank you."

"I'm glad we found you."

"I'm glad you found me too." I look up to find his eyes dark with emotion as he leans down and kisses me again.

CHAPTER NINETEEN

Crystal

Sitting on a tall chair in Sera's kitchen, I take cautious sips of something called 'coffee', which Linda insists helps to wake you up. She slept at Sera's house last night too. I'm not sure I need waking up. My heart hasn't stopped racing since Sera told me that everyone is on their way over and should arrive any minute. Flutters of excitement rise in my chest at the thought of seeing Dylan, but at the same time I'm terrified. What if he's changed his mind? What if he's realised how ridiculous it is? I take a deep breath and concentrate on the warm brown liquid in my cup.

"Oakstone's still out cold," Linda announces from the doorway.

Worry wraps cold hands around my throat. "Should I try and heal him some more? Do we need to call for human medical assistance?"

Sera chokes on her mouthful of coffee.

"Human medical assistance?" Linda pulls herself up onto a chair with a giggle. "That's brilliant."

"Don't worry, Crystal." Sera reaches out and pats my arm. "He was up really late working on the laptop, and he wouldn't have slept the night before either. He probably just needs rest."

I nod in agreement. The poor man has been through quite an ordeal. I know all too well what it's like to lose everything, forced to put your trust in a group of strangers.

The doorbell sounds and I jump out of my skin as Sera slides off her stool and goes to answer it. The next few moments are agony as I clasp my cup and listen to the voices moving down the hall.

The door swings open revealing Jordan holding Sera's hand with Eddie and Dylan behind, deep in conversation.

"Here's to another day of adventure," Jordan announces as he leaps up onto a stool beside Sera.

"Coffee's just brewed," Linda announces to the new arrivals. "Help yourselves."

Jordan catches my eye and closes one eye at me while smiling. I smile back in an attempt to hide my confusion. Why does he keep doing that?

"Good morning."

My senses are swept up in a mix of mint and freshly baked bread as Dylan's arms wrap around my waist, his lips brushing my neck. I inhale and try not to fall off my stool as happiness swirls through my body, my heart racing.

"Good morning to you too," I murmur, kissing his cheek.

"Right," Jordan booms, slapping his notebook down on the table. "Let's bring this meeting to order."

"Whoa," Eddie interrupts. "Are we seriously going to ignore what's going on here?"

I look around, my confusion mirrored on everyone else's faces. "What do you mean, Eddie?"

"You two." Eddie waggles his finger at me and Dylan. "What is *this*?"

My cheeks grow hot as Linda laughs and elbows her brother. "What does it look like?"

Eddie frowns and mutters into his coffee.

"Erm, Jordan?" Linda coughs. "I have something I'd like to start the meeting with, if that's okay?"

"I was only joking, Linda." He raises an eyebrow at her serious tone. "What's up?"

Something's wrong. I don't know Linda well, but I can tell from the way she's fidgeting that she's nervous. "Are you all right, Linda?"

"Okay." She takes a deep breath and sets her cup down with purpose. "I have a confession to make and you're not going to like it." She turns and faces her brother. "Especially you."

Eddie claws his hand over his face. "For crying out loud, Linda. What have you done now?"

"Remember when we went to look for Green Eyes and you and Jordan lost me for a while?" Linda fiddles with the edge of the table, her dark fringe hanging over her eyes. Despite her golden skin, she seems unusually pale. "Well, I wasn't exactly lost," she continues. "I found Green Eyes."

Everyone erupts into a chorus of raised voices and exclamations. Flinching at the sudden roar of noise, I watch speechless as the group leap from their stools and surround Linda, bombarding her with questions and berating her for her recklessness.

"Let her talk," I plead, but my voice is lost amongst the chaos. I try again, louder, but with no success.

Frustration fizzes in my limbs and I slip off my stool and shout at the top of my voice. Still nothing. In desperation, I find myself looking around the room for something—anything—to get their attention.

Spotting a jug of water sitting on the counter, an idea begins to form. I focus on my amulet, allowing the purple warmth to flow through me as I lift the water clean out of the jug. Moving the trembling sphere of liquid across the kitchen, I hold it—hovering—high above the squabbling group.

Wrinkling my nose in concentration, I begin to spin the orb around and around, faster and faster. As it spins, I loosen my hold just enough to allow tiny drops of water to spin out and rain down on them.

Sera notices first.

"Hey! Why is it raining in my kitchen?" She shrieks, trying unsuccessfully to cover her hair with her hands.

I keep my attention on the shrinking sphere until the last few drops of water spin out, landing with tiny splashes around the room. As the purple energy retracts, I exhale. I note with a smile that the shouting and arguing has stopped, but when I look at the group, I gasp, my hand flying to my mouth. Standing shocked, silent and bedraggled, everyone stares at me with looks of confusion and annoyance.

"Sorry," I mumble, biting my lip. "You were all shouting, and I couldn't get you to stop."

Jordan frowns. "I don't suppose your weird and wonderful powers can dry out my notebook?"

"I really am sorry." I shake my head, stifling a laugh. "I didn't think there was that much water."

"Let's take this outside," Sera suggests, tying her damp hair up in a ponytail. "The sun is shining, and we might dry off a little faster."

As people start to make their way to the glass doors leading to the seating area outside, I finally summon the courage to look at Dylan. He and Eddie seem to have taken the worst of the downpour. The water has darkened his hair and his t-shirt clings to his chest and stomach in a way that makes my heart skip a beat. I take a step towards him, hoping he's not too cross.

"Are you okay?" I reach up and run my fingers through his damp hair, tracing a drop of water as it runs down his cheek and tingling with the thrill of being allowed to touch him.

He grins and pulls me towards him. "Second shower of the day and it's not even lunchtime."

CHAPTER TWENTY

Dylan

"Eddie, mate. Sit down already."

I've been watching Eddie pace up and down the long patio, periodically shaking the droplets of water out of his hair, for the past five minutes. I'm worried about him. He can be so intense sometimes. Especially when it comes to Linda. They have a super weird dynamic that I still don't fully understand even after thirteen years.

With a reluctant grunt, Eddie pulls up a chair and sits beside me, folding his arms.

"Go on then," he says to his sister. "Tell us the tale of your lack of responsibility."

Linda shoots him a withering look before addressing the group. "Like I said, I found Green Eyes. He was down one of the alleyways and I confronted him." She pauses, looking warily at Eddie, who's staring at a fixed point on the ground. "His name is Jake," she continues. "He didn't know what an amulet was—and said I was talking nonsense when I suggested he might be from another planet—but he wants to meet you, Crystal."

My stomach twists and annoyance bubbles into anger. I'm about to speak when Eddie jumps to his feet.

"Are you kidding me?" he barks. "Of course, the strange psychopath wants to meet the mysterious girl from another planet. Of course, he told you *he*'s not from another planet. Why didn't you just give him all our social media passwords while you were at it?"

"Eddie," Jordan soothes.

I shake my head, in disbelief. "He's got a point, Linda. You've given him a lot of information that could put Crystal in danger."

"What exactly did you find out about *him*, Linda?" Eddie continues, batting away Jordan's attempts to pull him back down to his seat. "What does he want? Why was he watching us? Why did he attack you? Was he behind Oakstone's attempted murder?"

Linda has turned a curious shade of green and if I wasn't so disappointed, I might feel sorry for her.

"I didn't get a chance to ask," she mumbles. "You and Jordan came looking for me and I knew if you saw him, you'd overreact. I arranged a time for us to all meet up and left."

When Crystal stands, I let her hand slip from mine, realising how tightly I've been holding it. She walks over to Linda, placing a hand on her back.

"It's okay, Linda. You found a piece of the puzzle, which means we're closer to finding answers than we were yesterday. Thank you."

Eddie rolls his eyes. "So, when and where are we meeting this hardened criminal? Midnight in his secret lair?"

"Stop being such a jerk, Eddie," Linda bites back, tears forming behind her fringe.

As much as I wish she'd involved us sooner, Crystal's right. Linda was only trying to help, and this is the first lead we've had. Even if it's a dangerous one.

"When are we meeting him, Linda?" I ask, trying to keep the worry from my voice.

"Midday at Crestfield park."

Everyone but Crystal looks at watches or pulls out phones.

"Are you kidding me?" Eddie exclaims. "That's less than an hour from now."

I stretch, placing my hands behind my neck. "If we're going to make this meeting, we need to leave in half an hour at the latest. Which means, we need to start thinking of a plan—quick."

After twenty minutes of intense discussion, we've settled on a plan. There are a lot of ifs and buts, but we've got a back-up plan too. It's going to work. It's a good plan. I try not to wonder why it feels like I'm convincing myself.

"What do you think, Crystal?" I squeeze her knee. She's been really quiet throughout the whole discussion and I'm worried.

"Sorry," she says, her eyes distant. "I lost track of what you were saying."

I smile and rest my hand on her shoulder. "We were just saying we don't think you should come to the meeting."

"What?" She shrugs my hand from her shoulder, her eyes blazing. "Why shouldn't I go?"

I try and fail to find the words to explain. Because I want to keep you safe? Because I don't want to lose you? They all seem selfish and lacking in substance. I close my mouth.

"Because we don't know this guy," Jordan jumps in. "It's not safe. If he's connected to the guy who tried to kill Oakstone—"

"Then they were after your pod, and that means after you," I finish, giving Jordan a grateful smile.

"That is the biggest pile of glambak I've ever heard," Crystal fumes. Standing up, she fixes everyone with a furious stare. "Going down the alley looking for Green Eyes, or whatever his name is, was dangerous. Bringing Dr. Oakstone here was dangerous. Just being around me is dangerous. Things have been dangerous since you found me and that's not going to change until we find out what's going on."

I stand and take hold of her hands, which are balled up into tight fists. "I know, but that doesn't mean we don't want to keep you safe." I lower my voice and lean closer. "*I* want to keep you safe."

She sighs and her hands relax a little. "I understand why you're concerned. You're forgetting something though." She reaches inside her shirt and pulls out her amulet, the morning sunlight reflects off it, dazzling me. "I'm dangerous too."

"Morning, Doc," Jordan calls.

I turn to see Oakstone standing in the doorway to the kitchen, his hair dishevelled, and his expression bewildered.

He lifts a hand in response. "What time is it? I feel like I've been asleep for weeks."

"You were working on your computer for most of yesterday." Crystal steps towards him. "Did you find anything?"

Oakstone adjusts his glasses and frowns for a moment, as though trying to remember. Then his eyes light up as if someone flicked a switch. "I was mapping the data from when your pod entered Earth's atmosphere and comparing it to all the other data I could find from the last couple of decades."

"Ooh!" Jordan exclaims. "To see if any other ships have visited Earth before."

"Yes." Oakstone grins.

My heart is racing. "And?"

"And, I might have found something." He pauses, looking behind him at the kitchen. "Can I get a cup of coffee or something? I'm running on empty here."

Everyone stands in a chorus of scraping chairs and we traipse back into the kitchen.

"Did it rain in here?" Oakstone asks, looking around at the wet surfaces.

"Long story." I smile at Crystal, who turns pink.

Everything moves in painful slow motion as Oakstone fills a cup from the coffee maker and sips it. I'm itching to push for more information and suspense hangs in the air like static.

"So," he begins at long last. "According to my findings, it would appear that another similar entrance was made seven years ago."

"Another pod?" I ask.

Oakstone takes a deep swig of his coffee and nods. "It might not have been a 'pod' as such, but a craft of some description. Yes, I believe so."

Crystal's hand tightens around mine. "Could it have come from my planet?"

"There's really no way to tell." Oakstone smiles apologetically.

I watch as Crystal frowns and chews her lip. "I just don't understand it," she says. "Why would anyone come to Earth?"

"Thanks a lot." Sera snorts, flicking her long hair over her shoulder.

Crystal's eyes widen. "No, no! That's not what I meant."

I cough to hide the laughter bubbling in my throat. "What exactly did you mean?"

"I mean, we were aware of primitive life in this solar system, but we would never have visited for fear of interfering in your evolution. It goes against intergalactic code."

I cringe, secretly enjoying Crystal's attempt to dig herself out of the hole. "Primitive, huh?"

Crystal gapes at me and I laugh, pulling her against me.

"Intergalactic code?" Oakstone asks. "What do you mean?"

"It's called the Alayna Treaty," Crystal says. "It was agreed by twenty planets with advanced life scattered in and around several adjacent solar systems. There are many rules covering a lot of things, but the Alayna treaty was created because of one particular incident."

A hush settles over us. I have to resist the urge to pinch myself. I mean, I always believed there was life out there—you'd have to be arrogant not to—but to have it confirmed? To discover there are dozens of planets with treaties and spaceships? My brain aches at the concept.

"You see," Crystal continues. "Life originated on just two planets—the home planets—but eventually people looked to explore and colonise new ones. Usually, it was because they were fleeing war or persecution, but sometimes it was just for adventure. Finding an uninhabited planet capable of sustaining life is incredibly rare. Starlatten was one such planet."

"Elaini and Jetzia!" Linda exclaims.

"Exactly." Crystal smiles. "As people were searching for new planets to colonise, a group of exiles from one of the home planets travelled into a different solar system. They came across a planet inhabited by a primitive species. They were living in colonies, with language and trade, but were nowhere near intergalactic or even interplanetary travel. The people called themselves the Alayna. The exiles decided to try and integrate with the Alayna, who welcomed them with open arms.

"Unfortunately, the exiles transmitted some sort of virus to the Alayna, who didn't have the ability to treat it. When the first person died, they blamed the exiles and killed them before they could find a cure. Over 85% of their planet's population was wiped out over its next orbit."

"Whoa," I breathe. "That's awful."

Crystal gives a solemn nod. "It was because of that, that a treaty was signed by all advanced planets. No contact would be made with a primitive species. We'd leave them to evolve and develop until they could reach out to us."

"I can't even begin to process all this." Oakstone leans his elbows on the counter and runs both his hands through his mop of hair. "It's incredible."

"What happened to the Alayna?" Jordan asks. "What happened to the ones who survived?"

"The near extinction set them back thousands of orbits. They were monitored from a distance for a while, but once it was clear they weren't extinct, they were left alone." Crystal looks around the table. "I'm sorry. I really didn't mean any offence by calling you primitive."

"Don't worry," I say, pressing a kiss to her neck. "Compared to what you know, I guess we are primitive."

"So, you're saying that no one would come to Earth because of this treaty?" Oakstone asks, pouring himself another coffee.

Crystal nods.

"So, why would someone defy the treaty?" he mulls.

"Perhaps they wanted to hide?" I suggest.

Crystal turns to look at me, her eyes curious. "What do you mean?"

I pause—the thought still developing in my mind. "I mean, if I wanted to hide, I'd go somewhere I wasn't allowed to go. No one would bother looking here, would they?"

"Why would someone want to hide though?" Eddie asks. "Can you think of anything important or out of the ordinary that happened seven years ago, Crystal?"

"That's if the pod came from your planet in the first place," Oakstone clarifies. "It could be from any of the advanced planets you mentioned."

"I'm not sure what seven Earth orbits would be on Starlatten," Crystal says, "but there hasn't been any unrest for millennia. Starlatten is well known for being peaceful."

"Didn't you say someone attacked your ship?" Oakstone asks, his eyebrows raised. "Why would they do that if you're such a peaceful planet?"

Crystal tenses between my arms and I frown at the doctor. I know he doesn't really know us and he's being all scientific, but a little sensitivity wouldn't go amiss. Her fists have clenched again, her breathing is shallow. Gently, I unfold her fingers, circling my thumbs in her palms.

"It's okay," I murmur in her ear. "Breathe."

Crystal squeezes my hands and takes a shaky breath. "Zarbilian." She says the word as if it leaves a bad taste in her mouth. "They are the most recent planet to be colonised and they're the ones who murdered my family."

Realisation dawns on Oakstone's face. "I'm sorry," he says. "I got a little swept up in everything. It doesn't quite feel real. I'm so sorry for your loss."

Crystal gives a small smile. "Thank you."

"You never did tell us, Crystal," Jordan says, flicking back through his notebook. "Do you have any idea why they might have attacked your ship?"

Crystal shakes her head. "Zarbilian is one of our sister planets, colonised by people from Starlatten and under our rule. I'm not sure why, but they weren't happy about it. It was one of the reasons we were on our way to the peace talks on Ankaria. The morning of the attack, my father received word that an unknown people had joined the colony on Zarbilian, so perhaps that has something to do with it."

"More unanswered questions," I mutter, more to myself than anyone.

"I'm sorry to press you," Oakstone says, "but did anything happen with the Zarbilian a long time before the attack?"

Crystal closes her eyes in concentration for a moment before shaking her head. "I'm sorry. I can't think of anything."

"So, are we thinking it might be someone from Zarbilian, hiding on Earth?" Jordan asks, tapping the pen against his chin. "Could it be this Jake guy?"

"It couldn't be," Linda answers. "He'd have been a little kid seven years ago."

Oakstone nods. "If you're telling me he's around your age, it does seem unlikely. Perhaps it's the person that broke into my laboratory? That is, if it's even someone from Zarbilian or Starlatten. From what you've told us, it could have been a lawbreaker from any one of several planets."

My mind conjures images of alien fugitives hiding on Earth and the possible conspiracy theories. "I hate to say it," I sigh, looking at Eddie and grimacing, "but we need to go to this meet up."

"What time is it?" Linda gasps.

I glance at my watch. "Time to go. We're late."

Crystal reaches out and puts a hand on my arm. "I know you've already got a plan, but I think I might have another idea."

CHAPTER TWENTY-ONE

Jake

My neck cracks as I stand and stretch. I've been sitting on the rusted orange roundabout at the centre of the playground for almost an hour. I mean, it's not like I have anywhere else to be, but the waiting is starting to make my blood boil.

What I wouldn't give for four walls and a roof right now. I suppose I'm lucky it's summer otherwise sleeping rough would be very different. Glancing at my watch again through its cracked face, I see it's almost 1pm. My stomach rumbles as if to punctuate the point. I'm at the point of contemplating rooting through the trash when I notice two men walking towards me.

Where's Linda? Is this a set up? Of course, it is. *Aliens.* What a load of rubbish. I'm a complete idiot. Every muscle in my body tenses, ready to fight or run. I'm not sure which yet. Then I realise, I recognise the older man. I've seen his photo on the news. Oakstone—the man whose house I've been watching. I don't recognise the other guy and as they walk closer, I see he's around my age. What the heck is going on? I take a step back, ready to run.

"Jake?" the younger one calls. "We just want to talk. We're friends of Linda's."

My eyes dart side to side, assessing the quickest way out of the playground. "Oh yeah?" I call back. "Where is she? She's late."

Oakstone raises his hands too. "We're here to take you to her."

I laugh. "That's not what we agreed."

"Yeah, well *we* didn't agree to anything." The younger one frowns. "We need to know you're alone."

"Can you see anyone?" I scoff, gesturing around me towards the surrounding empty fields.

"Just because we can't see anyone, doesn't mean they're not there," Oakstone replies.

I stare them down, my chin raised in defiance. "So, I'm supposed to just trust you and do whatever you say?"

The younger one shrugs. "If you want to find out more about your amulet, then yes."

A dozen scenarios run through my mind, but in reality, it boils down to two: run away and face the wrath of my uncle when I return with nothing or go with these two and face whatever danger lies ahead. The real question is, which is the more dangerous option? These guys or my uncle? It's a no-brainer.

"Fine," I say through gritted teeth. "I'll come."

Oakstone and blondie glance at each other with what looks like relief. I take a few steps towards them and they reach to take my arms, but I shrug them off. I'm coming, but there's a limit to my cooperation.

We walk out of the park and down the path towards the road. As we approach, a shiny black Lexus with tinted windows pulls up. Who are these guys?

Blondie opens the door and pushes me towards the back seat. As I climb in, Oakstone swaps places with the driver, who I realise with surprise is Linda's brother. He opens the other back door and slides in beside me, his dark eyes filled with menace. Alarm bells scream inside my skull and my muscles tense in preparation to fight my way out of the car. Then the person in the passenger seat turns around to face me.

A girl with brown curls and big brown eyes gives me an apologetic smile as she reaches around her seat and touches my head. "Sorry…"

Darkness. Why is it dark? My eyelids have never felt so heavy. It takes all my strength to open them and I instantly regret it as bright light sears my retinas.

"Where am I?" I demand. I try to raise my arm to shield my eyes, but my hands are tied behind my back. "What the hell? Why am I tied up?"

"Precautions, mate. Can't have someone like you running loose now, can we?"

"I'm not your 'mate'," I bite back. From the sneering tone, I assume it must be Linda's brother.

"Will someone stop shining that bloody torch in his eyes?"

The light moves away from my face with a disappointed sigh. My eyeballs instantly relieved, I dare to open my eyes once more, but I'm not prepared for what I see.

I'm sitting on an office chair in a small square room with what look like metal walls, surrounded by stacks of books, boxes and odd-looking equipment. Eight people stand before me, their shadows giant on the walls behind them.

I recognise Oakstone, the tall blond guy, Linda's brother and ... Linda. She meets my gaze with an apologetic shrug. I don't recognise the others, although there's something about the girl with the long curly hair ...

"Hey!" I shout as the memory rushes back to me. "What did you do to me?"

The tall blond-haired guy steps in front of her. "Look, we didn't know if you could be trusted. We had to make sure you were alone and weren't being followed."

I snort. "So, what now? You're going to torture me?"

"Jake?" Linda steps forward and crouches down in front of me. Her brother steps forward too but she flashes him a look which makes him retreat. "I know you want to know what's going on just as much as we do. We need to trust each other."

I chew my lip as I study her face. Her dark brown eyes search mine looking for, what? Agreement? Understanding? I want answers. Something seriously weird is going on and somehow this lot have some of the missing answers.

"Fine." I sigh. "What do you want to know?"

"We want to know how you got this." The girl with the curly hair steps forward, this time holding something shiny up to the light.

It's my necklace. "Hey! Give that back!" I struggle against the ties around my wrists, my teeth grinding. "How dare you take my stuff!"

"Jake," Oakstone soothes. "We only wanted to confirm what we think it might be. You can have it back once we've talked."

"And what do you think it is?" I spit. "It's just a necklace."

"It's not just a necklace, Jake." The curly-haired girl pulls a similar looking purple necklace from her top and holds it up for me to see.

"Oh." I raise my eyebrows. "You're the alien, huh?"

Everyone turns and glares at Linda, who picks at something on her jeans.

"Jake," the alien girl steps closer, "can you tell us anything about your amulet?"

I watch in disbelief as one of the other guys takes out a notebook and pen, watching me expectantly.

"Sure, Veronica Mars," I scoff. "I was given it by a magic fairy in the woods after I saved a gnome from a gingerbread dragon."

Linda sighs from where she's still crouched. "Please?" she pleads. "We'll tell you everything if you'll just tell us what you know."

"Fine."

"Can we untie him?" Linda asks. "He's going to cooperate and it's not like he can go anywhere."

"Absolutely not," Eddie barks. "Seriously, Linda? He's not a stray puppy. If you can't keep it together, you can go and wait outside."

"Jake?" Curls interrupts. "You were going to tell us about the amulet."

"Sure." I smirk. "I found it in a box in my uncle's kitchen. I liked it, so I stole it. The end."

Disappointment flashes across her face, but she shakes it off. "Who is your uncle?"

How do I answer this? I decide there's no harm telling them the truth. "He's not a nice man. He wants you guys."

"Why does he want us?" she asks.

"You tell me."

Oakstone pulls up another chair. "Your uncle. Do you live with him?"

"Yes."

"Where are your parents?"

His question catches me off guard. I should tell him it's none of his business but the truth trips off my tongue before I can stop it. "I don't know. I don't remember them. Spare me the look of pity," I snarl at Curls. "I'm a big boy."

"A very sad story." Linda's brother sighs. "Look, this is getting nowhere fast. I thought we were going to get answers?"

"Jake?" Curls asks. "Will you let me touch your head?"

My eyebrows shoot up at the unusual question. "Sure thing, love." I look over at Blondie and wink for good measure. "However you get your kicks."

She frowns at me and steps closer. "Just stay still, okay?"

CHAPTER **TWENTY-TWO**

Crystal

It happens quicker than before. This time, it's not like Linda's memory. It's so much more confusing. It's dark, and everywhere I look, I see ghostly flashes of different memories. I realise I haven't told him what to think about. Perhaps it's for the best. Concentrating my efforts, I stare at the blurry image in front of me until a hard shove knocks me forward.

I'm up against a wall, my feet off the ground as invisible hands grip my throat. Every fibre of my being resonates with icy fear as the man in front of me comes into focus, his awful tawny eyes boring into my soul like hot coals. I gasp and struggle, desperate to get away.

He releases me and I'm on the floor. I'm running. I'm so sad, scared and lonely all at the same time. Another hard shove pushes the breath out of me as I fall back into darkness.

Poor Jake. That terrifying man must be his uncle—the man who tried to kill Oakstone. Who is he? How is he using powers like mine? Is Jake's amulet his? I need more information. A flash of green catches my eye and before I can focus on it, a shove pushes me through.

An old box is in my hands. The amulet. Something calls to me. I need to take it. There's something ...

Before I can even focus on where I am, the shove knocks me back into the swirling mix of memories. I frantically scan the flashing images around me, but there's too many. It would take forever to go through them all. I'm losing focus. Everything's getting fainter. The next shove knocks the air out of me, and I fall backwards.

"Crystal!"

I blink, finding myself in Dylan's arms.

"What happened?" he asks. "Are you okay?"

I can't answer him. The emotions I felt in Jake's head are still swirling around my bloodstream like a mix of ice water and flames. Instead, I turn to Jake. "You recognised it didn't you?"

He frowns. "What are you talking about?"

"The amulet. When you opened the box, it called to you."

"What the hell?" His green eyes flicker with anger and disbelief. "You've been inside my head?"

"Jake, I'm trying to help you." I step away from Dylan's arms, the room spinning a little as I do. "That's why you took it. You knew it didn't belong to him."

Jake's face is dark as he slumps against his restraints. "It's just a stupid necklace."

"Please let me try again," I ask, an idea forming in my mind. "I think I can get you answers. I just need more power."

I wait until he looks at me.

"Fine," he mumbles. "What do I need to do?"

I take Jake's amulet from my pocket. "I need you to wear this and try to remember as far back as you can. Try and think about your earliest memories of your uncle. Try and think about your parents."

"I told you, I can't remember them." He flinches as I fasten the amulet around his neck.

Placing one hand on Jake's head, I touch the other to the amulet resting below his collar bone. His heartbeat pulses against my fingertips. "Just try, okay?"

I have no idea if this will work, but I close my eyes and summon the purple energy—hoping.

This time it's different. The flashing images are gone, and I'm surrounded by a thick yellowish fog. It obscures my vision like it's trying to actively creep in and block my other senses—to conceal. I'm aware of something ... a voice? A smell? Something, just on the other side of the fog, always just out of reach. It reminds me of the shadow I felt when I landed on Earth and dread fills my bones.

Come on Jake. I will him to concentrate harder and my heart fills with pity. How awful to not remember your parents. I push the thought away before my own grief can wrap its ice-cold claws around my heart. Instead, I concentrate on my amulet and the gleaming, warm, pulsing purple light emanating from inside me. It seems so clear and sharp compared to the fog.

No sooner have I thought it, the purple light seems to throb, spreading out around me like an aura, dispersing the dense yellow and sending it fleeing into the dark corners. Feeling more confident, I push through the now depleted fog towards the sounds I'm sure I heard.

As the scene comes into focus, my eyes open wide and my breath catches in my throat. Starlatten. It's not somewhere I recognise, but the three moons and purple grass are unmistakable. I'm filled with euphoria at seeing my home but wracked by a wave of homesickness and loss as I wonder whether I'll ever see this place again.

I realise with a jolt, that unlike my previous mind explorations, I'm not seeing this memory through someone else's eyes. I can't smell or touch anything. I'm a ghost on the outside of a scene playing out.

Standing in front of me are a couple dressed in the robes ambassadors and members of the government wear. The man is accompanied by two tall, red-robed Dyja and as I look closer, I see the adornment on his robes to signify he is indeed an ambassador. I step closer still to get a better look at his face. I know him, but from where?

"How long will you be, Father?"

I turn and see a young boy between ten and twelve orbits old, standing just behind his mother. He has wavy, sandy blonde hair and piercing green eyes with thick dark lashes. Jake!

My gasp is so loud, I worry for a moment the people in front of me will hear. Oh, my stars ... Jake is from Starlatten. I really did smell prasalia flowers when I saw him in Linda's

memory. I still can't make sense of it though, so I push the puzzle from my mind and concentrate on the memory in front of me.

"I'll be back as soon as I can, Jaik," the ambassador says, his face filled with sadness. "I'm sorry I have to leave again so soon, but there's talk of an uprising on Zarbilian and we just can't let that happen."

The woman with long wavy hair the same colour as Jake's puts a hand on both her husband and son's shoulders. "We understand. Just stay safe."

The words have no sooner left her lips when the Dyja to the ambassador's left crumples to the floor, right by my feet. I jump back in surprise, but before anyone can react, the other Dyja crumples in the same way. There's something about the grotesque way they lie there on the floor that tells me they're dead. Jake's mother screams. I clap a hand over my mouth and I'm not sure if it's to stop me screaming or being sick.

Two hooded figures appear, their faces concealed as they grab hold of mother and son and I watch in horror as they strain against them, shouting against the gloved hands covering their mouths. Jake's eyes flash with fear and anger as he tries to break free.

"You will meet our demands," the taller of the two masked figures growls. "Or you will never see your family again."

Jake's father puts out his hands to plead, but before he can utter a word, a blinding light flashes behind the masked men, forcing me to shield my eyes.

When I open my eyes again, I'm back in the fog. No! I need to find out more. My heart racing, I look around, pushing out beams of purple. When I hear sobbing, I take a deep breath and step towards it.

I'm in a dark room. It's damp, cold and definitely not Starlatten. Earth? My brain throbs with the pressure of staying in Jake's head and the relevance of the information I've discovered but I have to stay focused for just a bit longer. I need to know what happened next.

The sobbing is coming from Jake. He and his mother are tied to chairs, back-to-back as she frantically tries to free his hands.

"When you get free," she whispers, "you have to run. Run fast and far. Use your amulet to send an emergency signal. Someone will find you."

"I can't leave you." Jake sobs. "I can't."

I'm standing so close to them I can see the tears streaming down Jake's cheeks. I almost reach out to help but stop myself. There's no point. This all happened many orbits ago. My own eyes sting with tears as I look at Jake, so young and helpless.

With one final grunt of effort, Jake's mother gets him free. He leans forward and unties his feet, before standing and trying to untie his mother.

"There's no time, Jaik!" she hisses.

He kneels by her feet, putting his head on her knees. "I can't ..."

"Look at me," she pleads. "If he comes back and finds you free, he'll kill you. You have to run."

Wiping his tears on the back of his sleeve, Jake stands and kisses his mother on the forehead. No sooner has he taken a step towards the door however, it flies open, filled *by a tall dark figure with broad shoulders and chilling amber eyes.*

"Going somewhere?"

Jake freezes. The only sound is the pounding of my heart. The man steps forward, menace oozing from every atom.

"I was wondering if you were stupid enough to try and escape. Now I have my answer." He pauses, touching something around his neck.

I notice his yellow amulet for the first time.

"Your father is just as stupid," he continues. "It seems Ambassador Bazanat is unwilling to negotiate."

Bazanat. I frown. I've heard that name before. Of course, it's not unlikely. With my father being king, I'm familiar with most of the ambassadors.

"Don't you dare hurt him, Cadicus!" Jake's mother yells.

"Me? Hurt a child?" He smiles cruelly. "Do you think I'm a monster?"

Frozen with horror, I watch as the man clenches his fist in the air. Jake's mother gives a strangled gasp before flopping forward—her body limp and lifeless. Jake screams a scream that tears right through the centre of my soul. He flings himself on her body, howling between heart-wrenching sobs.

Tears blur my vision as I look at the man called Cadicus standing calm and emotionless by the door.

"Hopefully this will be the incentive your father needs," he says as he turns to leave.

I can't take any more. I cover my face with my hands and the scene disappears. The yellow fog is gone, replaced with cold, dark emptiness.

Dylan's voice sounds as though it's miles away. His arms stop me from floating away, but I'm still lost in darkness. Sounds and senses are disjointed, as if I'm a dozen broken pieces all floating in nothingness, trying to find each other. I must have pulled back from Jake's memories too fast.

Oh Jake. My heart could burst with sadness. Even in the darkness, my eyes are hot with tears and the lump in my throat erupts into sobs.

"Crystal? What's wrong?"

I want to answer Dylan, but I can't. I'm not there—the sound of his voice still muffled. Slowly, the pieces of Jake's memories start to fit together in my brain. Jake is from Starlatten. *Jaik*. His mother had called him Jaik. It's a slight difference in pronunciation but …

My eyes fly open and I sit up. "Jaik Bazanat!"

Blinking away my tears, I see several pairs of confused and concerned eyes, but I'm not looking for them. I'm looking for a particular pair of green ones.

Jaik is sitting much as I left him—tied to the chair, head down. I begin to stand, to make my way towards him, but Dylan tugs me back.

"What's going on, Crystal?" he asks, trying to move into my line of sight. "What did you see?"

I glance at him for the briefest of seconds before turning back to Jaik. "We need to untie him."

"What?" Eddie splutters. "I don't think so."

I could tell them, but it feels wrong. I need to speak to Jaik first. I need to be there. I just … The pain. I felt it all. I stare at Eddie, my eyes pleading. "Trust me."

"I trust you, Crystal," Linda announces with purpose. "I trust Jake too."

Before anyone can stop her, Linda starts untying him. I watch as he moves his hands to his lap, rubbing where the ties have dug into his skin, his head still down.

"Jaik?" I move to his side and kneel before him, placing my hands on his. "Do you remember?"

He gives the slightest of nods.

"I remember you," I whisper. "I couldn't put the pieces together at first, but I remember now. It's me, Crystal Akinara. Do you remember me?"

He frowns, seeming to sift through his memories. Having experienced the dense yellow fog inside his head, I know first-hand just how difficult that is.

"We spent the summer together when we were children," I continue. "Your father invited us to stay in Galeania for a few weeks." I pause and my stomach lurches as I realise the ugly truth. "I asked about you when we returned, but my parents said you were sick and avoided the question.

"I stopped asking after a while, as I could see they didn't want to tell me. I thought it was politics and our fathers had fallen out. In fact, I did try to reach out to you once or twice using my amulet, but it didn't work. Now I know why."

"I do remember you," he says, his voice hoarse. "I remember everything."

He stands so abruptly, the chair goes flying and I topple backwards, catching myself with my hands. The sound rattles around the storage unit and everyone moves forward. I scramble to my feet, holding out my hands to keep them back as Jaik strides to a corner, swiping at his eyes with the back of his hand.

"Can someone please explain what the hell is going on?" Eddie demands.

Oakstone steps forward, placing a hand on Eddie's shoulder. "Crystal? Could you please share what you've discovered?"

I glance over my shoulder at Jaik and my heart shatters. His arms wrapped around his head, his shoulders shake with muffled sobs. I decide I should probably tell everyone what I know. If only to give Jaik some time to come to terms with his memories.

"Jake is actually Jaik Bazanat, son of the Ambassador of Galeania, which is one of the largest cities on Starlatten. We met when we were children, which explains why I found him familiar in Linda's memories. I never saw him again and now I know why." Recalling the memories causes my stomach to lurch and I clutch my arms around myself as I sit down on a wooden box. "It seems that not long after we met, Jaik and his mother were kidnapped by Zarbilian rebels. A man called Cadicus hid them on Earth."

Oakstone gasps. "The entry into our atmosphere, seven years ago."

"It would seem that way. When the Ambassador refused to negotiate terms, Cadicus killed Jaik's mother. I didn't know any of this until now and I don't understand how it's not common knowledge on Starlatten."

"That's horrendous," Linda exclaims, her wide eyes fixed on Jaik as he rests against the metal wall, his arms raised above his head.

"Why is Jaik still alive?" Sera asks.

Jordan looks up from where he's scribbling away in his notebook. "Good question. Did you see what happened after that guy killed his mum?"

"No," I say, looking at Jaik. "I may need to use my amulet again."

CHAPTER TWENTY-THREE

Jaik

"No!" I push myself off the wall and stride towards them, my face twisted with rage. "I can tell you exactly what that monster did next. He tried to get my father to negotiate, but he wouldn't. So, he told my father he'd killed me, but he didn't—he did something worse.

"He blocked my memories and pretended he was my uncle, when in reality I was his slave—an object that might come in useful again in the future." I clench my fists, looking around for something to punch. There's so much pain and anger building inside me and I don't know how to make it stop.

"I'm so sorry," Linda croaks, her dark eyes wet with tears. "I can't even imagine how awful that must be."

I watch, speechless, as she steps forward and wraps her arms around me, her tiny frame dwarfed against mine. I hold my arms out to the side in surprise, staring at her in shock. When was the last time someone hugged me? I try to remember but can't. She squeezes tighter and I relax my arms. It's actually kind of nice.

Blondie breaks the silence. "I'm really sorry about your family, man. Looks like we're all working towards solving the same puzzle."

"Indeed." Oakstone nods, taking off his cracked glasses and inspecting them. "I think it's safe to assume that this 'Cadicus' is the one who burnt my laboratory to the ground and tried to kill me."

"Yes." Crystal gasps. "I saw his yellow amulet in Jaik's memories."

"Wait," the guy with the notebook interrupts. "So, is Cadicus from Starlatten or that Zarbilian planet?"

Crystal pauses for a moment, before looking at me.

I shrug. "I honestly don't know. I assume he's from Zarbilian if he was trying to negotiate terms, but most of Zarbilian are originally from Starlatten."

"So, the Zarbilian rebels were trying to undermine the Starlatten government seven years ago?" Oakstone sits down and motions to the guy with the pen and notepad to take notes.

"It seems that way," Crystal admits, "but no one talked about the kidnapping and when they attacked our ship, it seemed to take everyone by surprise."

"Wait," I interject. "Your ship was attacked?"

She nods and her eyes flicker with grief. "Yes. They killed thousands of people, including my parents."

"I'm so sorry." I shake my head in disbelief. "So that's how you ended up here?"

Crystal wilts in front of me, I step forward and place my hands on her shoulders. She looks up and my heart aches at the tears brimming in her already red-rimmed eyes. So much pain. Pain I understand only too well.

The anger hasn't reached her yet, but it will. The tingling need for revenge already burns white hot in my veins. Crystal begins to shake, and I pull her to me, holding her firm against my chest. She's not alone and neither am I. The realisation makes me hold her tighter and she relaxes into me.

We're in the same position—stranded on an alien planet with parents murdered by the same evil bastard.

"Wait." I drop my arms and take her hands as another realisation takes hold. "The king and queen are dead?"

Her shoulders droop at my words, but I step back a little and lift her face, my eyes fixed on hers.

"You're the queen."

Before she can respond, I drop to one knee and raise my hand, five fingers splayed in the Starlatten salute. "Your Majesty."

The look of mortification on her face is almost hilarious. Her cheeks flame and she reaches up, trying to pull my arm down. "What are you doing? Stop it."

I look up at her and grin, my green eyes teasing for a moment before seriousness settles over me once more. "We need to get you home. We need to tell the people of Starlatten they still have a leader."

"I have no way of contacting anyone," she explains. "Cadicus destroyed my pod and there's no way my amulet is strong enough to send a signal."

I reach for my own amulet, holding it up between thumb and forefinger. "What about two of them?"

My memories are getting clearer by the minute. It's as if a fog is lifting. Even though my mind keeps replaying the image of my mother's crumpling body like a gif, I'm beginning to remember other things. Happy memories of my childhood in Galeania. Happy memories of Crystal.

I'd been so annoyed with my parents when they told me the royal family was joining us for the summer. I didn't care that the princess was a similar age. I had my own friends and hanging out with some spoilt royal brat was not in my plans.

Then she'd arrived, looking as miserable about the situation as I was. It had taken a couple of days, but then we'd started talking, realising we had more in common than we could have known. We practiced tricks with our amulets that we weren't allowed to do, chased greyare beasts, lay in prasalia-laced fields and watched the clouds cross the moons. It had been a pretty perfect summer. Until it wasn't.

"What are you smiling about?"

I blink, realising that Crystal is watching me. My grin widens. "Just remembering our summer in Galeania."

Crystal smiles back, but it doesn't quite reach her eyes. I make a silent pledge to bring joy to those eyes.

"Are you ready?" I ask. We're sitting cross-legged, our knees touching, on the cold floor of what I now realise is a storage unit. Quick introductions have been made and although Eddie is clearly not in a hurry to drop his guard, things are becoming a little more normal—if that's even possible.

I've never tried to send a signal using my amulet before, but I remember my parents teaching me how to do it in case of an emergency as a kid. I just hope it works.

"Do you think it will work?" Crystal asks, echoing my thoughts.

I shrug. "We can only try. I still can't believe your parents didn't teach you how to do it."

"I suppose as I always had Dyja around me, they didn't think the situation where I needed to would ever arise."

"What are Dyja?" Jordan calls out from nearby. "Sorry to interrupt ... Just curious."

Crystal turns to explain, a warm smile on her lips. "Dyja are guards. They protect our planet. They're extremely tall and they wear dark red, hooded robes."

"Right," I say, reaching out and taking her hands. "Are you ready?"

She nods and my heart pounds with excitement. I might be going home.

"Okay," I say, taking a deep breath. "We're going to focus all of our energy on our amulets." I'm explaining for my own benefit as much as anyone else's. "When we've pooled as much energy as we can, we're going to push that energy straight up into the atmosphere and hopefully, into space."

"Wow." Sera exhales. "Sounds like a long shot."

"Literally." Linda giggles.

I raise an eyebrow at them. "It's the only shot we've got."

"No pressure then." Crystal squeezes my hands. "Let's do it."

I close my eyes but my gut lurches as I realise that I haven't used my amulet since I was a kid. What if I can't remember how? What if this all falls apart because I've been here for so long without it? I'm about to open my eyes and voice my concerns, when I feel it—a warmth on my chest. The heat builds against my skin to the verge of being uncomfortable, but it never hurts. Green light seeps from the centre of the stone down my arms and into my fingertips, tickling and crackling like static electricity.

A rush of deep purple light bursts in through my fingertips, intertwining with the green and our combined energy seeps in and out between our fingers, pushing, pulling and connecting us. My breath catches at how intimate it feels.

Even with my eyes firmly closed, I can sense the swirling tower of purple and green energy building between us like a small tornado. It stretches and twists like it's alive, reaching up above us and I fight the urge to open my eyes to see if it's really there. My body buzzes with light and energy—euphoric and exhausting at the same time.

I'm just wondering how I'll know when I'm 'full', when a jolt knocks the breath from my lungs. It's as though a piece of elastic between the amulet and the swirling tower has snapped and as the last few droplets of power race down my arms and fingers, a burst of energy shoots purple and green light into the air and out of sight.

I'm thrown backwards and I try to hold on to Crystal's fingers, but the force is too strong. Instead, I watch in slow motion as she's thrown into the air in the opposite direction. I reach out, but as I hit the ground with force, exhaustion overpowers me, and my eyes close.

It's dark. Too dark. Too quiet. I open my eyes. Still dark. My heart begins to pound. Why can't I see? Dread gnaws at my insides. I rub my eyes and try to open them. Black. Has the amulet made me blind? Why can't I hear anything? I scream for help, throwing my arms out around me. My fingers find nothing. I hear nothing. My voice dissolves into the nothingness.

Hot tears burn my eyes. I finally get my memories back and now what? I'm dead? Maybe this is it. Forever. The lack of senses smothers me with a fear unlike anything I've ever known, seeping into every bone.

Then, I see it. Far away, in the distance. A very small light. I squint, peering at it curiously. So, I'm not blind and possibly not alone. Maybe it's Crystal? Maybe we're both trapped in this weird dark world. I hope she's not as scared as I am. I start running towards the light.

It's not a light. It's two lights. Two small orange lights. There's a brief, blissful second before I realise what I'm seeing—before my blood runs cold and ice shoots up my spine, knocking the air from my lungs. They're eyes. Amber eyes.

Panic exploding in my chest, I turn and sprint in the other direction. How has he found me? I'm not ready. In front of me, the darkness is thick and endless. Am I even moving? As if in answer, the eyes appear in front of me. I turn again, but there they are, again and again. They're everywhere. They're all around me. Amber eyes, glinting cruelly in the inky blackness.

"I see you."

I shout, but my voice is nothingness.

"I'm coming for you."

Something pulls me backwards. The eyes grow smaller and smaller. Then they're gone.

I open my eyes—my body doused in cold sweat. "Crystal!"

Pushing myself up, it takes a second to find her. She's sitting on the floor on the other side of the storage unit, a circle around her. Boxes and books are strewn across the container as if a small hurricane passed through.

She sees me awake and calls out. "Are you okay?"

"I'm fine," I reassure her, "but—"

"Do you think it worked?" she continues, her eyes full of hope. "It was a pretty powerful energy blast. Do you think anyone will sense our signal?"

Oh. Someone felt it all right. I struggle to find the right words. I've put everyone in danger. My stupid idea. I hold my head in my hands.

"What's wrong?" She's on her feet and by my side in seconds.

I shake my head. "I'm so sorry."

"What?" she presses.

"Cadicus. He's coming."

Watching from the outskirts, I linger as the group prepares to leave. Jordan seems to have secured himself a role as Oakstone's assistant—helping him pack his papers and laptop. Dylan is deep in conversation with Crystal and the others loiter nervously, going over the plan again and again.

"You okay?"

I look down to find Linda beside me. "Not really," I say honestly.

"I suppose it's a lot to take in."

"It's more than that." I shake my head. "When you guys brought me here, I was a completely different person—but not, at the same time."

"What do you mean?"

"When you guys kidnapped me—" I pause, raising my eyebrows at Linda's expression. "Oh, don't give me that look. You know you did. When you *kidnapped* me, I thought I was an unwanted kid living with an abusive criminal uncle. Now, I know I'm not even from this planet and I might still have a father out there in the universe somewhere."

"I guess that's a bit of an adjustment."

I snort at the understatement before nudging her gently with my arm. "Thank you."

"What for?"

"For coming back." I look down at her, my face serious. "If you hadn't come looking for me ... If you hadn't been brave enough to set up this meeting ..."

She shrugs and looks away, trying and failing to seem nonchalant. "You're welcome, I guess."

"Right," Dylan announces. "Let's get out of here. Now."

Oakstone unlocks the door to the storage unit and we pour out into the cool evening air. I blink in surprise at the dusk. I hadn't realised how late it was.

"Eddie?" Linda calls out as we begin to hurry down the long repetitive corridor of identical storage units. "We need to call Mum."

"I've already text her," Eddie replies without turning around.

My heart pounds with anxiety as we turn a corner. These guys don't know how dangerous Cas really is. I've lived with the monster for the past seven years and if he finds us, it will all be over.

The yard of storage units is like a maze, with hundreds upon hundreds of grey metallic boxes all in rows, like some sort of futuristic ghost town. When we reach a T-junction, we split. Crystal, Dylan, Oakstone and Eddie go left and the rest of us turn right. We decided that we should split up in case we're followed and have arranged to meet at Oakstone's aunt's house on the outskirts of town. Jordan suggested that Cadicus won't know Oakstone is working with us, so contacts of his are the safest. Plus, his aunt is apparently on a Caribbean cruise for the over-sixties for the next fortnight.

As our feet crunch the gravel, I realise just how eerily quiet the yard is. Just the sounds of our feet and breathing—not another soul in sight. I glance over my shoulder to see Linda jogging along behind us and I attempt an encouraging smile. In front of me, Jordan lurches forward, hitting the ground with a sickening thud.

I skid to a halt by his side as he rolls over gasping for breath. "What happened?"

"I don't know." He winces as Sera inspects him for damage. "I tripped."

My eyes scan the ground and when I see why Jordan fell, I motion for everyone to step back, my eyes darting from side to side.

"What's going on?" Linda demands, tugging at my sleeve.

I point at the ground—at the small, almost invisible wire stretched across the pathway. "We need to get out of here. Now."

Pulling Jordan to his feet, my blood freezes in my veins. They're here. They know where we are. It's too late.

As if conjured by my thoughts alone, two large men dressed in bulky black jackets rush out from a gap between the units, hoods up and their faces covered.

Linda opens her mouth to scream, but a gloved hand covers her mouth, another arm wrapping around her waist and lifting her into the air. I watch, frozen in horror as she kicks furiously against his grip. Another man grabs Sera in the same way and Jordan launches into action but the man lifts a knee and kicks Jordan so hard he's knocked right off his feet, smashing into a nearby unit. He slides to the ground, his head forward.

This is Cadicus. These men are here because of that monster. Rage pours through me and I leap forward, wrapping my hands around the throat of the man holding Linda. I squeeze, jumping at the chance to release some of my pent-up anger. Redness blurs the edges of my vision as the man chokes and gurgles, releasing Linda and trying to prise my fingers from his throat.

As the man grows limp, I realise Linda is shouting something. I blink, focusing on her tearstained face.

"Jaik! Please! They've got Sera!"

I let go of the man and he falls to the floor. The other man has made it to the end of the row with Sera—now drooping in his arms. I sprint after them, but it's too late. They're gone. I run down the path a little further and check down a few rows and then back the other way and try again. It's as if they've vanished into thin air. I run my hands over my face and trudge back to Linda and Jordan, my heart in my shoes.

"Jordan?" Linda shakes his shoulders. "Please be alive."

When he groans and rolls his head back, I realise I've been holding my breath.

"Where's Sera?" Linda looks up at me and then behind me as if expecting her friend to step out from the shadows.

I shake my head. "I'm so sorry. They'd disappeared by the time I got to them. I've looked, but there's no sign of them."

Linda covers her mouth as a sob tears from her and my hands ball into fists. "We're going to get her back," I say through gritted teeth. "I promise."

CHAPTER **TWENTY-FOUR**

Dylan

"It has to be him, right?"

I pause in the massaging of my temples to look at Jordan, who's standing, arms spread as he addresses the group. His eyes are wide, and I don't think I've ever seen him this scared. I don't have answers for him.

"It was him," Jaik says.

We've gathered in the living room of Oakstone's aunt's house with the flowered curtains drawn and just one small white candle for light, in an attempt to minimise attention. Linda relayed most of what happened through breathless sobs, but now, she sits in silence, knees to her chest and her face blank. I think she might be in shock. Jaik has been brooding in a corner since we arrived.

"Did you recognise the men?" Crystal asks.

"No, but what they were wearing and how they fought?" Jaik's eyes are dark. "They were his men."

Jordan flops down beside me. "We should have brought the one you took out back with us."

"What? And lead Cadicus straight to us?" Jaik scoffs.

"We decided not to, and it can't be undone," Crystal says, her voice quiet but firm. "There's little point arguing about it."

I reach over and put a hand on her knee. What if it had been Crystal they'd taken? My stomach turns inside out at the thought.

"I think it's time to call the police."

Silence echoes around the shadowed room as everyone turns to look at Eddie.

"What?" He holds his hands out in front of him, eyebrows raised. "Sera's been kidnapped. *Kidnapped.* God only knows what they're doing to her right now." He flinches and looks at Jordan. "Sorry, mate."

Oakstone gives a small cough. He's sitting in an oversized high-backed armchair covered in dark green leaves that look almost ghoulish in the flickering candlelight. "I think Eddie's got a point. This has all got out of hand. We're dealing with an established criminal gang so perhaps the best thing to do is to get more people involved."

I sense Crystal's eyes on me, seeking my reaction. What would be the downside of getting the police involved? Well, we wouldn't be able to tell them everything for a start, but what Oakstone said is true. We are in way over our heads. I glance around. We look lost—lost and weary. My mind dull and heavy, I can't think clearly at all. It's been a million years since I last slept, and my eyes are raw. If I think about too much, I reckon I could cry.

"Are you okay?"

I look down at Crystal's face, full of concern and force a smile. "I'll be okay when we get Sera back."

She returns my bravado with a smile of her own, but she looks exhausted too. Perhaps it's the shadows from the candlelight, but dark circles are appearing around her eyes and her light brown skin seems dry and washed-out. The last couple of days is taking its toll on us all.

"You should get some rest," I whisper, pulling her towards me. I stroke her hair as I lean back on the sofa, and she yawns against my chest.

Oakstone stands decisively and relief washes over me. I honestly just want someone to tell me what to do.

"Right. Here's what's happening," he says. "Three people try and get some sleep and the rest of us will keep watch and try to come up with a plan. We'll swap after an hour or so and gradually—hopefully—we'll refresh our minds and bodies."

Crystal mumbles something in protest, but it's unintelligible and within seconds, her breathing has become deep and steady.

"I'll take the first shift," Oakstone volunteers. "I need a lot less sleep than you young 'uns."

Jordan fidgets beside me. "I'll take the first shift too. I don't think I could sleep anyway."

I glance between Linda and Jaik. Linda is still sitting, staring into nothing, her face pale. "I think you should try and get some rest Linda. Crystal is already out for the count."

She says nothing, but Jaik nods in agreement and grabs a throw from the back of the chair she's sitting on, draping it around her. Her face unchanging, she turns to her side, still hugging her knees. I really hope she can get some rest. I don't think I've ever seen her this quiet and it's unsettling.

"I think it might be best for you to rest too, Dylan," Oakstone says, looking pointedly at Crystal. "If you move, she might wake."

Even though every atom is screaming out for sleep, I find myself arguing. "She's tired because of that signal. Perhaps Jaik should rest in case we need to use the amulets again."

Jaik watches me, his eyes narrowed. I'm pretty sure he doesn't like me, but I'm not entirely sure why.

"No, mate," he says. "You get some rest. I'm fine."

We stare at each other for a moment, both knowing how much each of us wants sleep. Jaik's eyes look barely able to stay open and I know the amulet will have taken it out of him. The fact is, neither of us want to miss anything.

Crystal stirs, her arms snaking around my waist as she snuggles her head against my chest. I tighten my grip on her just a little and the warmth of her body causes a fresh wave of exhaustion as I stifle a yawn.

"Jaik is right," Oakstone agrees. "It's only an hour or so. We'll compile everything we know and add what Jaik knows about Cadicus and his men. Okay?"

I open my mouth to protest but instead the yawn bubbles to the surface. I nod, heavy with sleep and then I'm gone.

There's a bee in my pocket. I know it's not real. It's an illusion caused by Cadicus and his yellow amulet. I try to stay calm, but it keeps buzzing and buzzing. There's something else—something I know I should have remembered. A small layer of guilt underneath everything. The bee keeps buzzing.

As the dregs of sleep fall away, I realise the incessant buzzing is my phone in my pocket. My eyes fly open. *Mum*. My stomach turns at the realisation. She'll be so worried. Linda and Crystal are asleep, and the room is dark. I don't know where the others have gone to talk.

Very carefully, I extract myself from underneath Crystal, who stretches out across the couch, her arms finding a small cushion. My phone has stopped vibrating and pulling it from my pocket, my fears are confirmed as a list of missed calls from home illuminates the room.

Voices drift in from the connecting kitchen, so I move to the stairs and find Oakstone's aunt's bedroom. Keeping the light off, my eyes adjust in the moonlight streaming through the open curtains and, heart pounding, I swipe to call her back, preparing for the onslaught.

"Dylan?"

"Hi, Mum."

"Where are you? Why haven't you been answering your phone? I've been calling for hours! I was about to call the police!"

"Mum!" I hiss. "Calm down. I'm fine."

"Where are you?"

I glance around the tiny floral bedroom. "I'm at Jordan's house," I start, the lie beginning to form in my mind. "We were playing a new game on his console and I fell asleep. I'm so sorry."

The silence on the other end of the line goes on for so long that I take the phone away from my ear to check she's still there.

"This is very unlike you," she says, her voice heavy. "I was really worried."

Shame presses down on my shoulders as I picture her alone—tired and sad. I've let her down.

"I'm sorry."

"You'll be back at five to help, right?" she asks, but it's not really a question. "I'll put the ovens on to warm at four, but I'll need you by five."

I can't. I just can't. How can I leave everyone in the middle of this mess? "Can Katie help you, just this once?"

"Katie's helping in the shop later."

"Please, Mum," I plead, trying to keep the urgency from my voice. I can't go home. "Just this once?"

"Fine."

Her short reply makes me flinch. "I really am sorry, Mum. I'll see you later."

The line goes dead, and I flop down on the bed, my head in my hands.

My heart is still heavy when I eventually make my way back downstairs. Everyone is exactly as I left them— oblivious to my angst. I wonder whether the others have contacted their parents. Crystal is still sprawled across the sofa. Not wanting to wake her, I lower myself to the floor and lean my back against the chair, resting my head near hers.

When I turn to look at her, her brow is creased and her eyes flicker behind her eyelids. I sit up. Is she having a nightmare? I'm debating whether to shake her awake, when she gasps and sits bolt upright causing me to fall backwards onto my hands.

"Jeez, Crystal," I breathe. "Are you okay?"

She looks around the room, her eyes wild. "Where is everyone?"

The door to the kitchen flies open and Jaik, Oakstone and Eddie spill into the room. Behind me, Linda starts to stir, blinking sleep from her eyes.

"What's wrong?" Jaik asks. Before I can get to my feet, he's sitting beside her on the couch, her hands in his. "What did you see?"

"Cadicus," she says, shaking.

Jaik pulls her into his arms, stroking her back. "It's okay. He can't hurt you. You're safe."

My teeth grind and my fingers claw into fists against the carpet as jealousy ripples through me. I force myself to shake it off. He's her childhood friend and I'm not going to be the jealous boyfriend. Wait. Boyfriend? *No.* I feel my cheeks heat at the ridiculousness of the idea. It's been a day. She's leaving as soon as she can. This is just ... fun? It doesn't feel like fun. Whatever it is, I can't help the overwhelming urge to rip Jaik off her.

"Crystal, what did you see?" I ask, in a shallow attempt to pull her focus.

My voice has the desired effect, and she leans away, her eyes wet and full of fear.

"It was awful," she says. "His eyes—those awful amber eyes. I couldn't speak. I couldn't scream or run. He was all around me. He knows who I am and that I'm here on Earth."

"Is Sera okay?" Jordan croaks. "Did he say anything?"

Crystal nods. "He says she's okay. For now. He said we need to meet him at 8am and that Jaik would know where."

All eyes turn to Jaik.

"The abandoned mill on Southland Street."

Oakstone already has his laptop open—the blue light illuminating his face in the dark room. "Are you sure?" he asks, turning the screen to face us. "This place?"

Jaik's jaw is clenched as he nods at the street view image of a dilapidated red brick factory building. Its walls are covered with graffiti and the windows that aren't boarded up are smashed.

"Looks delightful," Eddie murmurs.

"It's where Cas likes to do a lot of his dealings," Jaik explains. "It's too old to be demolished—something about town heritage—but it's too much of a wreck for anyone to buy. Cas makes sure squatters stay clear and no one else goes near it."

"What does he want?" Eddie asks. "He's not just going to give us Sera back, right?"

"Exactly," Jordan says. "What is he after? What's the point of all this?"

"Me," Crystal whispers. "He wants me."

I rise up onto my knees, taking her hands in mine. "Over my dead body."

Jaik exhales. "Crystal's right. He wants her. He couldn't get what he wanted by threatening my father but with the sole heir to the Starlatten throne ..."

"That's it. I'm calling the police." Oakstone's statement lingers in the darkness. "I think it's time we faced facts. We are dealing with murdering kidnappers. As the only adult here, I'm pulling rank."

Jaik stands to protest his adult status, but Oakstone holds up an apologetic hand.

"You know what I mean," he continues. "This is not about being over eighteen. This is about life experience and seeing the bigger picture. You'll get in more trouble if you don't involve the police than if you do."

Crystal squeezes my hands. "What do you think?"

I look up at her, wishing I had answers, but I honestly can't see a way out of this. "There's a lot we won't be able to explain," I start.

"Exactly. I'm on board with getting a little outside help here," Jordan chips in, "but how do we explain two aliens and a dead scientist?"

Oakstone claps his hands together in sudden inspiration. "We don't tell them about the alien part, and I'll feign amnesia."

"It's not that simple!" Jaik roars. "You don't know. You don't know *him*. He's not just a bad guy—he's pure evil. He won't show mercy. If he finds out the police are coming, he'll kill Sera without a second thought and they'll never find her body."

Jordan and Linda move to stand, but Jaik's face has turned a similar shade to his eyes and he runs to the kitchen door.

Crystal swings her legs off the sofa. "I'll go see if he's okay."

"No," I say—my own voice surprising me. "I'll go."

Before she can protest, I'm on my feet and pushing open the door to the cramped kitchenette. Jaik is still heaving over the sink when the door closes behind me.

"You okay, man?"

He looks at me sideways as he rests his head on the counter. "Yeah. Brilliant, thanks."

"Sorry." I look around and find a glass, holding it out to him.

Jaik fills the glass with water and turns, leaning against the countertop. "We can't call the police."

"Oakstone thinks—"

"I don't care what Oakstone thinks," Jaik bites out. "It's not worth the risk."

I blow out a slow breath and lean against the opposite counter. The kitchen is so small, our legs are almost touching. "He really messed you up, huh?"

Jaik grunts in response.

What am I doing in here? Maybe I should have let Crystal come after him. My initial jealousy seems stupid as I watch Jaik claw a hand over his face. I can't imagine how it must feel to forget your whole life and family, live an entirely different life and then try to merge the two.

"So," I say, trying to sound positive. "What do you think we should do then?"

"I'm not sure," he admits, placing the glass down and holding his head in his hands. "This is all my fault."

Not the response I was expecting. "It's not your fault. It's this Cadicus guy's fault."

"No. It's my fault." He looks up, his green eyes dark with regret. "If I hadn't gone back to that alley—if I hadn't met up with you guys ... I should have just run away."

"I'm sure if running away had been an option, you'd have done it a long time ago," I say. "I know I don't know the half of it, but I get the feeling Cadicus is a hard man to escape from."

"Perhaps," he admits.

"We'll get Sera back." I try and force confidence into my tone. "Good triumphs over evil, right?"

Jaik looks at me in disbelief. "Tell my mother that. Or Crystal's parents."

"Come on, mate." I sigh. "I'm trying."

"Well, don't," Jaik huffs. "We need to get back in there and figure out a plan that doesn't end in us getting ourselves killed."

Before I can respond, he pushes himself off the side and walks back through to the living room, leaving me with a darkness in the pit of my stomach that I can't shake.

CHAPTER TWENTY-FIVE

Crystal

Yawning, I take another sip of lukewarm black coffee. There's little else to drink in the house besides water and after a long night like last night, I need something stronger than water. A wave of homesickness washes over me as I long for the sweet but musky flavour of bahabo tea.

After staying up strategizing until the early hours of the morning, we ended up sleeping in the living room. Everyone except Oakstone. He put up a good fight, but we convinced him to sleep upstairs in the only bed. No one said it out loud, but I don't think any of us wanted to be separated after what happened.

Jordan slept in the chair after losing a game of something called 'rock, paper, scissors' with Eddie. Linda took the sofa. Jaik, Eddie, Dylan and I found spaces on the floor. It wasn't too bad. The floor is covered with a thick soft covering and we found a cupboard full of warm blankets. Plus, I got to spend the few hours' sleep we had in Dylan's arms. Waking up to his sleepy smile is something I could get used to.

"What are you grinning at?"

My smile broadens as Dylan sits down beside me with his second cup of coffee. "You."

"Oh?"

I open my mouth to tell him how happy he makes me, but Jaik stands and claps his hands together, calling our attention.

"Right. Is everyone ready for today? Everyone know their part?"

"Yes," I answer along with everyone else. I try to sound confident, but my insides are somersaulting at the thought of today more than the first time I travelled in a spacecraft.

"It's a good plan," Dylan murmurs at my ear, sensing my nerves. He moves into my line of sight, staring at me until I meet his gaze. "It will work."

I manage a small smile and try to breathe in his confidence. It might work, but there's also a lot that could go wrong.

It's a cold morning and the pale sun casts an eerie light on the deserted streets. As I stare up at the old building, the silence makes the hairs on the back of my neck stand on end. It's unlike anything I've ever seen before. Several stories high, it's covered with giant windows with a tall red brick tower reaching up into the sky.

Buildings on Starlatten are generally pale in colour with large windows—designed to blend in with their natural surroundings. There is nothing natural about this red giant. It looms over us, bringing nothing but a sense of foreboding.

Linda, Jordan, Eddie and I are crouched between discarded building materials, and something called a 'skip'. I shift position in an unsuccessful attempt to get more comfortable, watching as Dylan, Jaik and Dr. Oakstone make their way towards the building.

Last night, we decided either Sera is already inside the building, or they'll bring her here in time for the meeting. Either way, it's in our advantage to be here first. If she's already here, the plan is for Dylan and Dr. Oakstone to distract the guards while Jaik gets her out. If they bring her at the agreed time, Jaik will confront Cadicus and tell him that he's going to bring him to me. As soon as they leave, Dylan and Oakstone will free Sera. Eddie and Jordan are poised as back up, ready to help or call the police.

My stomach lurches at the thought of Jaik confronting that monster and we tried to convince him—tried to find another way—but he insisted.

Of course, things probably won't go to plan. Of this, we are all painfully aware. There are too many variables and even now—as I think it over—all I can see are huge gaping holes. This is going to be far from straight forward.

Beside me, Jordan looks at his phone for the hundredth time. Oakstone has set up a program using his computer that means when Jordan types a four-digit number into his phone, it will send an automated message to the police informing them of our whereabouts with as little information as we can get away with. Of course, that's only for if things go really, really wrong.

My gut churns as I watch Dylan, Oakstone and Jaik climb in through a window at the side of the building. Despite my protests, it was decided that I am to stay hidden at all costs and I'm not happy about it.

"I wish we could see what's going on in there," Linda whispers. "I hate this."

We agreed not to call or text each other in case the notification alerts someone it shouldn't, and I bite my lip hard, as I nod in agreement.

After a few minutes, Eddie shuffles closer and nudges me with his elbow. "Can't you send Jaik one of your psychic necklace messages? Get us an update?"

I blink in surprise. I haven't even thought about that. How strange. On Starlatten, talking telepathically is second nature. A handful of days on Earth and it's almost a distant memory. "It's worth a try I suppose. I don't know if he'll be able to respond though. It takes practise and he's only used his amulet once since getting his memories back."

"Please try," Linda pleads.

Jordan gives me a small smile. "What's the worst that could happen?"

I smile back, look towards the building and concentrate.

CHAPTER TWENTY-SIX

Dylan

Swallowing my nerves, I try to ignore my heart pounding in my ears as I watch Jaik lead the way. He seems so comfortable in his role—hiding in the shadows and then motioning for us to join him.

"Move it," Oakstone hisses, tapping me on the shoulder.

I lift my hand in apology and continue through the maze of dark, cold empty rooms trying to remember why I volunteered for this. The air smells of damp and something else I can't put my finger on—something I know I don't want to recognise. I push the thought from my mind and join Jaik and Oakstone in a huddle behind a mass of overturned tables, boxes and pallets.

This must be the main room. Tall boarded windows fill its length and enormous pillars covered with peeling, faded green paint support the damaged ceiling, which sends shards of light slicing through the gloom, illuminating the dust and cobwebs in the air.

"This is the room he'll bring her to," Jaik whispers, his green eyes flashing with adrenaline. "I honestly thought she'd be here already."

"They'll be here in the next half an hour," I say, glancing at my watch. "If he keeps his word."

"Do you think he will?" Oakstone asks.

Jaik doesn't respond. His eyes have glassed over and he's staring at a space just over my right shoulder. I'm considering waving a hand in front of his face when the light returns to his eyes and he looks at us in surprise.

"Crystal just sent me a message," he breathes.

"Of course." Oakstone gasps. "The amulets."

My heart jumps at the mention of Crystal's name. I hate knowing she's out there without me. Not that she needs protecting, as she made abundantly clear when we were coming up with the plan. "Is she okay?" I ask. "What did she say?"

"She's fine," Jaik says. "They want to know what's happening in here."

"So, tell her," I say.

"I don't know if I can." Jaik picks at the dusty floor. "It's been years since I used an amulet for communicating."

Oakstone frowns. "You used it in the storage unit, to send for help."

"I didn't really have to do anything," he mumbles. "Crystal channelled the power from both our amulets."

"Well, it's time to figure it out." I place a hand on his shoulder. "We need a line of communication—and you're it."

Jaik gives the smallest of nods before reaching under his black long-sleeved shirt for his amulet. He holds onto the green stone and closes his eyes.

"Put her in the middle."

I freeze and Jaik's eyes fly open. They're early.

Trying not to make a sound, I turn in the direction of the voice. Footsteps echo across the concrete floor accompanied by a screeching noise that makes my teeth hurt. They're dragging something across the floor. Crouching low between Oakstone and Jaik, I'm acutely aware of the volume of my breathing.

Jaik rises a little and peers over the pile of pallets. After a moment, he signals for Oakstone to take a look. I wait, swallowing as his face changes to match the look of dread painted on Jaik's. With a deep breath, I take my turn.

There are at least fifteen men, all dressed in blacks and greys. Some have their faces covered, but more worryingly, all of them are wielding weapons. The object I'd heard being dragged across the floor must have been the chair which has been placed in the centre of the room. My eyes widen as I look at Sera, hands and feet bound with plastic ties, her usually bright blonde hair hanging limply over her face as she slumps forward over her knees. Someone tugs on the back of my shirt and I crouch back down.

Oakstone shakes his head and when I look at Jaik, I see my own despair and hopelessness reflected. There are too many of them. We'd only expected three—four at most. There's no way Sera is going to be left alone and we can't take them all out. Unless Oakstone is a secret black belt, Jaik is the only one who knows how to fight.

My stomach churns so violently, there's a very real chance I might vomit. This is such a bad idea. It's time to signal the police. We just have to get a message to Jordan.

"Jake?"

A deep, booming voice echoes around the room and all colour drains from Jaik's face.

"Then again, I suppose it's Jaik now? I know you're in here, so you may as well save me the job of finding you and come out."

Cadicus' cruel, rumbling tones bounce from wall to wall. Each lingering syllable causes Jaik to shake as though someone is hammering nails into his body. He clenches his fists so tight the skin turns white, his teeth gritted. What do we do? We didn't plan for this.

The silence is deafening.

"Okay, okay." Cadicus sighs. "I'll send my men to find you. But know this: if they find anyone with you," he pauses. "Well, I think you know me well enough to know what would happen to them."

I watch, my heart attempting to beat its way out of my chest, as Jaik crumbles before me. We're dead. We're all dead. Jaik takes a shaky breath and tucks his amulet back inside his shirt. My eyes widen and I wave my hands wildly at him in protest. Oakstone reaches out to try and tug him back down as he starts to stand.

"It's just me," he calls out.

His voice echoes around the empty room.

CHAPTER TWENTY-SEVEN

Jaik

"How wonderful." Cadicus turns to face me, his face twisted in a wry smile. He waves an arm for me to come and join him like we're old friends.

I make my way towards him, glancing at each of the men surrounding us as I pass. Some I recognise. Pete, Aaron and Tom have all been on jobs with me before. They struggle to meet my eyes.

"Where is she?" Cadicus raises his eyebrows as he glares down at me. He's a monster of a man both inside and out.

I shake my head, feigning confusion. "Who?"

"You know who." Cadicus spits. "The princess."

I keep my face blank. "The what?"

Before I can react, Cadicus' arm swings out, the back of his hand meeting with my face and sending me flying backwards to the floor. The concrete knocks the breath from me, scraping the skin from my right elbow and my back.

"Don't play games with me, boy!" he roars. His voice seems to shake the walls, his eyes burning a dark orange beneath his heavy brows.

"I don't know what you're talking about!" I shout back as I scramble to my feet.

Cadicus clutches his short greying dark hair in rage and yells—actually yells. I stand in shock as the cry reverberates around the room before echoing into nothing.

Around me, the men shift in their places, fidgeting with their weapons. I take the opportunity to look at Sera, realising with relief that she's unconscious but alive.

Standing, eyes closed, Cadicus takes a deep breath. "If you want something done …" His eyes snap open but as he fixes me with his amber stare, I know the words that follow are not meant for me.

"I know you can hear me. Come out from wherever you're hiding or Jaik dies. Don't take too long. I bore easily. Although, perhaps watching my men take turns practising their skills on him might keep me amused … for a while." His eyes never leave mine. "See you soon, Your Majesty."

Despite the cold breeze whistling through the cracks in the boarded windows, beads of sweat drip down my back and trickle along my hairline. Crystal can't come in here. She can't. But then, what will happen to me and Sera? Cadicus doesn't say anything he isn't willing to follow through with.

Cadicus gives a theatrical yawn before waving a hand at one of the men to my left. "You. Go."

My breath catches in my throat as I turn to see one of the men rushing towards me, a knife glinting in his hand.

CHAPTER TWENTY-EIGHT

Crystal

"You can't go in there," Eddie hisses.

I shake my head as I get to my feet. "What choice do we have?"

"Eddie's right," Jordan whispers. "The plan was to keep you safe no matter what. This is definitely not keeping you safe."

"We have no idea what you're walking into. Please don't," Linda pleads. Her fingers clutch mine as she tries to tug me back down to our hiding place.

A while ago, a vehicle pulled up at the entrance to the building, blocking our view. We were unable to see who got out of it and, although we can't be sure, it sounded like more than a few people. What I do know is, if I don't go in there, Jaik dies.

The situation swirls around my head like a storm, bringing flashes of pain like lightning with each possible scenario and outcome.

"If I stay here, Jaik and Sera die," I say. "It's me Cadicus wants. If he has me, he might let you all go."

Linda pulls harder at my wrist. "You're the queen of a bloody planet! We're not going to let you sacrifice yourself."

"It's not your planet," I say, unpicking her fingers as I pull away. "You didn't know other worlds existed before you met me and, once I'm gone, nothing will change for you." I raise a hand as Jordan opens his mouth to interrupt. "I appreciate everything you've done for me, but I've brought you enough trouble and for that, I'm sorry. This is my war, and it ends now."

Shouts and yells bounce across the floor towards me from the end of the short corridor and I push the final rusted door open, unprepared for the sight that lies before me.

The first thing I see is Sera's long blonde hair, cascading to her knees as she droops forward on her chair. Beside her, the towering frame of Cadicus, arms folded and a dark smile playing on his lips. He's even more terrifying in real life than Jaik's memories. He hasn't seen me yet though. He's too busy watching something happening in the middle of a ring of cheering men.

My hand flies to my mouth as I make sense of the scene in front of me. Jaik is in the middle of the circle, a knife in one hand, his left eye swollen and bloodied and a deep cut down his right cheek. He limps a slow circle with the other man, who is crouching, ready to pounce as he brandishes some sort of bat. Doused in the horror of what I'm seeing, the words leave my mouth in a yell before I can think.

"Stop!"

Weapons raised, the crowd turns to face me. My eyes find Jaik's and he shakes his head in anguish. I look away. The defeat and helplessness are just too much to bear. I need to believe that this isn't over—that it's going to be okay.

"Princess!" Cadicus raises his arms and takes a step towards me. "It's so nice to finally talk to you face to face."

I take a step backwards. "I'm sorry I can't say the same."

"Oh, I'm devastated. Especially after you turned up so soon, spoiling all our fun."

He gestures to Jaik, who is now being held by two burly masked men. Another man lies on the floor nearby, a pool of dark red liquid snaking out along the concrete from his stomach.

"Yes, Jaik won the first round, but we were so looking forward to seeing how he did in the second." Cadicus pauses as if realising something. "Perhaps we should continue? After all, you did miss an impressive fight, Princess."

My teeth grind together, and I attempt to swallow the rage building inside me. "Don't you dare," I manage to bite out. I nod towards Sera. "What have you done to her?"

"Oh her?" Cadicus strides over and grabs a fistful of Sera's hair, lifting her head so I can see her face. "She's fine. Just in a very deep sleep."

"Let her go."

Cadicus chuckles, raising his hands in mock surrender. In doing so, he lets Sera's head fall limply back to its downward position. "Okay, okay. Let's get down to business, shall we?"

"What business?" I hold my head high, trying to keep the tremors of fear from my voice. "You've got me, so let my friends go."

"Oh? You think it's that easy? You've created quite the mess by turning up here, Princess."

I frown. "You asked me to come."

"No, no. Earth, Princess. Earth." He sighs. "My plan may have failed all those orbits ago when I tried to infiltrate the Starlatten government through Jaik's father, but now—with my allies on Zarbilian—we are finally getting somewhere." He pauses, sneering down at me. "This, however, wasn't part of the plan."

I watch, as he paces back and forth, my heart pounding almost in time with his footsteps. He's aged since the memory I saw in Jaik's head. Grey flanks the sides of his short dark hair and peppers the stubble on his chin. His dark, heavy brows knit together as if he's working something out, but the deep wrinkles remain when his face finally relaxes.

"It's worked out for the best, however," he announces with a half-smile. "The government might not have been willing to negotiate for an ambassador's wife and son, but now they have witnessed the scale of our wrath, they will be desperate to comply and avoid further attacks. And if they don't—I have the heir to the throne."

I push the image of the *Galastasia* exploding into nothingness from my mind. "What are you trying to achieve? What do you want?"

Cadicus stops pacing and strides towards me. I start to back away and find myself blocked by two large men. They grab hold of my arms as Cadicus reaches out and fishes my amulet from my shirt.

"This!" he shouts. "This is what I want. All you idiotic people wandering around with one amulet each, putting it back when someone dies like it's all part of some ridiculous, romantic circle of life." He spits in disgust. "Do you have any idea the power these amulets actually possess?"

After a pause, I realise he's actually waiting for a response. I turn my head away from his ragged breath. "Yes?"

He lets the amulet drop back to my chest and raises his hands in exasperation. "This is the problem. One amulet has a phenomenal amount of power if used correctly. Imagine the power of ten ... A hundred ... A thousand!"

With a heavy thud, the pieces of the puzzle slot into place. He wants the crystals. He wants power. All of it. I've never seen the crystals of Starellia. My grandparents are still alive—or at least I hope they are—and I won't have to make the journey until I meet someone with whom I want to spend my life with. From what I've learnt in class and seen in pictures, however, and with the simple maths of knowing how many people live on Starlatten—there are an awful lot of crystals in that pool. The stories say millions, and that might not be much of an exaggeration.

"What would you do with them?" I manage to choke out.

Cadicus laughs and it chills me to my core. "Whatever I want, Princess. Well, perhaps not that frivolous. The people exiled to Zarbilian are deserving of so much more. More than a meagre existence on a barely inhabitable rock. Returning to our rightful home is top of the agenda. Oh, and revenge. Of course."

"Exiled?" I shake my head in confusion. "What are you talking about?"

"Exiled, Princess," Cadicus snarls. "As in banished. Evicted. Have you ever been to Zarbilian? There is nothing there. It is merely a prison colony, existing only to contain us."

I try to make sense of his words. There is no prison colony. "The Zarbilian people chose that planet." My voice is barely a whisper. "They chose to leave Starlatten."

Cadicus' laugh is hollow as he looks me up and down. "You are so naïve, Princess. Soon, the Zarbilian people will be free. Free to take back what's ours. Free to find new planets to make our own."

"You can't just go wherever you want."

"If they haven't evolved fast enough, then they don't deserve to," he sneers. "We have been silenced for too long. Using your amulet, I will be able to guide ships here to take me back to Starlatten, where you will help me bring any remaining government to its knees."

"Never!" I scream, my face hot with anger.

Cadicus' laugh fills the room—every cavity of my soul, echoing in my bones—until suddenly, it stops.

"Oh! Look what we have here."

I follow his gaze to the back of the room as the crowd of men part to make way. My lungs are filled with rocks, as I try to breathe, the weight almost pulling me to my knees.

Four men drag Oakstone and Dylan towards us. They must have been searching the building while Cadicus was talking. As I meet Dylan's terrified stare, the world falls away at my feet. This is not how it was supposed to happen. This is all so wrong.

"I knew you wouldn't have come alone, Jaik, but Dr. Oakstone? What a turn of events! I thought I'd already killed you." Cadicus claps slowly in appreciation before turning to one of the masked men. "Kill him."

Before the intake of breath needed to form my scream is complete, the masked man raises his gun and pulls the trigger.

The scream tears from my throat, and I pull and struggle against my captors as Dr. Oakstone crumples to the ground. His unkempt hair falls forward as his glasses shatter on the concrete—his eyes frozen wide with surprise.

"Why?" I scream at Cadicus. I can barely breathe as I choke on my sobs and damp curls stick to my face as I continue to pull against the iron grips on my arms.

He shrugs. "Why not?" Then he turns towards Dylan and opens his mouth.

Time stops. Everything is sharp. Clear. I inhale through my nose and the terror and pain melt away. Determination steels in my bones—I'm in control. I close my eyes, reaching with my mind for the amulet around my neck and the purple energy races through my veins, mixing with adrenaline, and filling me with renewed purpose. When I open my eyes, I fix them on the man holding Dylan.

He flies back as though hit by a meteor, slamming against the wall several meters behind, where he slides to the floor. Not daring to look at Cadicus for his reaction, I slide my eyes to the three men standing to my right, my body pulsing with power. The man who shot Oakstone still has his weapon raised and he turns it towards me. Before he can complete the turn, I lift all three of them, screaming, up into the air—high up towards the towering ceiling. Then I let them drop.

As the men meet the ground with sickening thuds, the arms holding my arms loosen their grip. I shake them off and face them, my eyes sparking with electricity. Almost tripping over each other, they turn and run.

Rage ripples through me like I've never felt before and I seek out the two men holding Jaik, but he's already taken advantage of the diversion and knocked one man to the floor, delivering the knock-out punch to the other as I watch. His knife clatters to the floor as the room falls silent.

The sound of clapping brings me back to reality.

"Oh, bravo, Princess." Cadicus chuckles gleefully. "Do you see now? Do you see? Look at what you accomplished with just one amulet. And you are just an amateur." He casts a glance at the fallen bodies of his men. "They were really only for show, if I'm truthful. I can manage perfectly well on my own."

Keeping his eyes on me, he nods his head towards Dylan and Jaik. I watch as they stand panting, tensed for whatever comes next. Nothing can prepare me, however, for what does.

Using his amulet, Cadicus raises the knife from the floor and hovers it in front of the two boys. "Hmmm. Which one shall we deal with first, Princess?"

The blood drains from my face as the knife glides through the air, dancing between Jaik and Dylan. "Please, Cadicus," I plead. "No one else needs to get hurt."

Even as I say the words, I know it's useless. Jaik was right. He's pure evil. There's no reasoning with evil.

He steps closer, his amber eyes appearing as orange as flames as he fixes me with his heartless stare. "Oh, but they do, and they will."

Without a backwards glance, Cadicus sends the knife flying at speed. It meets Dylan's chest with such force, it knocks him backwards to the ground, where he lies motionless, blood seeping across his shirt like a sunrise.

I scream.

Jaik drops to Dylan's side, shaking his shoulders and calling his name. I try to run to him, but I can't. I'm frozen.

"Oh, you're not going anywhere," Cadicus snarls.

I tear my gaze away from Dylan—limp, pale and bloodied—fighting back the sobs beginning to shake my body.

"I think you can see now, there's no point resisting." Cadicus smiles. "If you hand over your amulet, I might just let you and Jaik live a little longer."

I can still hear Jaik talking to Dylan, trying to get a response, even though I know it's no use. I'm numb. Dr. Oakstone. Dylan. My parents. All the innocent men, women and children on board the *Galastasia*. Gone. It's too much. Too much death and no hope. I reach for my amulet, ready to hand it over.

As my fingers touch the smooth surface, I swear it pulses. Purple swirls through my body, as if refuelling me, giving me hope. A rush of regret wraps itself around my heart. If only I'd tried harder in lessons instead of pushing against tradition, refusing to learn to use my amulet properly. In just the last few days, it's become so much easier—an extension of me. In a way it always has been. It's been on my skin—against my heart—every day since I was born.

I almost choke on the realisation. This is why the stones have to be returned to the pool—cleansed when their wearer dies. Just as I've been learning how my amulet works, my amulet has been learning from me. Our connection is stronger, quicker. I thought I was getting better at using it, but now I realise it's also the bond between us that's strengthened.

Taking a deep breath, I embrace the now familiar deepening purple filling my mind and body. Narrowing my eyes, I concentrate on Cadicus. This is going to end. Now.

"Oh?" Cadicus smiles, his amber eyes flashing. "You want to take me on?"

I say nothing, concentrating on the power pulsing through me and push it out towards him as hard as I can.

He wavers a little, as though a strong breeze has caught him, a maniacal laugh on his lips. "You are no match for me, Princess."

A cold grip wraps around my throat and the purple energy drains from me. The ground beneath me falls away as I'm lifted up into the air, my feet kicking—searching for something to grip. Even though I know it's pointless, I lift my hands to try and prise the invisible fingers from around my neck.

"Put her down!"

I watch in horror as Jaik launches himself at Cadicus, who raises a hand as if swatting an insect, sending him flying across the room where he lands in a crumpled heap. I try to call out, but I can only splutter as I fight to get air into my lungs.

Struggling to get to his feet amongst the crumpled bodies of his former captors, Jaik looks just like the terrified boy I saw in his memories. Fear and hopelessness shine in his green eyes as he stands, watching.

Summoning every last ounce of strength, I use my amulet to call out to him. *Jaik. You have to do something.*

I can't.

The reply comes back in a heartbeat, and I see the surprise register on his face.

You can, Jaik. You didn't think you could use your amulet, but you just have.

He's too strong, Crystal.

My eyes grow heavy, my vision darkening as the lack of oxygen begins to take its toll.

CHAPTER TWENTY-NINE

Jaik

My eyes sting with tears. I'm no stranger to violence, but it's never involved people I care about. Not since my mother. My face and head throb with pain from where I've been sliced and punched, and my leg sends shooting pains up my spine when I put weight on it. This is all too much. Dylan and Oakstone's blood pools beneath my feet. Cadicus is too strong. I tried to tell them—to warn them.

I watch as Crystal's flailing legs begin to slow. It's like my mother all over again. I hadn't been able to stop him then. What's different now? The agonising ache of loss twists in my gut and I double over in pain.

Be strong, Jaik.

As the barely-there message echoes in my mind, my amulet pulses against my heart sending warmth across my chest. I force myself to look at Crystal, hanging limply in the air.

What's different now? I'm not a scared little boy anymore, that's for sure. I might not have had a lot of practise with my amulet, but at least I have it. I clench my fists as I realise Cadicus doesn't know. I have the element of surprise and even if I don't try, Cadicus will kill me anyway.

If I'm going down, I'm going down fighting.

Blinking back the pain, I concentrate on the emerald stone against my skin, trying to recall the sensation from the storage container. It roars through my bloodstream, almost knocking me off balance with its force as it swirls inside me, refreshing my muscles and giving me strength.

Concentrating the energy, I focus it on Cadicus and release it with an almighty roar. He staggers backwards, his eyes wide in shock and Crystal falls to her hands and knees, spluttering and gasping for air.

Keeping my eyes firmly fixed on Cadicus, I stride towards him, the green light gushing and pulsing inside me. I remember my mother and the utter disregard he showed as he snuffed out her life. I'm not even thinking—the green light swelling inside me telling my body what to do. Lifting an arm, I raise Cadicus up off the floor.

If I wasn't so angry, I might have relished the look of surprise on his face a little more, but all I can think about is the last seven years. The mental and physical abuse. The lies. Seven years of being made to feel worthless and unloved. Seven cold and lonely years, constantly hungry— not just for food but for human contact. It would have been kinder for him to kill me after my mother. Perhaps that's why he didn't. Cadicus Kain is never kind. He raises his own hand and I put one foot behind me to steady myself as he tries to fight me.

I realise he's trying to speak, but the grip I have around his neck is too tight. I almost lessen it, but there's nothing he can say. There are no words I want to hear from him.

The weight of holding him in the air lessens and I realise Crystal is standing beside me, her hand lifted too. Keeping my own hand raised, I step closer to him. His face is a picture of twisted rage.

"It's over," I growl through gritted teeth.

Cadicus holds my stare and for a fleeting moment, I think I see something, but he turns his livid gaze to Crystal.

Have you ever stopped to wonder why Starlatten is in charge?

I glance between them in surprise as his message reaches us both.

Have you ever stopped to wonder why everything is so peaceful? Are people really happy or are they scared? Scared of what will happen to them if they speak out.

"Enough!" I shout out loud. I don't want him in my head—in Crystal's head. Nothing he can say will change what I'm about to do. Reaching up with my other hand, I rip the yellow amulet from his neck. "This ends now."

Without a second's hesitation, I reach inside Cadicus Kain and sever his life, just as he did my mother's.

CHAPTER THIRTY

Crystal

"We need to get the others."

Jaik's voice sounds muffled and distant as I look away from where Cadicus' lifeless body lies at my feet.

"We need them to send the message to the police," he murmurs, his eyes still on Cadicus. "Then we need to get out of here. There's no way we can explain this."

My eyes brimming with fresh tears, I turn and look at where Dylan and Dr. Oakstone lie—my heart swollen and numb.

"I'll go and get them." Jaik takes my hands and squeezes them, before pulling me into a hug. I can't take my eyes off the bodies. "We'll need to get Dylan out of here."

I pull back from the hug and open my mouth. I'm not sure whether it's to question or protest. "Where would we take him?" I finally ask. Jaik has already gone.

Standing alone, I survey the sea of bodies around me. *Dylan*. I pick my way over to where he lies, each step pure torture. I feel raw—like someone has peeled away my skin. Lying on his back, one arm is draped across his chest, blood trickling along it and splashing a steady rhythm on the floor beneath his elbow. Dropping to my knees, I take in the knife still embedded in his torso before tracing the side of his face and gently pushing his hair from his eyes.

"I'm so sorry," I manage to choke out. "I never ... I wouldn't ..."

Words fail me as tears race down my cheeks, weaving fresh pathways along skin already tight with dried salt. I lean forward and press a kiss to his lips. They're still warm. I linger as his breath tickles my skin. My heart stops.

"Dylan?"

My hands shaking, I feel for a pulse. It's faint, but it's still there.

"Sera!"

I flinch as Linda's shout echoes around the cavernous room. Closely followed by Eddie and Jordan, they skid to a halt as they take everything in, a limping, bloodied Jaik just behind them.

"Oh my god," Eddie croaks. "Dylan?"

I'm unable to speak as they stand, horrified and unsure what to do next. Jaik spurs them into action.

"Jordan? Untie Sera. She's okay, just in a deep sleep." He puts a hand on Jordan's shoulder, giving it a gentle shake.

"Are you okay carrying her? Linda can give you a hand if you need it."

Linda stands motionless, hands over her mouth and silent tears streaming from her eyes.

Jordan nods, but his glazed eyes are fixed on the doctor's blood-soaked body. "What about Oakstone?"

Jaik shakes his head. "Oakstone is linked to this. There are pictures of him all over Cadicus' house. If he stays here, it'll be clear he was murdered, and his family will get his body. I know it sounds harsh, but it's for the best. Besides, there's not enough of us to take them both."

I'm behind a thick window watching the scene unfurl—everything muffled and far away. The meaning of Jaik's words hits home and Jordan finally seems to see Dylan's body. He doubles over, his hand over his mouth.

Jaik tugs a dazed, pale Eddie towards us. I glance down at Dylan's pallid body, noticing that my own clothes are now stained with his blood. There's so much blood.

"Eddie? I'm going to need you to help me carry Dylan's body out of here."

"He's alive." I swear I mean to shout it, but it comes out as a whisper.

Jaik doesn't hear me and continues to give Eddie directions on how best to lift him, but it's clear he's not taking it in.

I stare up at them and it's like my ears have popped. Everything is clear and sharp again as I shout. "He's alive."

They both stop and stare as my words hit them a little louder than I intended.

Eddie drops to my side. "Are you sure?"

I nod. "We need to try and save him. I'll need your help, Jaik." I try to force confidence into my words.

"Well," Jordan calls over as he finishes breaking the ties around Sera's ankles. "Whatever you're planning on doing, you need to be quick because the police will be here any minute."

Jaik holds his hand out to me. "Let's give it everything we've got."

Taking his hand, I shove all other thoughts from my mind as I focus on the purple light—willing it to flow one more time. I hover our hands just above Dylan's chest, pushing the purple energy out, feeling it swirl and twist with Jaik's green.

I have no idea how to heal a wound this severe and with every fibre of Dylan we fix, it seems to strip away one of mine. As the energy drains from me, I sway, struggling to keep hold of Jaik's hand. Still, I focus the light on the only boy I've ever loved with everything I have.

Love. The word takes me by surprise, but it feels true in my heart. We may have only known each other a few days, but I know I love Dylan with all my heart. I can't lose him. I can't. I screw my eyes tight and give it every last drop of energy I possess.

"Crystal!"

Someone tugs at my hand. I try to ignore it.

"Crystal!"

I open my eyes to tell whoever it is that I'm trying to concentrate, but it's Jaik, holding my hand with both of his. I blink, confused.

A bemused smile plays on his lips. "We did it."

"What?" I gasp, looking down at Dylan.

The knife lies at his side and the tear in his t-shirt soaked with blood, but the wound itself is just a light pink scar. He's breathing properly and his eyes flicker behind his eyelids as if he's dreaming.

I make a sound that's half laugh, half shriek as Jaik hauls me to my feet.

"Can you walk?" Jaik asks, looking pointedly at my quivering legs.

"Yes," I say, although I'm not actually sure I can. My eyes keep flicking back to Dylan.

"Go! Go! Go!" Eddie shouts.

The sound of sirens grows closer and I take a few steps forward, my head spinning. Jordan rushes past me, Sera slumped over his shoulder with Linda following close behind. Eddie and Jaik lift Dylan between them and follow suit. Tripping over my feet, I stumble after them, ignoring my body's pleas to collapse.

As we make our way out of the room, I steal a last look over my shoulder at the sprawled figures of Dr. Oakstone and Cadicus Kain. Police cars screech to a halt by the entrance and we make our way out of the window at the back of the building and away into the still deserted streets.

CHAPTER THIRTY-ONE

Crystal

I can't stop staring at my fingers. Splattered with blood, I still can't quite comprehend what happened. We came back to Dr. Oakstone's aunt's house. No one could think of anywhere else we could go, but it only makes it all the more real that he's not here with us.

My eyes flicker to the heavily patterned chair he was sitting in just a few short hours ago and my throat tightens. Such a clever and kind man. He survived death, only to arrive at the same end regardless.

"We need to wake Sera up."

I blink at Jordan's voice, sounding so far away, when in reality he's sitting beside me on the floor leaning against the sofa.

"I don't know how to even begin to explain what happened," he continues.

I'm unsure if the statement is directed at me, as he stares into the distance and I look around the room in a daze. Jordan, Jaik, Eddie, Linda and I sit slumped on the floor, bloodied, silent and tearstained. He can only mean me or Jaik, and I'm the only one out of the two of us that has any idea how to wake her up. That is, if Cadicus used the same mindsleep technique I did when we kidnapped Jaik. I try not to think about what will happen if he's done something else—something I don't know how to undo.

Wincing, I heave my aching body over to where Sera's lying on a makeshift bed, still gloriously oblivious to the hell we've all just endured.

I place my hands on either side of her head and will the purple light to flow through me once more. The sheer exhaustion of it almost makes me cry out. As soon as Sera's eyes open, I sink back down and wrap my arms around my knees.

"What's going on?" Sera asks, clutching her head as she sits up. "Where am I?"

Jordan pulls himself over to her and clutches her to his chest. "I'm so glad you're okay," he breathes. "You missed a lot."

"I can see that," she says. "Is he okay?"

I don't need to look at her to know she's talking about Dylan, lying on the sofa behind me.

"Cadicus tried to kill him. He almost died, but Crystal and Jaik saved him," Jordan explains.

"Oh," Sera breathes, her eyes wide. "What about Oak—"

"

"Oakstone's dead," I interrupt, my voice hollow. "Cadicus murdered him."

"There was nothing you could have done."

I stare at my knees, ignoring Jaik's attempt to reassure me. I can't bring myself to look at his bruised and battered face. Not yet.

Sera takes a wary intake of breath and I know which question is coming next.

"And Cadicus? What—"

"No longer a problem." Jaik cuts her off.

I look across at him, immediately wincing at the slash across his cheek and his swollen purple eyes and nose.

"We need to fix your face," I say, getting to my feet again. The room sways and I hold onto the arm of the sofa to steady myself.

"You need to take it easy." Jaik frowns, wincing at the movement. "My face will still be a mess after we've got some strength back."

Now I'm on my feet, I'm filled with the urge to get out of this room. I'm not sure whether it's the metallic stench of blood or the crushing weight of Dr. Oakstone's absence, but I can't breathe.

"I need some air," I mutter, before turning and stumbling towards the kitchen.

I use the small back door to let myself out into the tiny garden and the crisp morning air. Slumping down on the cold, stone step, my knees send jolts of pain through my body. They smashed hard when I fell from Cadicus' grip and I haven't the energy to heal them yet.

The sun has started to warm the breeze and I close my eyes, allowing it to caress my skin. I can't relax though. Even though it's all over, Cadicus' last words have been playing on a constant loop in my mind since we arrived back at the house. What did he mean?

Adored by the people, the royal family have always ruled with compassion and trust. Ambassadors are elected by the people and meetings are held regularly within different cities for people to raise their issues. Elaini and Jetzia founded Starlatten after fleeing a cruel and murderous regime on their home planet and with this in mind, they swore never to travel down the same path, ensuring a planet in harmony with its people.

If Starlatten is so bad, why do people still choose to live there? And as for Zarbilian being a prison ... I shake my head as the words prick the inside of my head like spikes. He was clearly out of his mind. Cadicus was the delusional leader of an uprising who wanted power to spread fear and destruction. I groan as I realise, I never asked about the other race that have supposedly settled on Zarbilian. Who are they? What part do they have to play in all this?

A small creature lands on my shoe. It rests there, opening and closing its delicate white wings. I stare, transfixed and unmoving.

"It's called a butterfly."

As Linda perches beside me, I keep my eyes fixed on the tiny creature.

"Are you okay?" she asks, giving me a gentle nudge. "Jaik's been filling us in on what happened inside."

I continue to stare at the butterfly, mesmerised by the opening and closing of its wings. I can hear people talking as they walk by on the street outside. Everything is carrying on around us as if nothing extraordinary happened this morning. I can't decide if it's comforting or infuriating.

"It sounds like you kicked ass," Linda tries again.

As the butterfly finally grows bored and flutters away towards some flowers, I break my stare and turn to look at Linda. "I kicked what?"

Linda chuckles, although the mirth doesn't quite reach her eyes. "It's an expression. It means you're a badass."

I continue to stare at her in bewilderment.

"You fought with impressive strength?" Linda tries again.

"Ah." I give a small, fleeting smile. "I suppose you could say that. I've certainly never used my amulet like that before." I hope I never will again.

Linda wraps an arm around my shoulders and squeezes. "If you hadn't, it's safe to say it wouldn't just be the Doc missing now."

At the mention of his name, a sombre silence falls over us. The image of Dr. Oakstone lying in his ruby puddle, looking so young and innocent, will haunt me for the rest of my days.

"Crystal! Linda!"

We turn in unison to find Sera standing over us in the doorway.

"Dylan's awake."

My heart pounds as I pull myself up, stumbling back towards the living room. Leaning against the doorframe, I find Dylan sitting up on the sofa against a flowery pillow. He's pale, but oh so gloriously alive. I realise I've not been allowing myself to think about him waking up. What if he hadn't? What if we hadn't been strong enough? I stand frozen in the doorway, staring at him—alive.

"I thought you were dead," I whisper.

"Nope," he says, looking down at himself with a small smile. "Definitely not dead."

He lifts a hand and I stumble forward, my eyes filling with tears of relief.

"Hey, don't cry," he soothes, wrapping his arms around me. "I'm okay, thanks to you."

As he strokes my back, I notice the rip across his blood-stained shirt. I touch my finger to the hole, tentatively running my fingertip over the pink silky scar tissue.

"How do you feel?" Jordan asks.

"Like I've been hit by a bus." His deep voice rumbles against my ear and I wrap my arm tighter around him. "Although," he continues. "Jaik looks like he actually was."

"Thanks, mate." Jaik raises a hand from where he's sitting. Someone's given him a bag of something, which he's holding over his swollen eyes.

"Seriously," Dylan says. "Thank you, Jaik. Thanks to both of you."

Dylan's fingers lift my head from his chest, turning my face to his. A myriad of emotions flash through his eyes as he looks at me. I wonder absentmindedly what I look like. When I talk my skin is tight, but whether it's blood, tears, sweat or all three, I have no idea. He traces his fingers down my cheek and I close my eyes. I thought I'd lost him forever.

My eyes open as I remember my realisation. I love him. My heart beats unevenly as the thought swells in my mind. Dylan's eyes widen a little and I wonder whether he can sense my thoughts as his thumb finds its way to my lips, brushing against them.

Sera coughs loudly from where she's leaning in the doorway. "So, I don't think I'm the only one who needs a shower."

My cheeks burn as she looks pointedly at me and Dylan before inspecting her dusty hair with disgust.

"Now that Cadicus is no longer a problem," she continues. "Why don't we go back to my house and get cleaned up?"

Linda leans back against the door with a groan. "That sounds like a fantastic idea. I'm so over this place."

Dylan shifts beside me. "Are we sure it's safe?"

Jordan shrugs. "I guess so. I mean, Cadicus' men aren't interested in us without him, right?"

"Even if they were," Jaik smiles wryly, "I think Crystal scared them good and proper."

Dylan nods. "Let's do it then."

"There's just one thing." Linda steps out of the kitchen, looking around with a frown. "I hate to say it, but people are going to ask questions if the seven of us wander across town covered in blood."

"Okay. Well, we could use the bathroom here to wash our faces and clean up a bit," Dylan suggests.

"Perhaps there are some clothes or coats we could borrow in the wardrobe?" Eddie adds.

"Great." Jordan pulls out his notebook from his back pocket. "I'll make a list of everything we take, so we can clean it all and bring it back before the aunt comes back from her cruise. She can't ever suspect we were here."

"Right." I stand and face Jaik with renewed determination. "Let's sort out your face."

Jaik smiles and pulls a long chain from his pocket, holding it aloft so the shimmering yellow stone glints in the light from between its ornate casing. "And later, we'll send another signal."

CHAPTER THIRTY-TWO

Jaik

My ankles are showing. I tug at the waistband of the dark blue jeans Sera has borrowed from her dad's wardrobe, but it makes little difference. I mean, it doesn't matter if the jeans are a little short. Not in the grand scheme of things.

Staring at myself in the full-length mirror in one of Sera's guest bedrooms, it's just nice to feel clean again. Crystal healed the gash on my cheek right down to a white-pink line and although my eyes are sore, they're no longer bruised and bloodshot. The hot shower stung, but it was a welcome relief.

I throw myself down on the bed and place my hands behind my head, staring up at the black jewelled chandelier dripping from the ceiling. The soft duvet envelopes my weary limbs like a deep pink swirling marshmallow and the warm breeze licking the curtains makes me smile with every caress against my skin.

When is the last time I felt this comfortable? It's been far too long since I felt any sort of comfort. Memories are still coming back to me all the time. Memories of home. Memories of my family. I realise things must have changed loads in the last seven years. Is my father even still alive? He might have been on the *Galastasia*. I close my eyes. A feeling I don't recognise washes through my body with every breath.

"Jaik? Are you okay?"

Linda's voice on the other side of the door forces me to open my eyes and sit up out of my marshmallow. I reach for the clean t-shirt Sera found for me. "I'm fine. Come in if you want."

As Linda opens the door, I stifle a grin as her eyes bulge at the sight of me shirtless. "Are *you* okay?" I ask, pulling the shirt over my head.

"Yeah. Of course. Fine."

My grin develops into a full smile. Linda is weird and adorable all rolled up into a neat little package. I stand and walk over to her, slinging my arm around her shoulders. "Come on. Let's get Crystal and send this signal."

I practically bounce down the stairs to the others and inhaling deeply, I manage to place the feeling I couldn't identify. It's hope.

When we reach the kitchen, Crystal's nervous disposition pricks at my good mood. I skid to a halt, forcing the smile to stay painted on my face.

"Are you ready?" I rub my hands together and sit on the stool beside her at the breakfast bar.

"As I'll ever be, I suppose."

My smile slips, replaced by a frown. "Why aren't you more excited?"

Crystal struggles to meet my eyes. "It might not work," she mumbles.

My heart sinks. This has to work. If it doesn't, I'm stuck here. We're both stuck here. Although, I now realise, perhaps that's what she wants.

"I mean, of course we'll try," she adds as she notes the steel in my eyes. "I just don't want you to get your hopes up."

Panic tickling my lungs, I reach out and spin her chair to face me, causing her to cry out in surprise. I place my hands on her shoulders and put my face close to hers. "Hope is all we have, Crystal."

She wriggles out of my grasp and I'm aware that Sera, Jordan and Eddie have stopped their conversations, staring at us curiously. Linda hovers somewhere over my shoulder.

"It's a little different for you," Crystal says, her voice tight.

I sit back on my chair and fold my arms. "Oh? How so?"

"If this signal works, we might get to go home," she says, "but your home is very different to mine."

I frown. Is that it? "We've both suffered losses, Crystal."

She closes her eyes and rubs her temples as though struggling to explain something simple to a toddler. Irritation causes me to grit my teeth and tighten the grip on my arms.

"When you go back, you can continue your life," she explains, staring at the ground. "You can rekindle friendships and hopefully find your father. I'm the queen.

I'm going back to deal with the biggest attack in our planet's history and the Zarbilian uprising. I have no one."

Tears form on her dark lashes as the words tumble from her lips. The silence is deafening, and I have nothing to say. All I can do is watch.

Crystal slips off her stool and walks to the door. "I'm going to check on Dylan and then we'll send the signal."

The kitchen door has barely swung closed before I'm off my stool, chasing after her. I find her collapsed, a couple of steps up the staircase, her fists balled in her eyes as though attempting to push the tears back in.

"Oh, Crystal." I sigh, sitting beside her. "I'm sorry."

She says nothing, her head still down.

"I'm just so excited at the thought of going home," I explain, slipping an arm around her shoulders. "I suppose I didn't think about what that meant for you."

"It's fine."

Resting my head on hers, I exhale. "I forget sometimes when I'm with you. It's like I'm still the Jaik you knew on Starlatten and this whole Earth thing has just been a dream. Although, nightmare would be more accurate. I never really dealt with what happened. Cadicus took my memories before I could grieve for my mother and I don't know how to process how I feel about something that happened seven years ago."

Crystal raises her head and I lift my own out of the way, taking in her damp, red eyes. "I don't know how long ago my parents died."

"What do you mean?"

"How long does it take to get from our solar system to here?" she asks. "Because I have no idea. In a large ship would be one thing, but in a tiny one-person escape pod? It might have happened an orbit ago. The control panel wasn't working when I woke up. I don't know whether it was one orbit, two orbits … I might have lost a huge chunk of my life." Her eyes open wide. "I don't even know how old I am. Maybe Starlatten isn't even there anymore. Maybe Zarbilian won and destroyed our planet."

My mouth falls open as Crystal spews the contents of her mind before me. I hadn't even considered half these things. No wonder she seems so tense. I'm not sure whether to shake her or hug her.

"Look," I try. "Cadicus seemed to be in the loop. If Zarbilian had won, he wouldn't have been so eager to get your amulet, right? There'd have been no point."

"Maybe …"

I reach out and wipe a tear from her cheek with my thumb. When I look in her eyes, I'm a kid again, lying in the grass, carefree, happy and buzzing from a day of mischief.

"Crystal … What you said before about having no one. You have me. I know it's not much, but you do."

"Thank you. It's okay," she says, sitting up a little straighter and wiping the remaining tears away with her palms. "I'll be okay."

She stands and before I can stop myself, I grab hold of her hand, my eyes still fixed on hers. The way she makes me feel … it's like everything makes sense.

"Let go, Jaik," she says, trying to shake off my grip.

I don't know what I'm doing. I just know I don't want her to leave.

"Jaik," she says, panic rising in her voice. "Let me go."

I blink and let my hand fall, watching as she runs upstairs without a backwards glance.

CHAPTER THIRTY-THREE

Crystal

"Dylan?"

My heart is pounding as I reach the room he's using. I lift a hand to knock on the door, but it opens before I have the chance and I step back in surprise.

"Are you okay?"

I open my mouth to reply but the words stick in my throat. Dylan stands in the doorway, his eyes narrowed with concern and his hair dark with water. My eyes follow the droplets as they pool on his bare shoulders, making tracks down his muscled chest, past his scar and down his stomach.

"I'm just getting dressed." He pulls the white fluffy towel tighter around his waist and steps backwards into the room. "Come in."

Swallowing hard, I step into the room decorated with dark green leaves and brightly coloured orange flowers. I'm unsure what to do with myself. I haven't felt this awkward around Dylan for a while. I'm not sure where to look.

"Let me throw some clothes on and we can talk."

He grabs some clothes from the back of a chair and disappears into the bathroom. I look around for a moment before deciding to sit on the bed to wait. I don't have to wait for long as it's mere seconds before Dylan emerges—his t-shirt wet in places where he's not dried himself properly. He rubs at his damp hair with the towel and sits down beside me.

"Have you been crying?" he asks, although I know it's not really a question.

I force a smile. "I'm fine. I'm just finding it hard to cope with Jaik's newfound enthusiasm."

Dylan tenses. "Why? What's he done?"

"Nothing really," I say. "It's just hard to figure him out. It's like he's three people: Jaik I knew from orbits ago, Jake the guy who attacked Linda in the alley and now Jaik whose only goal is to get home no matter what."

Dylan raises his eyebrows in surprise. "Did he say that?"

"Not quite," I admit. "He's just very excited about the possibility."

Dylan watches me, his eyes flickering over my face. "And you're not?"

I groan and look away, studying the thick green carpet instead. I sink my toes into it and consider my answer. "It's not that I'm not excited or looking forward to it. It's just that it might not happen. The chance of our signal reaching the right people is minute at best."

"But it might."

"It might."

He sighs and lies down on the bed, his hands behind his head. "What if it does?"

"I don't know—"

I gasp as Dylan's hands reach around my waist, pulling me down onto the bed beside him. He pulls me to his chest and wraps his arms around me from behind. A smile warms my face as I relax into the embrace and cover his arms with mine. This feeling—this sense of belonging that I get when I'm with Dylan—it feels a lot like being home.

"Talk to me," he murmurs in my ear.

Staring at the long curling leaves painted across the walls, I try to organise my thoughts. "I'm just not ready," I admit with a sigh. "I'm not ready to go back and lead an entire planet. It sounds ridiculous even saying it. Being queen was always so far away—something to worry about in the distant future. I never bothered to learn or pay attention. I wasn't the best in any of my classes and now I'm supposed to decide the fate of hundreds of thousands of people?" I shudder at the thought and Dylan presses a kiss to my neck. "I miss Starlatten terribly, but the Starlatten I knew is gone. Most of my friends and family are dead and I can only imagine the mess the planet is in after the attack. It may never be the same. Am I awful for being scared of going back to that?"

I wait in agony for Dylan's response, feeling the warmth of his breath against my ear and the thudding of his heart against my back. What if he thinks I'm a coward? Any relief I felt by sharing my concerns is overshadowed by fear of judgement as I wonder whether he'll think less of me for considering running from my responsibilities.

Just as it's becoming too much to bear, I hear the intake of breath I know will carry my answer. But the answer never comes.

Instead, Dylan pulls out of our embrace and turns me to face him. He stares at me for a moment, his lips parted as if on the verge of saying something. Then he seems to change his mind, choosing instead to cover my mouth with his.

My head swims as I inhale the citrus scent from his still damp hair. Our kiss deepens and he rolls on top of me. My heart contracts and I gasp at the sensation of his weight pressing down on me. His kiss sets fire to my blood and when he pulls back, I moan in disappointment.

"Don't go," he breathes, kissing my earlobe.

My heart stops. "What do you mean?"

Dylan props himself up, his breathing shallow as he stares into my eyes. "Don't send the signal. Stay here—on Earth. With me."

I open my mouth a few times to respond but any words I catch hold of, slip away. Nauseated by the flurry of emotions running through me, I push him off me and sit up.

"Please say something." Dylan swings his legs over so he's sitting next to me. He tries to take my hand, but I flick him away.

As the swirling emotions settle, I realise which one lies closest to the surface. "How could you?" I snap.

Dylan blinks in surprise. "How could I what?"

"How could you make things even harder for me?" I demand. "How could you be so selfish?"

His mouth sets in a firm line. "Maybe I shouldn't have said anything."

I stand and make my way to the door, my already sore eyes filling with angry tears. My hand on the handle, I pause, unable to look at him. "No. Perhaps you shouldn't."

We assemble in the living room and I find myself sitting cross-legged once more in the centre of the room with Jaik opposite me. Looking around, I can't believe it's only been a couple of days since we last sat around this very room after the incident with Eddie. The black television on the wall looms over us in silence. No one is brave enough to switch it on.

Sera sits sideways on Jordan's lap in a large soft chair. Her head nestled on his shoulder, they're engrossed in entwining and untwining their fingers. Eddie sits next to Linda on the sofa. He gives me an encouraging smile as our eyes meet. Linda, however, is chewing her nails, her eyes fixed on Jaik.

I have to twist around to find Dylan and for a moment I think he's left the room. But he's still here, standing by the door, arms folded and a foot resting against the wall, his face unreadable. He blinks and looks away a millisecond after our eyes meet and my heart plummets to the carpet.

"Let's do this." Jaik rubs his hands together and reaches into his pocket, pulling out Cadicus' amulet.

As he dangles it in the space between us, I can't hide the repulsion that rolls over me like a wave, forcing me to edge away from it.

"It's okay." Jaik reaches out and places a hand on my knee. "He's gone. He can't hurt us anymore."

Despite Jaik's words, I can't tear my eyes away from the yellow stone. Spinning on its chain, it disperses the rays of sunlight coming in through the partially drawn curtains into rainbow streaks across the room. How can something so beautiful have caused such evil? Every now and again, I catch a glimpse of amber within the smooth teardrop shape of the stone and my heart jolts as I recall those vile soulless eyes. Eyes which shone with delight as they murdered Dr. Oakstone and almost killed Dylan.

I force myself to look away. "Let's just get this over with."

Jaik clutches the amulet in his left hand before reaching for me. I take a shaky breath and take hold of his hands, trying to touch as little of the yellow amulet as possible.

Jaik raises an eyebrow at me. "Are you ready?"

"Yes," I reply with as much enthusiasm as I can muster.

Closing my eyes, I slow my breathing and focus on the warm purple crystal on my chest. My body floods with the glistening violet energy with barely any effort and I smile— filled with confidence.

After a moment, the now familiar rush of Jaik's green energy mixing with mine seeps in through my fingers and pulses along my arms causing my skin to tingle. Why have I not noticed before how intimate this is?

His energy is stronger this time, confidence glowing in every emerald curl as it entwines with mine. Stroking, searching, the green light moves as though it has a mind of its own.

My cheeks grow warm and I consider stopping, but before the thought fully forms, a blast of bright yellow energy shoots down my right arm and through my chest, knocking the breath from my lungs.

It takes everything I have not to open my eyes as I fight to hold onto Jaik's hands. Multi-coloured energy swells between us like a storm and I'm almost certain I'm being lifted up off the ground. Jaik's grip on my hands tightens. It's a signal. We have to push this energy up and out as far and high as we can. This is it. This is our chance for rescue. Our chance to go home.

The force of the upwards pour of energy seems to suck the air from the room and I screw my eyes tight and hold on to Jaik in fear of being pulled into the spiralling stream of colour.

After only a few seconds, the last of the energy snaps away from me with such force that I fall backwards, my tumble softened by the cushions pre-emptively scattered around us. I open my eyes, gasping in shock as my heart tries to hammer its way out of my chest.

Around us, paintings are askew on the wall, the lamp has fallen to the floor and the carpet is littered with the many magazines and books which previously adorned the low table near the sofa. Slowly, my friends lower their arms from shielding themselves from what appears to have been an actual hurricane.

Eddie whistles. "Well, that was different."

Linda fights to brush her windswept hair from her eyes. "Yeah ... it didn't do that last time. I mean, it was a bit windy, but nothing like that. At least you two didn't go flying this time."

Cadicus' amulet was so powerful, the sensation of yellow energy lingers inside me, and as I sit up, I shiver, repulsed by its presence.

"I guess that means it must have worked." Jaik pushes himself up from where he's fallen and grins, his eyes shining with joy.

His excitement is contagious and a smile spreads across my lips. "So, we did it?"

"We did it." Jaik reaches out and pulls me into a celebratory embrace.

It catches me off guard and I topple forward, tipping us both to the ground. The energy in the room is one of success and celebration and I allow myself to be swept up by it as Jaik kisses me on the forehead. When he bursts out in booming laughter, I find myself joining in.

We lie there in a heap of tangled limbs, my curls wrapped around my face as I laugh like I haven't since I left Starlatten. The stress and trauma of the past few days melts away as I lie in a pile of cushions laughing with people who mean everything to me. *Dylan.* I sit up and swipe the hair from my face, but the space by the door is empty.

"So, what now?" Eddie asks as he heaves himself off the chair and begins picking up the debris. "How will you know if someone gets your message?"

"Yeah." Sera slips off Jordan's lap to pick up the fallen lamp. "How do they know what the message is? Did you guys mentally shout 'help' as you sent the signal?"

Jordan cocks his head thoughtfully. "What if another alien race picks up the signal? Is that possible? And how would they get a ship into our atmosphere undetected?"

"What if it takes years?" Linda muses, eyes wide.

My confidence falters and I turn to Jaik for reassurance.

"It's not really something that's done very often," he tries to explain. "It's sort of an SOS. I'm assuming only people from Starlatten will be able to detect or read the signal as it would be transmitted or translated through their amulets. As for how long it might take … I have no idea."

Jordan pauses in his straightening of pictures on the wall. "Well, if you consider the speed of light, your energy must be as fast, if not faster. What we also need to consider is whether someone is already closer than Starlatten."

I frown. "What do you mean?"

"He means search parties." Jaik snaps his fingers and Jordan nods in agreement. "You're the queen, Crystal. They must have people out looking for you."

He reaches out and squeezes my shoulder, but I shrug it off. "They probably think I died on the ship."

"No." Jaik shakes his head. "They'll know. I remember when there was an accident back home in Galeania. There was a bad storm and a building collapsed. Several people were killed, but the rescue teams knew people were still alive because they could sense the power from their amulets."

"It's still rather unlikely though." I stare at the cushion I don't remember picking up, fingering the red fringe around its edges. "Earth is a long way from Starlatten."

"I'm beginning to think you don't want to be rescued."

My head snaps up at Jaik's accusation. I open my mouth to protest but find I'm not sure what to say. He's right. Part of me doesn't.

"Right. This has been the longest day in history." Sera sighs as she picks up the last fallen magazine. "I think we need some rest and some space. Boys? It's time to go home."

There's a reluctant murmur of agreement as people begin to gather their things.

"Erm, Sera?" Jaik scratches his head. "Have you got a sleeping bag or something similar I could borrow? I'll find somewhere to kip."

Sera palms her face. "Sorry, Jaik. I completely forgot."

"It's okay." Jordan smiles. "Come crash at mine. My folks are so used to Eddie and Dylan practically living there, they won't even notice."

"Thanks, mate." Jaik slaps him on the back as they start towards the door followed by Eddie.

"Are you coming, Linda?" Eddie calls as he scrolls through his phone. "That's weird."

"What?" I ask, my eyes focused on the glow of his display.

"Dylan's already gone home. Says he'll ring me tomorrow."

I try to keep my face neutral, even though every atom is trembling.

"I didn't even see him leave." Jordan pulls his phone from his pocket and stares at it. "I guess a near death experience deserves a bit of alone time."

"Fair point," Eddie agrees.

"I'll catch you up, Ed," Linda calls as the boys make their way out the door and into the hallway.

Eddie rolls his eyes and shuts the door behind him. "Don't be too long."

As we stand alone in the middle of the room, I'm struck by how much bigger it seems without the boys. I look from

Sera to Linda as the silence takes on an air of awkwardness, although I'm not entirely sure why.

Sera begins to back away towards the door that leads to the kitchen. "I'll give you two a minute."

I frown in confusion, turning to ask Linda what's going on, but she beats me to it.

"What's going on between you and Jaik?" she demands.

I stare at her, my eyes wide. I was not expecting this. "What do you mean?"

"I saw you," she says, lifting her chin. "On the stairs, earlier."

"Nothing is going on, Linda," I say, flinching at the memory of the awkward encounter. "We were just talking. He saw I was upset and was trying to comfort me."

Even as the words leave my lips, I know there's more to it. I've been trying to ignore it, but there's something in his eyes when he looks at me. Something … more.

I press my fingers to my eyes. "I know Jaik's a bit overfamiliar sometimes, but I think it's just because we're from the same place. We have a shared history. I think he feels safe with me."

Linda looks down at the floor, kicking at the carpet with her toes. "Yeah, I know. Anyway, it's not like we're together or anything."

I smile. "You like him, don't you?"

"It doesn't really matter. You guys will be back up in the stars soon."

My stomach somersaults and my face drains of colour.

"I'm sorry." Linda cringes. "I got so caught up in watching you and Jaik, I forgot about Dylan. Have you guys talked about it? What are you going to do?"

I take a breath, unsure of whether to confide in her about what happened upstairs, but the words fall from my mouth before I can make the decision. "He asked me to stay."

"He *what*?"

I turn with Linda to see Sera standing in the doorway, aghast.

Linda rolls her eyes. "So much for giving us a minute."

"This is huge!" Sera waves a hand at her in dismissal. "What did you say?"

I flop down on the sofa, pulling a green velvet cushion to my chest. "I told him it was unfair to ask me, and we haven't really spoken since."

"Ah." Linda sits down beside me. "That's why he was being all moody before he disappeared."

"I thought he was in a huff because he was sick of watching Jaik fawning all over you," Sera muses before looking sideways at Linda. "Sorry."

"Do you think Dylan's noticed Jaik's behaviour?" I ask, although I already know the answer.

Linda laughs. "I'd say so."

Burying my face in the plushness of the cushion, the swirling hurricane of thoughts in my mind turns into a thudding headache. Sera places her hand on my back.

"What are you going to do?" she asks.

I lift my head from the cushion to meet her sapphire blue gaze. "There's nothing I can do. We just need to wait and see what happens with the signal. Whether I stay or go isn't even really my choice at the moment."

"What are we going to do about Jaik?" Linda asks.

"Oh, don't worry about that." Sera grins, her eyes sparkling with mischief. "I already text Jordan and told him he has to ask Jaik what's going on between him and Crystal."

As the chatter swims around me, I sink back into the sofa. Guilt washes around my gut and my fingers dig into the cushion. I'm so tired of feeling guilty. Guilty for what happened to my family. Guilty for Dr. Oakstone. Guilty for not knowing what happened to Jaik. Guilty for pushing Dylan away. Guilty for obsessing over an Earth boy when my entire planet might be a mass of empty cold debris floating through the solar system.

As my eyes prick with tears, I bite my lip, hard. I'm sick of crying. I inhale a slow breath through my nose, trying to quell the shouting in my head. What do I want? What do I truly want? Dylan? I shake my head at the uncertainty of it all.

We could have a day together, a week—a lifetime. How long do people from Earth live? I force my brain back on track. Would it be better to stop now—to prevent the ache already in my heart from worsening when the time comes to leave? Or would it be better to savour every moment, enjoy each second we're given, but risk a devastated heart? When I picture Dylan's face, my heart shatters into a galaxy of stars.

But, I also want to go home.

CHAPTER THIRTY-FOUR

Dylan

It's strange to be home. Lying on my bed, my fingers keep sliding under my shirt to touch the silken scar on my chest. Mum tore pieces off me when I walked through the door, but I just stood there and took it, too tired to try and give excuses.

Eventually, her onslaught slowed and fear that something was wrong crept into her eyes. Finding the energy to assure her everything was fine and avoid the fact that I almost died this morning was exhausting but somehow, I even made it through the family meal. As soon as I'd eaten enough to satisfy, I excused myself to my room where I finally collapsed.

I have very little memory after the force of the knife knocked me to the floor. Drifting in and out of a haze, I remember sensing light and voices as I felt the life draining from me, blood gushing from me with every exhale.

My mind replays the image of Oakstone crumbling to the ground like a pile of Jenga bricks beside me. The whole gruesome scene is there every time I close my eyes like a desktop wallpaper I didn't ask for. We never had the opportunity to chat to the guy and I didn't feel like Oakstone wanted to discuss his personal life, but he didn't wear a wedding ring and he seemed too young to have a family. Certainly, no one else was living at the house Cadicus blew up. I wish we'd known more about him. He was a brilliantly clever man with his whole life ahead of him. What a waste.

Which is exactly why I don't want to waste any time. Why bite your tongue or play it safe when your life could end tomorrow? I know it seems like a cliché, but everything seems so much clearer now. Every day is precious and I'm not going to waste time doing things that make me miserable.

I want to live. To do. Despite my exhaustion, determination trickles in my bloodstream and the conversation I need to have with Mum about the bakery lies heavy on my mind.

Crystal had certainly not appreciated my carpe diem attitude. I rake my hands over my face as I replay the image of Jaik pulling Crystal on top of him. Of him kissing her—his hands always finding a way to touch her.

Maybe I should shave my head. Maybe that's what Crystal prefers. As soon as I think it, a snort of laughter bursts from my nose. I know Crystal likes me, not Jaik.

My heart swells, my breath hitching in my throat as I think of the way she kissed me at Sera's house. Then I opened my big mouth and ruined it all. I know it's me she wants. In my heart, I know. Knowing is useless, however, because I've blown it.

The second she walked out the door, I'd cringed at the selfishness of my words. She'd just confided to me her fear of going home and I'd thrown my own stupid feelings into the mix. She's a queen. My cheeks redden as I replay the scene in my head. I asked the queen of an entire planet to give it all up, for me.

Rolling over I bury my face in my pillow with a groan. How could she possibly stay? *Where* would she stay? I mean, we've known each other less than a week. I just ... I just don't want it to end. The thought of never seeing her again hurts more than Cadicus' knife.

What's worse is I understand how conflicted she is. Obviously, it's on a much smaller scale, but I understand the battle between desire and duty. Responsibility for my Mum and sister is what's stopping me from doing what I really want, and meeting Crystal has confirmed the whispers I've been ignoring in the back of my brain. I want to see the world. I want to travel. I send another groan into the pillow.

So now what? Do we all get together tomorrow? Is this whole thing over? Does life resume as normal? Questions swirl around my brain until I'm dizzy. Does Crystal even want to see me again? What if the signal takes months to work? What if it doesn't work? What if it works tonight? Tomorrow?

My heart begins to pound with a newfound urgency. I have to fix this. I can't waste another second with her angry or disappointed in me. If she doesn't want to see me, at least I'll know. But I need to know.

Grabbing my phone, I creep out of my bedroom, carefully navigating the creaky steps on the stairs and slip out the back door.

Waiting in the darkness of Sera's garden, my phone warm in my hand, I'm not sure if this is more Romeo or stalker. Sera replied to my text to say she'd speak to Crystal, but it was ages ago and my neck is starting to ache from staring up at her window. Are the curtains twitching? My eyes have adjusted to the dark, but I'm not sure.

The curtains pull apart, revealing a flood of warm yellow light from within and the silhouette of exactly who I'm hoping to see.

Crystal fiddles with the lock on the window before opening it and staring down at me, her eyes wide. "Dylan? What are you doing here?"

"I had to see you," I call up as quietly as I can. "Will you come down so we can talk?"

She pauses for what is probably a couple of seconds, but it feels like hours. Then she's gone, the window empty. I wait, my heart pounding, until a light turns on downstairs and the double doors leading from the kitchen slide open.

Crystal peers out, a blanket wrapped around her shoulders. "Why don't you come inside?" she calls. "It's warmer."

"I want to talk to you away from prying eyes and ears." I nod towards the house knowing full well Sera will be listening somewhere.

Crystal shivers and pulls the blanket around her as she walks out onto the cold grass towards me. "What would you have done if I wasn't awake? Or if Sera had been asleep?"

"I'd have thrown stones at your window until you woke up." I grin as she reaches my side. My heart grows ten times larger at the sight of her. "Come on, I've seen the perfect spot at the bottom of the garden."

I lead the way down through a small group of fruit trees to a clearing with a small fountain and a white painted metal bench. When I glance back, I can see only the very tip of the roof above the trees.

"See?" I nod. "Private."

Crystal moves to sit down on the bench, but I stop her. I pull my navy-blue hoodie off over my head and hand it to her, taking the blanket from around her shoulders and laying it down on the grass.

"Won't you be cold?" she asks, the sweatshirt hanging in her hands as she hesitates.

I roll my eyes and lie down on the blanket, placing my hands behind my head. "It's not even that cold. I'll be fine."

Crystal stares at me until a gust of cool evening breeze makes her shiver and pull the sweatshirt on over her head. Sitting down beside me, she pulls her knees to her chest. She's so close, but also so agonisingly far. Behind us, the fountain splashes and the drone of the occasional car can be heard in the distance. Other than that, it's eerily still.

"I'm sorry," I say, breaking the silence. "Perhaps it was the near-death experience or maybe it was just me being an insensitive jerk, but either way, I shouldn't have said it. I should never have asked you."

As my apology hangs between us, I sit up and take hold of her hands, tugging them until she raises her eyes to meet mine.

"I know we've only known each other a few days," I continue, stroking the backs of her hands with my thumbs, "but it's like you've always been here. I can't imagine life without you and the idea of you leaving forever? It kills me." I drop my gaze to our hands, aware that I'm presenting my heart to her on a platter for her to potentially destroy. "All I know is, if you'll let me, I want to spend as much time with you as I can before you leave. I couldn't cope knowing I'd wasted what little time we have left."

The silence is agonising, watching her thinking things over, and as she reaches out a hand to push the hair from my forehead, I'm sure my heart will burst. When I look into her eyes, it's like toppling over the edge of a cliff—falling and falling and never stopping. She traces her hand down my jaw and I move my face into her palm and kiss it. Reaching out with her other hand, she runs her fingers through my hair, and I close my eyes with a sigh. I'm not sure if it's a sigh of relief or happiness.

When she leans forward and places her warm lips on mine, I know it's both. My heart shatters into a million happy pieces as I reach out and wrap my arms around her, pulling her close. My eyes warm with joy, I pull back and kiss the tip of her nose.

"Does this mean you're in?" I ask. "For however long we have?"

Crystal smiles, her eyes sparkling in the moonlight. "For however long we have."

CHAPTER THIRTY-FIVE

Crystal

Smiling, I snuggle into Dylan's shoulder. Lying side by side, the stars above us glisten in the velvet darkness and for a moment, I think I can make out a couple of familiar constellations. I blink and they're gone.

"You know," I whisper. "On Starlatten, we have three moons."

"Whoa." Dylan chuckles, kissing me on the top of my head. "I'd love to see that."

A thought pops into my head and I sit bolt upright making Dylan flinch at the sudden movement.

"What's wrong?" he asks.

"Perhaps you can." Excitement courses through me, warming me despite the chilly evening air.

Dylan shuffles back up to a sitting position. "What do you mean?"

"I'm not sure if it works this way round," I say almost to myself, "but it should."

Before he can question further, I place my hands on either side of his head. Closing my eyes, the purple stone heats against my skin allowing the sparkling energy to flow through me and out of my fingertips.

Mauve fog clears, replaced by a blinding white light. I raise my arm to shield my eyes, aware of Dylan beside me doing the same. As my eyes adjust, I lower my arm, blinking to focus. I say Dylan's name, but no sound leaves my lips. I can only watch as he stares in awe out of my bedroom window. When I reach out to touch him, my hands move through him like a hologram.

I smile at the look of disbelief on his face as he takes in the towering glass walls framing the enormous white sunstar and our three moons. Anjar, the largest, is pale grey and ten times larger in appearance than the sunstar, so close you can see the craters and grooves. I smile as a handful of ships move in front of it, all enveloped by the beautiful pale green sky.

I inhale, grinning at the expanse of soft purple grass as it stretches out before us, edged with plants and trees in various hues of violet and blue. Below the trees, colourful flowers twist and bloom amongst delicate sculptures all enclosed by glittering grey walls.

Beyond the palace gardens, small clusters of buildings made of glass and shimmering stone glint in the sunlight, stretching out until they meet the shadows of the giant purple-grey mountains in the distance. Every now and again the white light of the sunstar reflects off landcraft as they hover between the buildings. I wonder whether I ever really appreciated how breathtakingly beautiful this was before.

Before I can think about what I'm doing and how this is working, my mind flicks to the throne room. I choke out a silent sob as the room materialises around us and I catch sight of my mother and father on their thrones.

My father stands, his arms outstretched, and for a moment I think he sees me, and I raise my arms in response, but of course, he hasn't. This is my memory of a brilliant speech he gave on our planet's civilisation anniversary. Standing proud, his dark skin contrasting with his pale robes, his eyes find mine across the crowded room and he smiles. I almost slump to the floor under the weight of my heart. Beside me, the ghostly image of Dylan watches, his eyes bright with wonder. I try and focus. This is for him—to show him where I've come from.

Forcing the grief from my mind, I picture my mother in our gardens—her favourite place. The memory shifts and I find myself standing above her crouched frame as she tries to teach me about the different plants in our gardens and the healing properties they have. Her soft curls fall down the back of her light blue robes as her delicate pale fingers run across the petals and leaves.

It's all too much and a wash of sadness makes me shiver. Before I can stop it, the memory starts to dissolve, rippling like a puddle into faint violet fog.

Silent tears stain my cheeks as I let my hands drop from Dylan's head. I wipe them away with the sleeves of his sweatshirt as he opens his eyes and stares at me in disbelief.

He opens and closes his mouth to speak several times, before shaking his head.

"Was it too much?" I ask, doubt stirring in the back of my mind.

"No," Dylan exclaims. He reaches forward and takes my hands in his, bringing them to his lips. "I'm glad you showed me. It's just a lot to take in. I mean, purple grass?"

My doubt turns to laughter as I relax into the smile playing on his lips. "So, what did you think? Honestly."

"Honestly?" He scratches his chin. "I mean, it's incredible. In fact, I'm even more in awe of how you've coped these last few days. Earth is a huge culture shock for you."

"It's certainly different." I move to lie back down on the blanket, pausing as I see Dylan watching me. "What's wrong?"

"I'm trying to decide if you look more like your mother or your father." He smiles and before I crumble, he reaches out and takes my hand. "I'm so sorry. You must miss them so much."

My throat is a lump and all I can do is nod.

After a moment, Dylan lies back on the blanket, pulling me down beside him. I watch him as he stares up at the night sky, memorising his profile. Every now and again, I reach out and stroke his face as if to check he's really here.

He turns his head toward me, and I note his serious expression, his eyes a million light years away.

"What's wrong?" I ask.

"I've had a lot of realisations today," he says, his eyes glistening with sadness. "I've decided I'm not going to take on the bakery. I hate getting up at four and five in the morning and I hate scraping dough out of my fingernails all day."

He sits up, plucking blades of grass and examining them before throwing them into the breeze.

"What are you going to do?"

He laughs bitterly. "Break Mum's heart. Tear my family apart."

"Will she not understand?"

"I honestly don't think so. She clings to the bakery as though it will bring Dad back. Maybe that's one of the reasons I don't want anything to do with it. As far as I'm concerned, his legacy doesn't deserve to be continued."

I watch him, my heart aching in sympathy. "I know it's different, but I understand how you feel."

"What do you mean?"

I pull my arms around my legs, resting my chin on my knees. "My path has always been laid out before me. I never asked to be a princess and I've never felt comfortable receiving special treatment. Back home, I'm not even allowed to pour my own drinks. I just want to be treated like everyone else."

"What would you be if you didn't have to be a princess?" he asks.

I raise my eyebrows, considering his question. "Do you know? I've never even thought about it, because it was never an option."

"Could it be an option?" he prompts. "What if you abdicated?"

My blood runs cold at the thought. Turning my back on over a thousand orbits of my family ruling Starlatten? I might not have chosen the path for myself, but the thought of running away from it ... it makes everything clear. Despite the fear of what lies ahead, it's something I need—something I want—to do.

My mother's voice weaves its way into my thoughts. As she held me in her arms amongst the terrifying chaos of the evacuation deck, her beautiful face streaked with tears and dirt, she'd told me that sometimes we don't get to create our own path. Sometimes we have to carve our own truth into the one that's been chosen for us.

I never wanted to rule but it's the right thing to do. I want to put things right. I want my home back.

"If there's a planet left to rule," I say with growing determination, "I want to be the one to do it." I turn my head to look at Dylan, my heart buzzing with the exhilaration of accepting my fate. "Thank you."

"For what?"

"For helping me realise that it's okay to accept my path, even if I didn't get to choose it."

Dylan gives me a small smile before standing and reaching out a hand to me. "You're welcome. Come on, let's get you back inside. You need a good night's sleep after today."

When we reach the sliding glass doors that lead to Sera's kitchen, Dylan leans forward and kisses me, squeezing my hand as he pulls back. "I'll see you tomorrow, okay?"

I notice that his smile fails to reach his eyes.

"See you tomorrow," I echo as he turns to leave.

I wait until he's disappeared into the darkness before I close the doors, only then realising that I didn't give him his sweatshirt back.

After tonight, I feel closer to him than ever, but as I turn and head back upstairs, I can't shake the feeling that somehow, I've pushed him away.

CHAPTER THIRTY-SIX

Jaik

After the third sigh from Jordan, I place the chemistry textbook I've been flicking through down on the cluttered desk and swing the chair round to face him.

"What's with all the sighing?"

Jordan looks up from where he's lying on his bed, his phone bright in his hands. As he glances between me and the screen, it's clear he's trying to decide whether to say something and I swear he changes his mind at the last second.

"It's just been a hell of a day," he says, placing the phone, screen down, on the bed. "I can't imagine what it must have been like inside the warehouse."

"Yeah. It wasn't fun."

"It must have been terrifying." Jordan shakes his head and sits up, leaning back against the headboard. "I mean, there was so much blood. And the bodies ... I can't shake the image of Oakstone face down, his glasses cracked on the floor and Dylan lying there, that knife in his chest like a flag in a sandcastle. The blood ..."

I lean back in the chair and survey him with a frown. Violence has been such a huge part of my life for so long. Sure, today was particularly gruesome, but I've seen worse. I haven't really stopped to consider how it might affect the others.

"First time you've seen a dead body?" I ask.

Jordan nods. "I'm guessing it wasn't your first time?"

I shrug.

"I can't help thinking," Jordan mutters, his eyes fixed on his hands, "if we'd come in a little sooner—"

"You'd have been dead." I cut him off. "Cadicus killed Oakstone in a split second. Even I didn't see it coming. If you guys had stormed the warehouse, you'd have all been part of the body count."

Jordan doesn't respond, his stare distant. I'm about to turn back to my book when his phone beeps, illuminating the bedcovers, despite being facedown. He sighs again.

"Seriously, Jordan?" I press. "Who is it? What's going on?"

A small smile appears on his lips. "It's Sera."

"Ah." I lean back and fold my arms behind my head. "And she's making you sigh like that already? You two been together long?"

"We've known each other for years, but we've only been together," Jordan pauses, surprise lighting his face. "two days."

"Two days?" I raise my eyebrows. "You seem pretty serious."

"It's been a pretty serious couple of days."

I snort as Jordan taps out a response to Sera, the phone giving his dark brown skin a blueish tint. My heart beats a little faster as I realise the next question I'm about to ask. "How long have Crystal and Dylan been together?"

Jordan's head snaps up fast enough to give him whiplash.

"Erm, same as me and Sera to be honest," he says, trying to hide his reaction to my question by rearranging the pillow behind him. "We got together the same evening."

"Seriously?" I scoff. "Two days? What is it with you lot and super serious relationships? What do you do after a week? Get married?"

Jordan pulls a face and shakes his head. "Hilarious. Anyway, Crystal only landed on Earth, what … five days ago?"

My hands drop to my lap in shock. "What? Five days? I thought it had been a couple of weeks, or longer. No wonder she seems so bewildered all the time." I swivel on the chair and gesture around Jordan's room. "I can't begin to imagine how weird all of this stuff must be to her."

Jordan sits forward in interest. "Pretty different where you come from, huh?"

"Oh man." I laugh. "You have no idea. I mean, all of this is normal to me because I lived with Cas for so long believing Earth was my home. Now, when I think about my life before? It's laughable. I don't mean to offend, but you guys are so—"

"Primitive?" Jordan offers.

I hold my hands aloft. "You said it, but yeah. Primitive."

We sit in silence for a moment and I think back to Starlatten, wondering how much it's changed since I've been gone. I wonder if my home is still there. Is my father there alone? Did he remarry? My heart contracts as I imagine him living in our home with a new family as though we never existed. I force the image from my mind.

"You okay?" Jordan asks.

"Yeah." I smile. "Just thinking about purple grass."

"Purple grass?" Jordan's eyes bulge at the thought.

"Yep. And three moons. Oh, and the plants are blue, and the sky is green."

"You have three moons and purple grass?" Jordan exclaims. "Purple freakin' grass? It sounds like something out of a Dr. Seuss book."

"Just imagine how bewildered Crystal is."

Jordan blows a slow whistle through his teeth. "Jeez. I bet she thinks Earth is so ... bland."

I laugh harder. "Don't be so harsh. Think about the rainforests. Tropical islands. There's some pretty incredible beauty on this planet."

"So, back on your planet—I will never get used to saying that," Jordan laughs, "—did you live near Crystal?"

"Her palace was about a day's journey away by landcraft. My place was really nice, but the royal palace?" I shake my head, remembering the glistening white walls and sprawling gardens. "You wouldn't believe it."

"It really sucks what happened to you," Jordan says out of the blue. "I'm sorry."

Jordan's words take me by surprise, and I can only meet his sympathetic stare for a second before dropping my gaze to my shoes with a shrug.

"How old were you the last time you were on Starlatten?" he asks.

"I suppose around eleven or twelve in your years?" I swivel back and forth on the chair. "I can guarantee things have changed quite a bit in the last seven years though."

"What do you mean?"

"Technology, fads, fashions," I explain. "Think of how many things exist on Earth that didn't seven years ago."

Jordan considers this for a moment. "I'd imagine even more so on your planet as you're so technologically advanced."

A comfortable silence settles over us and I turn back to the stack of textbooks on Jordan's desk.

"I wonder if Crystal's told Dylan about the three moons and purple grass." Jordan muses, his phone back in his hand again.

My jaw clenches and my shoulders stiffen as I flip the pages of the history book I've selected, trying to shake the frustration in my fingertips. Five days. She's been here *five days*. Anger churns and bubbles in my gut until finally, it erupts. I slam the book down on the desk and turn to face Jordan.

"If you ask me, Dylan's taking advantage."

Jordan flinches but doesn't speak.

"I mean, she crash-lands on a strange planet after losing her entire family, and he makes a move on her? Are you kidding me?"

My skin is red hot and I want to crush something in my fists. At the same time, however, it's so good to get this off my chest. It's like a weight has been lifted.

"It's a bit more complicated than that," Jordan mutters.

"Is it though?" I demand, leaning forward. "Let's face it, Crystal is extremely vulnerable and Dylan's taking advantage."

"Hey!" Jordan shouts. "Dylan isn't like that. He really cares about Crystal. He'd never do anything to hurt her."

I open my mouth to reply, a pile of spiteful retorts on my tongue, but there's no point. Jordan is Dylan's best friend. He's never going to take my side. Exhaling in frustration, I lean back in the chair.

"You really care about her, don't you?" he asks.

"Of course," I snap. "She's my only link to home. She's one of my last memories of who I was."

"Were you and Crystal ever more than friends?"

Jordan's question comes quietly and stops the breath in my throat. A memory of lying side by side in lilac grass, breathless from running and laughing, fingers touching. Staring up at the moon, she'd started counting the craters and I'd taken her hand in mine. She'd turned to look at me, her brown eyes large and sparkling. I remember finding it harder to breathe. It was the last time I saw her.

"No," I say, shaking the picture from my head, surprised at the clarity of the forgotten memory. "I'll admit, when we spent that summer together, I started to hope we might become something more, but we were so young. I thought we had time."

"What about Linda?" Jordan asks.

My head snaps up and I frown. "What about her?"

"I don't know." He shrugs. "You two seem pretty close."

"I guess." I smile at the thought of her face when she came to check on me earlier. "She's pretty great and I owe her a lot. She was so brave coming to find me after I ... well ... after how we met."

"So, there's nothing romantic going on?"

"Romantic?" I echo, unable to keep the smirk from my face. "No. If Crystal and I go home, there's no point. I'll never see her again, so why break her heart?" I look pointedly at Jordan, who shakes his head. "Why are you suddenly master of questions anyway?"

He ignores my question. "What if you don't go home?"

I stand and lift the curtain, staring out the window at the empty sky. "Nothing we can do but wait."

CHAPTER **THIRTY-SEVEN**

Crystal

I wake how I've woken every day since the explosion—with a hard knot in my stomach, wondering where I am. What horrors might today hold? As the sunlight filters through the curtains, my eyes focus, and I remember. Sera's house. Safe. Sighing with relief, I snuggle into my pillow and pull my covers around me, enjoying the warmth of the bed.

A familiar scent winds its way to my nose and I open my eyes to find I'm clutching Dylan's sweatshirt to my chest. I smile and bring the soft blue material to my face, inhaling deeply. The knot in my stomach starts to unravel, giving way to hope—and hunger.

Stretching, I swing my legs over the bed and motion to the clothes piled on the chair. They drift across the room and into my open arms. *Oh.* I stare, astonished, at the clothes in my hands. It's the first time I've used my amulet so casually since the ship and it brings with it an uneasiness I can't quite place.

By the time I arrive downstairs, Sera is munching on some toast and nursing a cup of coffee.

"Hey." She grins, her blue eyes sparkling with excitement. "Tell me everything."

I slip onto a stool, keeping my face neutral, and pour myself a glass of orange juice. "I have no idea what you're talking about."

"Oh, come on, Crystal. Don't make me beg. What's going on with you and Dylan? Did you sort everything out?"

"I suppose so." I give her a small smile. "We've decided we're going to make the most of whatever time we have."

"Aww, that's sweet," she says, before adding as an afterthought, "well, bittersweet I guess."

"So, what's the plan for today?" I ask, changing the subject. "What do people do when they're not running from murderous rebel leaders?"

Sera laughs, sending her long golden tresses in ripples across her shoulders. "Something fun. I've already messaged everyone to meet here when they're up."

I glance around for a clock, even though I haven't quite got the hang of Earth time. "What time is it?"

"It's almost midday," she replies, shaking her head. "It seems we've all had a bit of catching up to do in the sleep department."

As I consider this, there's a knock on the glass double doors. My heart jumps into my throat as I turn to see who it is, but sinks with a wave of guilt as I see Linda and Eddie waving to be let in.

"Morning!" Linda grins as Sera opens the door. "Did you sleep well?"

I nod. "Very well, thank you. And you?"

Linda shrugs and pulls up a stool. Sera called Linda last night immediately after Jordan had told her about his conversation with Jaik. Perhaps it's for the best that Jaik isn't interested in Linda that way. Eddie is a long way from forgiving him for the whole 'attacking his little sister in an alley' situation.

"Are you okay, Eddie?" I ask as he props himself up at the table.

"Right as rain," he says. "Which means good."

I smile gratefully for the explanation. "We were just discussing what we're going to do today."

"I've been thinking about that too," Linda blurts. "You need to experience some proper Earth culture before you go back."

"Please, not a museum."

I turn at the familiar tone to find Jaik standing at the open doorway, Jordan by his side.

Jordan heads straight to Sera's side, wrapping his arms around her with a tender kiss and I smile at the sight of their happiness. Jaik is still leaning against the doorframe, his tall broad figure filling the space. He must have borrowed the black long-sleeved t-shirt he's wearing from Jordan, because it's tighter than anything I've seen him wear, showing off his muscular arms and chest. His green eyes gleam like precious stones in the morning light and I find myself trying and failing to find the young boy I held hands with so many orbits ago.

"Museums are boring," Jaik continues, locking eyes with me. "I should know. I've slept in most of the ones around here."

"You poor thing." Linda pats the stool beside her and Jaik pushes himself off the doorframe and makes his way over. "Did Cadicus kick you out a lot?"

He shrugs. "If I didn't come back with enough information, money or goods, he'd make me stay out until I did. I got quite good at sneaking into places until they shut."

"So, it's a no to museums then?" Jordan jokes.

"As if I would suggest a museum." Linda laughs. "I was thinking the cinema and perhaps the zoo."

Chatter flutters around the group as they discuss the idea and I watch, sipping my orange juice, quite content. I have no idea what 'cinema' or 'zoo' mean, but everyone seems quite pleased with the suggestion.

"There's a decent film on in town at one," Eddie offers, already tapping away on his phone.

Sera swipes something on her phone. "That means we'll still have a couple of hours for the zoo if we still want to go. Perfect."

Jaik leans over to me, whispering conspiratorially in my ear. "The cinema is giant moving pictures telling a story and the zoo is where they keep different types of animals from around the planet."

I smile at him in thanks and he closes one eye in a gesture I've now been told is called a 'wink'. Turning away, I stare out of the window to the garden. Where is Dylan? Why isn't he here yet?

A black hole opens in my stomach. What if Jaik and I didn't do a good enough job of healing him? What if we missed something? What if started bleeding in his sleep? What if he's dead? I picture him, lifeless and pale in a pool of blood, and find I can no longer breathe.

"Has anyone heard from Dylan?" I choke out.

The chatting stops as everyone turns to me.

"Are you okay, Crystal?" Jordan asks. "You look like you've seen a ghost."

I try again, cold fear making every fibre of my body shudder. "Has anyone heard from Dylan?"

Eddie holds up his phone. "I'll call him."

Linda reaches across the table and places a hand on mine. "What's going on?"

I force myself to utter my worst fear. "What if the healing didn't work? What if we missed something? What if he's—"

"Late?"

I spin around on my stool to see Dylan standing by the doors. I leap from my stool, and fall towards him, wrapping myself against his chest. "I thought something had happened to you."

"Whoa!" he exclaims as I almost knock him back through the doors. Relaxing into my embrace, he rubs my back and kisses my hair. "I'm fine. I just needed a nap between opening up the bakery and coming here. I'm exhausted." He tips my face and winks. "Must have been the late night."

"You opened the bakery this morning?" Eddie gawps. "You almost died last night."

Dylan loosens his embrace, lifting his head from mine. "I couldn't exactly explain that to my mum, could I?"

I wonder whether I'll still be here when he tells his mother his decision about the bakery. As I picture him, heartbroken and wracked with guilt, a lump forms in my throat and I reach up to stroke his face. I want to be there for him, but the cold reality is that I probably won't.

"Right." Jaik smacks his hands down on the breakfast bar with such force it makes me jump. "I'm off. Have fun kids."

Linda's face falls and she reaches up to place a hand on his arm. "What? You're not coming?"

"Nah." Jaik stands and gives her shoulder a squeeze. "I'm going to swing by Cadicus' place to see if the police have found it yet. I want to see if I can find any useful information. He might have kept some of my mother's stuff too."

"Be careful," I offer as he walks towards the door.

He stops right in front of me, his green eyes intense as he stoops and gives me a kiss on the cheek. "I will."

Lifting a hand to the others, he steps outside, knocking Dylan's shoulder on his way out. I wince, but Dylan says nothing, his mouth set in a firm line as his fingers tighten on my shoulders.

"Right." Sera dusts the crumbs from her fingers and finishes the last dregs of her coffee. "Let the day of fun begin!"

I'm so happy I could burst. As I snuggle down into the seat next to Dylan with my second slice of pizza, my face aches from smiling. I don't know many Earth foods, and as pizza was the first one I tried, it seemed like a fitting choice tonight when they asked me what I'd like to eat.

In the furthest corner of my mind, a small knot of nerves glows like a distant beacon, but I've covered it in so many layers of happy, I hope perhaps it will fade away.

Today was an incredible experience. When Jaik described the cinema as moving pictures, he hadn't prepared me for the overload on my senses. We watched a film about two people racing to save the city from a villain. Dylan explained that the people on the enormous screen were called actors and most of the things happening had been added later by computers.

I mean, Starlatten has art, stories and music, but nothing like that. It was so loud and powerful. I laughed and cried, completely exhilarated by the end. It also gave me a glimpse of other countries on Earth and I'm in awe of the diversity spread across such a small planet.

After the cinema, we made our way to the zoo. It was very busy and filled with herds of small children, which I admit I enjoyed immensely. I haven't seen much of normal Earth life and it answered several of my questions. Oh, and the animals ... What amazing and incredible creatures. My favourite by far was the giraffe. Dylan had to pull me away from their enclosure. I read every single fact plaque for every exhibit, lapping up information until the crowds waned and the air took on the chill of late afternoon.

Finally, exhausted, we made our way back to Sera's house to order pizza and go over the events of the day. Dylan hasn't left my side. I can't describe how much I've enjoyed being close to him. Holding his hand and relishing the warmth of his arms slipping around me—the soft brush of his lips on my skin when he kisses my neck.

There were a couple of times today, however, when I caught him staring at me with a sad, distant look on his face. I tried to ask him about it, but every time I did, he dismissed it with a kiss, telling me he was just admiring how beautiful I am. Of course, I know it's something more than that.

"I hope Jaik's okay," Linda says through a mouth full of pizza.

I look away from Dylan. "I'm sure he is."

"Could you find out?" Linda asks, peering out from beneath her lashes. "You know, with your amulet?"

"I'm sure he's fine," Dylan grumbles. "He'll show up at some point."

Linda stares at me, her eyes pleading, so I finish my bite of pizza and wipe my hands on a napkin. Closing my eyes, warm, purple glittering energy fills my mind. I concentrate on Jaik, trying to picture him neutrally, but I keep coming back to the brooding image of him in black, leaning against the doorway earlier today.

Are you okay? I push the message out and he replies almost instantly.

Yeah, I'm fine. Did you enjoy your 'day of fun'?

The sarcasm hanging on every word irks me, but I shake it off. *It was very nice, thank you. Are you coming back to Sera's? We have food.*

There's a pause. *Do you want me to come?*

I frown. *Whether I want you to or not is irrelevant. We're here. There's pizza. Are you coming or not?*

Calm down. I'm coming.

Opening my eyes, I end the communication before he can add anything else. Linda stares at me expectantly. "He's coming."

She smiles and returns to her pizza.

"Great," Dylan mumbles.

When the doorbell rings half an hour later, Linda leaps up to answer it and I share a look of concern with Sera. Jordan told Sera that Jaik thought Linda was nice but there was no point getting involved, which Linda seems to have taken as a positive sign to pursue something. Sera has tried to steer her away from the idea several times, but she doesn't seem to be listening.

Linda drags Jaik into the room and on to the sofa beside her.

He gives a collective greeting and grabs the slice of pizza we saved for him. "So, did you all have a good day?"

"It was brilliant." Sera smiles. "You should have come."

"Did you have any luck at Cadicus' house?" Jordan asks.

"Oh, yes." Jaik says, looking at me. "I found my mother's amulet."

My mouth falls open. "That's amazing. I suppose that's how he was able to keep in touch with Zarbilian."

Jaik pulls a glistening blue amulet out of his pocket, holding it aloft. "We can try sending another signal tonight if you want?"

"Do you not think it could be dangerous, using too many amulets?" Dylan says. "The aftermath of the last attempt was pretty intense."

Words stick in my throat as Dylan and Jaik stare at each other, the underlying aggression palpable. I kiss Dylan's cheek, drawing his attention away. "We can think about it and weigh up risks. There's no rush."

General chatter resumes as Eddie and Sera go to fetch some more drinks. I breathe a quiet sigh of relief but as I watch Jaik, I can see the anger rippling just under the surface. The crust of pizza he's holding is mush beneath his clenched fist.

Are you okay?

He doesn't even look in my direction. *I just want to know I've done everything I can.*

I'm about to respond when Linda echoes my question, unaware of our silent conversation.

"I'm okay, thanks," Jaik says, putting an arm around her and pulling her towards him. "Thank you for looking out for me."

Linda smiles up at him. "Any time."

He bends and kisses her on the cheek, then—with a quick glance at the kitchen door—he lifts her face and kisses her on the lips. I'm not sure if it's me or Linda who gasps.

As they pull apart, Jaik leans back on the sofa, his arm draped around a beaming Linda. My fingernails dig into my palms and my teeth grind together as I glare at the side of his face. I know he can feel me staring but he ignores me.

What in Jetzia's name are you doing?

For a moment I think he's going to ignore my message too, but then the petulant reply comes.

Well, if no one cares about getting me home, I might as well make the most of my time on Earth.

A frustrated growl rumbles in my throat and Dylan looks at me, his eyebrows raised, but I grit my teeth and focus on my empty drink. When Eddie and Sera return, they both freeze, staring at Jaik and Linda as though a wild creature has wandered into the house and joined us. Eddie looks as furious as Sera does thrilled, but neither of them say anything as they hand out drinks and take their places.

I resume my glaring. *You'd better not hurt her. You'll break her heart.*

This time, Jaik turns to look at me, his green eyes dark and defiant as he slides his gaze down to Dylan's arms wrapped around me.

He narrows his eyes and shakes his head. *You mean, like you're going to do to Dylan?*

I look away.

CHAPTER THIRTY-EIGHT

Dylan

"Do you know what's going on with Jaik and Linda?"

Crystal pulls away in surprise at my question. Everyone has long since gone and the sun has dipped below the horizon, leaving Crystal and I saying our goodbyes in the hallway. Although, these are the first words either of us has spoken.

"I think he's trying to prove a point," she says, trying to resume our kiss.

I lift my chin, putting my mouth out of reach. "What do you mean?"

She sighs, her eyes looking everywhere but at me. "Jaik's convinced I don't want to go home."

"What? Why?" I lean back so I can see her face. "Because you didn't jump at the chance of using his mum's amulet?"

My shoulders stiffen and I try to breathe out the tension. I get that Jaik's been through a lot, but man he can be so dramatic. Crystal's eyes look sad and distant now and I curse myself for causing it. I shouldn't have said anything.

Tucking a curl behind her ear, I lift her chin and press my lips to hers. I swear I'm addicted. Every time I'm near her, my blood lights on fire, my heart aching with an insatiable need to touch her, to be close to her. It's never enough.

Today has been brilliant and I'll admit I enjoyed every second of watching the childlike wonder on Crystal's face as she took in even the most common sights. Now I've seen what Starlatten is like, I'm beginning to see Earth through her eyes and it's definitely making me see things I take for granted in a new light. It's also cemented the gut-wrenching realisation I had last night—she can't stay. We have to get her home, where she belongs. Keeping her here on Earth would be like capturing a rare and beautiful bird and keeping it in a cage.

Also, there are the practicalities. We don't even speak the same language. What would happen if her amulet broke, or stopped working? I mean, how long do people from her planet live? How old is she, really? She looks my age, but we haven't had time to do the maths to work it out properly. I must remember to ask Jordan about it tomorrow.

Crystal's fingers find their way under my t-shirt and I push the thoughts of her leaving back into the furthest corner of my mind where they've set up camp, and try to pretend they aren't there.

I'm too late, however, as Crystal breaks the kiss, staring up at me in concern. "What's wrong? What are you thinking?"

I smile and try to resume the kiss, but she leans back, her hand on my chest.

"Don't try and distract me with a kiss or tell me how beautiful I am." She frowns up at me. "I want a proper answer."

I study her face, trying out several answers in my mind before the simple truth finds its way to my lips. "I was just thinking how unfair it is."

She stares at me, waiting for more of an explanation.

With a reluctant groan, I let go of her and turn to lean against the wall beside her. I push my hair back from my face in an attempt to buy more time to cope with the words I don't want to make real by admitting them.

"It just seems like everything I want at the moment means hurting people. I want to travel instead of taking on the bakery, which will hurt my mum. And ..." I pause, my heart aching as Crystal looks up at me, her big, brown eyes wide and innocent. "I want you, but I can't keep you."

"Oh, Dylan," she says, her voice breaking as her eyes sparkle with tears.

Guilt floods through me, my heart hanging like a bag of wet sand in my chest. "See? This is why I didn't want to say anything. I didn't want to ruin this perfect day with my pathetic pity parade."

Standing on her tiptoes, she pulls my face to hers, softly kissing my cheeks, my nose and finally my lips. "Don't think about the end. We might have many more days like this, and while I'm here, you have me. All of me."

For a heartbeat we stand there staring at each other, but then my hands are on her waist as I press her against the wall, kissing her like it's the only thing keeping me alive. Crystal's heart thuds in time with mine against my chest as my hands move up to her face, tangling in her curls. As she pulls me closer, the softness of her lips, the warmth of her mouth causes everything, every bit of common sense— everything other than my need to be with her, touch her— to fade away. Crystal's fingers find their way under my shirt again, her thumbs sliding up my stomach and it takes more willpower than I thought I was capable of, but I pull away, my breath ragged.

"I should go."

Disappointment flits across Crystal's face and I smile, despite my frustration, at how beautiful she looks.

"You don't have to go," she whispers.

"Trust me, I really don't want to," I say, straightening my shirt and hair, "but I do. I have to be up at four."

Every thud of my heart screams at me to stay—to make the most of every single second we might have—but instead, I take her fingers and lift them to my lips.

As I close the door behind me, the cold night air smacks me across the face—a stark contrast to the heat of the last hour. Lightheaded at the memory of her touch, my fingers trace my swollen lips as the real reason I left echoes along the empty street with every step. I've fallen. Hard. When the time comes to let Crystal go, it's going to shred my heart into a tiny million useless shards and I'm not sure I'll survive.

CHAPTER THIRTY-NINE

Crystal

With a glance at the light switch by the door, the room clicks into darkness and I pull the covers around me. Holding Dylan's hoodie to my chest, I inhale his scent and close my eyes. My body tingles at the memory of our last moments, my breath catching in my throat as I replay our last kiss. A delicious end to a perfect day. Highlights dance through my mind and wonder which Earth experiences might be suggested for tomorrow.

As I lie there contemplating travelling to Africa with Dylan to see giraffes in the wild, sleep wraps its tendrils around me, and I slip into the comforting darkness with a smile.

I'm woken by a swirling silver mist brushing against me, wrapping itself around my limbs, nudging me and whispering my name until I sit up.

"Hello?" I call out.

Peering through the grey mist, the mattress beneath me shifting as I turn, I wonder whether this is a dream or really happening? My senses are disorientated but this sensation is familiar …

Fear squeezes the air from my lungs, and I swing my legs over the side of the bed, preparing for the amber eyes I'm certain are going to appear.

"Princess Akinara? Can you hear me?"

I gasp, turning a slow circle, searching for the source of the voice. It's not the deep, arrogant tones of Cadicus. My fear melts into confusion as I squint into the mist. The voice sounded muffled, as though coming from another room. I decide to reply.

"Who are you?"

"We have received your signal and located you, Your Majesty. We will come to you at nightfall at the top of the large landmass near your location. I'm afraid we don't have names for the geological locations on this planet."

I freeze. "Tomorrow? Who are you?"

"The Royal Guard, Your Majesty. May the stars bless you."

Before I can respond, the silver mist thins as though being sucked from the room, until I'm left alone in the dark.

I open my eyes and sit up gasping, searching the room for signs of silver mist as my heart slams against my ribcage. Sinking back down onto my pillow, I exhale. It was just a dream.

What if it wasn't? How can I possibly tell? I wonder whether they've contacted Jaik. Before I can decide whether it's a good idea or not, I reach out to him.

Jaik? Are you awake? Jaik?

I am now. His voice is filled with sleepy concern. *What's wrong?*

Has anyone contacted you? I ask.

What do you mean 'anyone'?

I sigh with frustration. *Anyone from home.*

No. A pause. *Have they contacted you?*

I'm not sure, I admit. *It might have been a dream. That's why I thought I'd see if you'd been contacted too, so I can be sure.*

What did they say?

I think back to the mist and try to recall the details. *They said they were the Royal Guard, and they have my location. They want to pick me up tomorrow night at the top of a large land mass.*

A large land mass? What? Like a hill?

I roll my eyes—glad he can't see me. *How am I supposed to know? They didn't say.*

We'll have to go tomorrow night and see then! This is brilliant news.

I can't help but smile at his enthusiasm, but I don't share it. In fact, I'm a little numb.

See you bright and early, he says.

As Jaik's final message gives way to silence, I wander over to the window. It's still dark outside and from the lack of noise, I can tell it's still the middle of the night. Pulling the curtains apart, I stare up at the silent sky and a handful of stars blink back at me. Rescue. I should be thrilled.

If this is real, I'll get answers. How long ago was the *Galastasia* attacked? What's happened to Starlatten? Do they know Cadicus is dead? Are my grandparents still alive? My heart warms at the thought of seeing them again. Every question, however, spawns a thousand more. What if everything I know is gone?

I stare up at the sky until my eyes are sore and my toes are numb.

"Wake up, sleepy head."

I try to open my eyes at the sound of Sera's voice but fail. After an awful night's sleep, my body is heavy with exhaustion.

"Is everything okay?" I mumble. "Did I miss anything?"

Sera chuckles and the bed sinks as she perches at the end of it. "No. It's still morning. Jaik and Jordan are downstairs already though and Jaik really wants to talk to you."

I pry my eyes open to see Sera watching me, her eyebrows raised. Last night's dream-message comes flooding back and I pull the covers over my head with a groan.

"You can't avoid him forever." Sera laughs. "Plus, Dylan's on his way over too. Jaik told Jordan to text everyone. If you thought he was excited the other day, well ..."

I push the covers back and sit up. There's no hiding from this. Better to get it over and done with. Besides, perhaps it really had been a dream after all.

Twenty minutes later, I walk into the kitchen to find Jaik pacing, as everyone else perches on stools around the breakfast bar wearing similar expressions of curiosity and confusion.

"Finally!"

Sidestepping Jaik, I cross the room to where Dylan's waiting to pull me into his arms. I inhale the scent of soap, bread and something spicy that makes me deliciously lightheaded and kiss him. What happens next could change everything and perhaps it's selfish, but I want to hold on to the way things are until the very last second.

"Crystal?" The impatience in Jaik's voice rises. "Are you going to tell them, or should I?"

Pulling away from Dylan, I smooth away the crease that's formed between his brows with my thumb, before turning to Jaik.

"Tell them about the message," he says.

"So, last night, I dreamed I received a message from the Royal Guard." Dylan's arms tense around me and I swallow. "They said they were coming to collect me from a large landmass nearby."

A tense silence follows, punctuated by the shuffling of Jaik's feet as he shifts from one to the other. Jordan is the first to speak.

"So, was it a dream or not?"

"I honestly don't know for sure."

"When did they say they would come?" Dylan asks.

The tightness in his voice is nothing in comparison to the fear in his eyes when I turn to face him. "Tonight."

He swallows, holding my gaze, and it's pure agony. My eyes blur and I bite down on my tongue refusing to let the tears form. If I cry, I don't think I'll be able to stop.

"Well," Dylan says, his eyes still fixed on mine, "we're going to have to find out where they mean and be there just in case."

"Yes." Jaik claps his hands together in agreement. "Exactly. Let's talk large land masses."

"Edgemont Hill?" Eddie offers.

Jordan shakes his head. "It's barely a hill. This needs to be something that can be seen from space, I guess."

"If they meant mountain, they'd have said mountain," Jaik dismisses with a wave. "We have mountains on Starlatten."

"Oh!" Linda gasps. "What about Huntingdon Pike? It's less than an hour from here and it's much taller than a hill."

Jordan mulls this over before nodding his agreement. "I think you might be right."

"So, a spaceship is going to descend on Huntingdon Pike tonight and beam Crystal and Jaik up?" Eddie scoffs.

"This isn't one of your stupid sci-fi shows." Jaik sneers. "They'll transmit a team down from the ship which will be just in Earth's orbit. Then they'll take us back up with them."

"Teleportation?" Jordan gasps.

"Sort of, I guess," Jaik admits. "To be honest, I don't completely understand how it works."

Eddie snorts. "Sounds like beaming up to me."

I watch the exchange in silence, pulling Dylan's arms tighter around me and nuzzling against his neck. Just a few more days—that's all I wanted. Even as I think it, I know it's a lie. No amount of extra days would have ever been enough.

CHAPTER FORTY

Jaik

My blood is electricity in my veins. As we discuss logistics, I fear I might explode with the anticipation of leaving this prison of a planet and going back where I belong. My eyes keep flitting to Crystal. She looks awful. I'm torn between pity and anger as I watch her try and block out what's going on. I get that she doesn't want to go, but staying is not an option, so she needs to get over it and get on board. Even Dylan's doing a decent job of pretending he's okay with what's happening.

I'm aware of Linda, loitering near me. With the message and possible rescue, I completely forgot about yesterday's kiss. A wave of guilt swells in my chest. I shouldn't have done that. It wasn't fair on her. I catch her eye and give her a smile, which she returns, looking up at me from behind her fringe. I'll have to talk to her before tonight's plans unravel.

"So, camping?" Eddie echoes.

"Sort of," I say. "We might only be there a couple of hours, but it makes sense to prepare for the whole night, just in case."

"We'll take the supplies up during the day," Jordan agrees. "We won't be able to climb the pike in the dark, so getting there and waiting sounds like the best plan."

I nod in agreement, trying to keep the excitement from my face. "How long will it take us to get to the top?"

"If we set off at midday, we could be at the top by three-ish?"

"Wait," Linda interrupts, pulling a face at Sera. "Doesn't the sun set at like eight at the moment?"

Jordan pulls out his phone and checks an app. "Twenty minutes past eight tonight."

"So, what exactly are we doing for five and a half hours at the top of Huntingdon Pike?"

Silence breezes around the group as Linda chuckles to herself in what appears to be disbelief. Sensing my irritation, she places a hand on my arm. "Look. I know you guys are super excited but getting there sooner isn't going to make the sun set any earlier."

I stare down at her, attempting to convey the importance of this expedition. "We need to be there early enough to survey the area and prepare."

"Yes," Linda agrees. "And two hours will be plenty of time."

Sera grins. "So, we set off from here at 3pm?"

I look between the two girls, wondering what I've missed. I'm about to ask as much when Linda spins her stool to face Crystal and Dylan, who haven't moved a muscle for at least ten minutes.

"Hey, you two," she calls out, waving her hands at them. "You've got five hours. Go make the most of it."

Crystal gives her an uncertain smile before looking at Dylan.

"Go!" Linda shoos. "Get out of here."

This seems to have the desired effect and Dylan slides off his stool, leading Crystal out of the room. I try to catch her eye, but she doesn't so much as glance in my direction. I'm wondering whether I should send a message to her when Linda claps her hands together beside me, making me flinch.

"What about everyone else?" she asks.

"Well." Sera gives Jordan a sheepish smile. "With all the drama, Jordan and I realised last night that we haven't even had a proper date yet. I was thinking perhaps we could go for a little lunch date?"

Jordan wraps his arms around her and squeezes. "Sounds good to me."

Linda turns to her brother next. "What about you?"

"I have a date too." He smiles, waggling his eyebrows.

"What? Who with?"

"My PlayStation." He laughs. "I've not been online in a week. I have friends who are going to think I've died."

Linda turns to me, mid eye roll. "What about you, Jaik?"

I look down at her expectant face and realise she's hoping that we can do something together. "Why don't we go for a little walk?" I suggest, holding out my hand.

As she slips down from the stool, I meet Sera's eyes and I can tell she knows exactly what's going on. I feel downright rotten as I look away and lead Linda through the door, closing it behind us.

Once we're outside, we wander down the lush, manicured gardens towards a little white bench. Putting my hands in my pockets, I kick at the grass. "You know, back home the grass is purple."

"Really?" Linda raises her eyebrows. "What colour is the sky?"

I smile. "Green."

"Oh, come on. You're winding me up."

"No, really." I hold my hands up. "And we have three moons. Two of them are enormous compared with yours."

"You're really excited about going back, aren't you?" Linda sits down on the bench and squints up at the bright blue sky.

There's not a cloud to be seen, which is excellent news for our trip later on today. I sit down beside her and take her hand.

"I am," I say. "I need to find out if my father is still alive and what happened after my mother and I were taken."

We sit for a moment in silence, listening to the chirping of the birds as they flit amongst the branches beside us.

"Linda—"

"You want to talk about the kiss, don't you?" She cuts me off. "Don't worry. It's fine."

I pause, a mouth full of excuses and apologies ready to unload.

"Seriously," Linda continues. "Don't worry about me and my heart. We had an intense couple of days—and yes, you're super-hot—but I'll carry on living after you've gone."

I stare at her in disbelief for a moment and then laughter erupts from my lips. Of all the ways I thought this conversation would go, this is definitely not one of them. It takes a minute or two for me to regain control, my sides aching as I wipe a tear from my eye. Beside me, I notice that Linda's cheeks are tinged with pink as she watches me.

"You're incredible, Linda." I exhale and shake my head. "In another place and time, we might have had a really good thing."

"Yeah." She gives me a rueful smile. "It could have been awesome."

Even though she's making light of it, I know she's upset. Of course, she is. I used the spark of chemistry between us to lead her on. To ... I find myself trying and failing to grasp a decent reason. To get back at Crystal? To make Crystal jealous? Why? What would be the point in that? I think back to when Linda forced that first hug on me at the storage unit. Maybe it was just to feel something—anything—that wasn't hate, anger or fear.

"What are you going to do with yourself today then?" she asks, pulling me from my thoughts.

I shrug and drape my arms over the back of the bench. "Nowhere to go, no one to see." I pause, looking at Linda out the corner of my eye. "You know, I've never actually been to the cinema. Do you want to see a film? As friends?"

"You've really never been to the cinema? In all the years you've been on Earth?"

"Excuse me," I protest. "I was enslaved by an evil fake-uncle. Do you really think he let me go to the cinema?"

"Sorry." Linda looks mortified.

"It's okay." I wink. "I'm 'super-hot', so I can handle it."

As Linda groans and covers her face, her blush bright enough to be seen from space, laughter bubbles in my throat once more.

CHAPTER FORTY-ONE

Crystal

Hauling the heavy backpack onto my shoulders, I follow the others to the door. Everyone else has bags filled with snacks, blankets and useful supplies. Mine is filled with memories.

Everyone suggested or offered things for me to take back to Starlatten to remind me of Earth and I've got clothes, books, magazines, trinkets, a shell, cinema tickets and a leaflet from the zoo to name but a few. During my morning with Dylan, we used something called a 'photo booth'. One of the strips of pictures it produced are wrapped up in his sweatshirt, which he said I could keep.

Jordan took a photograph of all of us together and printed it on a computer at Sera's house, who then used one of the many frames in her bedroom to put it in. I think it might be one of my most favourite things I've ever owned. I joked that it was all going to be a bit unnecessary if this was all a dream, but now with everyone swathed in sombre silence as we prepare to leave, it seems so final.

The bus ride to the bottom of Huntingdon Pike seems to take forever. Linda and Jaik chat about the film they watched earlier today on the seats in front, while behind me, Eddie, Sera and Jordan talk about how they're going to spend the rest of the summer holidays before returning to school. I smile as I hear Jordan discussing a possible switch to astrophysics and astronomy. Dr. Oakstone would be proud.

Dylan sits next to me in silence, squeezing my hand every now and again with an encouraging smile. Although I smile back, my heart is numb. It's not that I don't want to go home, it's just I don't want to go back to a home that's potentially in tatters. A home where I won't be Crystal, but 'Your Majesty.'

"Right." Jordan stands as the bus crawls to a halt. "This is us."

I file off with my friends and find myself standing at the bottom of a hill so huge, I can't see the top. The sky is a clear expanse of warm sapphire—its perfect surface marred only by the blazing golden sunstar. Squinting up at the tall trees, the huge leaves shuffle in the breeze like waving hands and I close my eyes, the summer sunshine warm on my face. I desperately try to commit everything to memory. Just in case.

"Are you ready?"

Opening my eyes, I find Dylan watching me and I nod, but I can't bring myself to smile.

"Right, people. Let's go," Eddie declares, marching up the dirt path towards the trees.

As we trudge up the path after him, the weight of the bag on my back grows heavier with every step. It matches my heart.

After two hours of steep twists and turns, towering boulders and small paths over babbling brooks, we round a corner and find ourselves staring at the summit. A steep path of uneven rocks leads up to a small stone building at the top of a tall slope with several walkers milling around, taking photos of the view.

"So, do we go up?" I ask, a little breathless from the climb.

Jaik chews his lip, frowning as he scans the surrounding area. "Yeah, I think we should go up and see what it's like up there. We can make a better decision then to decide where the best place to lie low until dark is."

Eddie is already marching up the path. "Come on, people. Final stretch."

I have to press my lips together to stop from calling out for him to slow down. Why are we racing ahead? The sunstar is already lower in the sky and I find myself out of breath by the top of the steep, stony path.

It's all forgotten, however, as I straighten and look around me. I can see to the horizon in every direction with small villages, large towns, huge metal buildings, farms and even mountains in the distance. Roads weave in and out amongst the expanse of green, the vehicles like small insects crawling through the undergrowth.

"It's beautiful," I breathe. "I didn't think we'd climbed this high."

"Deceptive isn't it?" Jordan inhales deeply. "Just imagine the view from an actual mountain. Huntingdon Pike is only 360 meters high. You'd need to almost double that to classify as a mountain."

"You always know how to spoil a moment with science, don't you?" Eddie laughs, clapping him on the back.

"Geography, actually," Jordan mutters.

Jaik shifts the bag on his back and surveys our surroundings. "I think we should head to those trees down the other side."

I follow his pointed finger to a cluster of trees further down on the opposite side of the summit to the one we've just climbed. Walkers are sticking to the path, so once we're in the trees, we should be quite hidden.

Long grass and hidden holes make the climb trickier than we anticipate, but we soon find a clearing and begin spreading out groundsheets and blankets.

As everyone settles down and starts chatting, my attention is drawn back to the way we came. It feels like such a waste to be hidden in the trees when such a spectacular view is nearby.

"Would it be okay if I went back up to the top to see the view again?" I ask.

"I don't see why not." Dylan stands from where he's been straightening the blankets. Tilting his head, he studies my face before asking, "Can I come with you?"

I blink, as if him not coming would be an option. "Of course."

Together, we hike back up the steep slope to the old stone building, where I run my fingers over the names and numbers carved into its surface.

"What do these mean?" I ask.

"They're names and dates of people who've been to the top," Dylan explains, running his fingers over some particularly ornate letters. "You're not supposed to, but a lot of these are really old. Vandalism laws were a bit different a hundred years ago."

I nod, pretending I've understood half of what he's just said, and choosing a grassy spot by the side of the building, I sit down and look out at the rolling hills. Now orange, the sunstar is lower still and the breeze is already colder than when we started our climb. Reaching out I take Dylan's hand, bringing his fingers to my lips.

"Thank you," I say with a sigh.

"What for?"

"For finding me. For helping me. For ... everything."

Dylan leans over and presses his forehead to mine, closing his eyes. "I'm so sorry, but I'm really hoping it was a dream."

"Me too," I admit.

"I'm also sorry you can't go back to your life the way it was." He strokes my cheek. "And I'm sorry I made it all about me when you told me how scared you were about going back."

Shaking my head, I squeeze his hands. "Stop apologising. No one was thinking straight that day after what happened. Besides, you've more than made up for it by listening to me talk about it all day today."

It really has been another perfect day. Dylan took me to some nearby gardens to show me different types of flowers and plants. We sat in the sunshine and talked for hours about our past, present and our hopes and dreams. As we discussed our mutual fear of the future and the forces dragging us towards it regardless of our wishes, I felt closer to him than ever. We would have forgotten to eat, if it hadn't been for the loud rumbling of his stomach.

"Crystal?"

"Hmmm?"

Taking my hands in his, he shifts his position so he's facing me properly. "This has been the most incredible week of my life. I honestly can't see how anything will ever come close to this again."

I open my mouth to speak, but he shakes his head before taking a breath and continuing.

"If it wasn't a dream and you really are being whisked away across space and time tonight, this will probably be the only chance I have to say this."

My heart beats simultaneously in my stomach and my ears. I study his face, his eyes flecked with brown and copper beneath thick dark lashes, the way his hair always seems to fall forward across his brow in soft strands of gold and bronze, his cheekbones, straight nose and strong jaw— those lips. I swallow, my mouth dry, as he reaches out and caresses my face, his eyes fixed on mine.

"I've never felt this way about someone before. You make me feel ..." he fumbles for the words and I smile at the frustration on his face.

"Centred," I say. "Like everything makes sense. Strong and grounded but also lighter at the same time."

Dylan's eyes widen, his mouth falling open. "Exactly," he says.

I smile, trying to ignore the warmth pooling at the back of my eyes.

He shakes his head in disbelief. "I'm so lucky to have met you, Crystal and I know how lucky I am to have been able to spend the time that we have, together. I know it's only been a week, but I don't care. I love you, Crystal Akinara. I love you with everything I am, and I don't think I'll ever stop."

My heart explodes into a galaxy of stars and I smile, crimson cheeked, as a tear trickles down my face. "Oh, Dylan. I love you too."

I put my hands over his and hold them against my face, closing my eyes to savour their warmth. When his lips brush mine, I relish every soft and tender touch, knowing it might be our last.

When we finally pull apart, I gasp at the ribbons of pink, orange and yellow strewn across the sky as the sun blazes low on the horizon. Dylan wraps his arm around my shoulders and pulls me close. Above us, the first pinpricks of light are appearing in the sky.

"I'm afraid we need to get back to the others." He sighs into my hair. "It'll be dark soon and they'll be stressing."

We both know who he means by 'they' and I know he's right, so reluctantly, I stand and brush myself off. As we make our way to where everyone is waiting, I glance back one more time at the horizon to see that the sunstar has all but disappeared.

CHAPTER FORTY-TWO

Crystal

There's no moon tonight and the darkness wraps itself around us like a thick blanket, blinding us and muting our senses. All the walkers have gone, and lights no longer bob up and down the hill. We sit in darkness, whispering nervously as though the woodland creatures might hear us. Jordan recommended we sit in darkness, as any light might draw unwelcome attention from people called 'rangers', who might want to see what we're up to.

I squeeze Dylan's hand and he squeezes it back. It's been dark for quite a while and the tiniest flicker of hope is beginning to burn within me that it might have been a dream after all. Jaik is pacing somewhere behind me, cursing intermittently as he collides with branches or inhales bugs.

Linda gasps a millisecond before I see it. A bright light flashes for the smallest instant at the top of the hill. It reminds me of the flash on Jordan's phone earlier today when he took our picture.

"Did you see that?" Linda hisses.

I nod, forgetting it's too dark to see.

Eddie feels his way forward to where I'm sitting. "Is that them?"

"I don't know," I murmur, squinting in the direction of the flash. I think I can see something moving, but it's hard to tell.

It is safe to show yourself, Your Majesty. We are waiting.

As the voice from my dream fills my head, the tiniest whimper escapes my lips, and my hands fly to my mouth. My stomach is full of rocks, pulling me down into the ground, filling me with darkness.

"What is it?" Dylan whispers. "Are you okay?"

"It's them."

Jaik crouches down beside me and reaches for my elbow. "Did they send you a message? What did they say?"

"They said they're waiting for me." I'm trembling.

Jaik squeezes my arm. "Have you told them about me?"

I shoot him a withering look through the darkness. "It hasn't exactly been a two-way conversation."

"Crystal?" Jordan calls out in a whisper as the rest of the group begin to rouse to their feet. "Perhaps it might be an idea to explain that there's a few of us. They're probably only expecting you."

I'm on my way. I have a few friends with me, as well as Jaik Bazanat of Galeania.

"What did they say?" Eddie asks after a few seconds of tense silence.

"Nothing."

"Perhaps they've gone?" Dylan makes no effort to hide the hope in his voice.

We are ready, Your Majesty. Please approach with your friends.

My hands pat the ground, searching for my backpack and I haul it on to my shoulders. "They say it's okay. It's time to go."

Adrenaline and curiosity push me forward on shaking legs, up the slope towards the stone building, which stands like a black void against the night sky. As we draw near, I can just about make out three figures and I know we've been spotted as two coloured lights begin to shine.

Growing steadily brighter, they illuminate the surrounding area just enough to allow us to see that the light is coming from amulets around the necks of two Dyja. They stand, distinctively tall in their deep red robes, behind a smaller dark-haired man I don't recognise, wearing black military robes.

As soon as they spot me, they drop to one knee, one hand raised with fingers splayed in the traditional Starlatten salute. I'm so used to seeing this when I'm with my parents that I almost look around for them out of habit. The only person who's dropped to their knee for me is Jaik, and he was half joking. I squirm, deeply uncomfortable and will them to stand up.

"Your Majesty." The man dressed in black lifts his head to address me. "I cannot express our relief and happiness to find you safe and well. I am Commander Risiki, Commander in Chief of the Royal Guard."

I clear my throat. "Please stand."

I've never heard of Risiki and senior positions within the Guard are held for decades. The Commander in Chief used to be a tall bald man called Cobbat. I think back to the last time I saw him and my stomach lurches as I realise that it was onboard the *Galastasia*. Another life lost.

"We are beyond relieved to have located you, Your Majesty." Risiki smiles. "Starlatten needs you more than ever."

It's still there. I'm surprised at the wave of relief that washes over me. I have a home to return to. Maybe things aren't as bad as I've imagined.

I motion for Jaik to step forward. "Commander, this is Jaik Bazanat of Galeania."

"We believed you killed by rebels." Risiki offers a small bow.

"Well, you believed wrong," Jaik replies, his voice dripping with accusation. "My mother was killed, but as you can see, I'm very much alive."

"We are very happy that you have managed to make the queen's acquaintance so that you might find your way home." Risiki nods. "Your father will be most pleased."

I gasp as Jaik looks at me and smiles.

"We must return to the ship, Your Majesty," Risiki says. "It will not be in optimal position for our return much longer." He glances for the first time at the cluster of people standing huddled behind me and Jaik. "I'm assuming you are the people who helped look after our queen. May the stars bless you all."

"I guess this is it then?" Jaik says, turning to the group.

I watch as he makes his way round everyone, offering back slaps, hugs and a kiss on the cheek for Linda. Even Eddie shakes his hand, I note with a smile.

"Thank you." I turn to face my friends. "Thank you for everything. I'm so incredibly lucky that you found me."

Linda throws her arms around me and squeezes me, joined after a second by Sera. We stand, swaying for a moment until reluctantly, they fall away.

"We'll never forget you." Linda sniffs, swiping at her eyes with her sleeve.

I nod, unable to find words sufficient enough to respond.

Eddie and Jordan take it in turns to envelop me in hugs so tight they make me gasp.

"You've changed our lives," Jordan says with a smile as he steps back. "I really hope things work out for you back home."

"Yeah. And hurry up and invent intergalactic email," Eddie scoffs. "You call *us* primitive!"

I start to laugh, but as I turn to face Dylan it dies on my lips. His face streaked with tears, he steps towards me and lifts me up off the ground into his arms. I'm aware of the Dyja altering their stance out the corner of my eye, but I don't care. Nothing is going to come between me and my last moments with the boy I love so much it aches.

When my feet find the ground again, I bury my face in his chest, my tears soaking his jacket. A sob shakes his shoulders and my heart cracks into a million splinters as I cling to him.

"I don't want to say goodbye," I whisper

Dylan pulls back and dips his head to kiss me, but as I bite back a sob, I find it's like trying to hold back a storm with my hands. I can't let go. I cling to him, my shoulders shaking with the force of my tears, as he murmurs that it's going to be okay and that he loves me, over and over again in my ear.

Risiki coughs. "I'm sorry, Your Majesty. We really must leave."

I draw a ragged breath and pull back to look up at Dylan's face for the last time. Words burst from my lips in desperation before I even know I'm thinking them.

"Come with me."

Dylan's eyes widen with surprise. "What?"

My mind whirls with desperate possibilities. "Come with me. You wanted to travel—come to Starlatten."

"I ..." Dylan shakes his head, looking between me and his friends. "Is that even an option? My family ... I haven't said goodbye ..."

"We have to go *now*, Your Majesty," Risiki repeats with more urgency.

"Crystal!" Jaik calls. "Come on. We have to go."

I want to shout at them to shut up, but I don't. Every atom of me is focused on Dylan and his answer. "Well?"

"This is a lot to spring on me at the last moment." His brow is furrowed, but there's something in his eyes that makes me think he's made up his mind.

"I know. I'm so sorry." My heart is pounding so loud it blocks out everything around me. All I can see is Dylan.

"Hey!" he yells, his eyes wild.

I can't understand why he's shouting until I realise someone has their hands around my arms, pulling me backwards. I struggle against them, looking back at Dylan just in time to see his outstretched hand disappear in a blinding flash of white light.

CHAPTER FORTY-THREE

Crystal

Pressing my forehead against the ship's window, I stare down at the blue and green sphere below me as it grows smaller and smaller.

"I had to," Jaik tries again. "We would have missed our chance."

I scrunch up my eyes, sending droplets of liquid to the floor. Curling my hands into fists, anger floods through me as I turn to face him. "He was about to answer."

Jaik shakes his head and groans, looking up to the metallic silver ceiling. "He was never going to come. You can't expect him to just leave all his friends and family forever to live on a different planet with no warning."

I glare at him, trying to convey every particle of anger and hatred burning within me, before turning back to the window. I know in my heart Jaik's right. It was too much of me to ask. Dylan might have said yes. He might have come. But it wouldn't have been fair on his family, his friends. Perhaps he would even have resented me for it in the future.

"Are you getting in?"

Still glaring, I turn and watch Jaik climb into the dark, metallic capsule, which will preserve us for the long journey back to Starlatten. I take one last long look at the patch of darkness dotted with lights I know contains Dylan and my friends, before making my way to the sleep chamber beside Jaik's.

Once we're strapped in, the capsules rotate to an almost horizontal position and two Dyja appear, securing the straps and pressing buttons. I stare up at the ceiling through the transparent casing, trapped within my own body.

My mind drifts back to the carousel we rode at the zoo the day before. It had been so much fun, and I'd been so sad when it had slowed to a halt. Right now, my life feels like a carousel that's never going to stop. A constant motion of up and down, but I can't get off or change direction. I just have to hold on and survive.

As the casing seals around me with a loud hiss, I turn and look over at Jaik to find he's watching me. He grins at me and raises his eyebrows, reminding me of the boy I'd once known all those orbits ago. Completely hollow, I can't bring myself to smile back. I don't think I'll ever be able to forgive him for what he did. Jaik's smile fades as he seems to realise this and I look away, returning my gaze to the ceiling.

As cool mist fills the chamber—the covers locking tight with a decisive click—I close my eyes and try to relax as the fog swirls around me, filling my lungs.

I'm going home.

CRYSTAL: BONUS EDITION 2020

Read on for Dylan's Exclusive Chapter

TWO MONTHS LATER

Dylan

I see her all the time. A few seats in front on the bus. Just ahead in a crowd. Turning a corner in a shopping mall. I hear her voice, her laugh, rising above the chatter. I feel her touch against my skin in my sleep and I wake with the taste of her on my lips.

For the first few hours, days—perhaps even the first couple of weeks—I hoped she might come back. I knew she wouldn't, but a tiny splinter of my shattered heart hoped.

The front door slams downstairs and I flinch. My mum was so worried about me when I got home that night. I couldn't talk to anyone for two days. Whenever I've been forced to watch chick flicks and romcoms by Mum and Katie, there was a part of me that would roll my eyes at how dramatic the characters would get when things went wrong, or they broke up—wandering the streets sobbing or locking themselves away. I get it now. Having felt a knife pierce my chest, I can honestly say that this hurts worse. Pity and concern ran out weeks ago though.

For the rest of the summer, I was a ghost. Mum let me off helping with the bakery for a day or two and then that was pretty much all I'd do. I would get up and help out and then go back upstairs to my room. Jordan and Eddie came round almost every day for a while. They'd chat near me and I'd ignore them. What could they say? What could they do, to make me feel better?

I was waiting. I was waiting for someone to say the words I knew they were all thinking. 'She's gone. Get over it.' My fists clench at the thought. Even worse, 'it was only a week' or 'how can you fall in love in a week?'

The answer is, I don't know. But I did.

Yesterday, after surviving the first week back at school, I told Mum that I'm not taking on the bakery. I told her I'd help out as I have been doing until June, but then … I don't know. This is the cause of the door slamming. Perhaps I should have waited until I figured everything out until I told her, but it was weighing on my already heavy chest and I couldn't keep it in any longer.

Someone knocks on my bedroom door and I frown. Katie doesn't knock.

"Erm, yeah?"

A familiar dark head of hair pokes around the door. "Hey. Can I come in?"

"Linda? Erm, yeah. Sure. Come in." I shuffle to sitting, giving a half-hearted glance around the room to check nothing embarrassing is lying out. I can't quite bring myself to care though.

She watches me for a moment before sitting down on the chair by my desk. Her eyes linger on my hands and I realise what I'm holding. With a sigh, I place the strip of photos from the photobooth on my bedside table and fold my arms, trying not to think about how pathetic she must think I am.

"What's up, Linda?"

She tilts her head and shrugs. "I just wanted to see how you're doing. I haven't seen you in ages."

"I saw you at school yesterday."

"A wave from across the corridor doesn't count." She snorts. "Seriously, Dylan. We're all worried about you."

A groan rises from my throat and I drag my hands over my face. "I'm fine."

Another snort from Linda. "Well, that's not true."

I sit forward. "What do you want from me? I'm going to school. I'm working in the bakery. What else do I need to do?"

"Live," she says. "She's not coming back."

Linda's words freeze the breath in my lungs and my fingers curl around the covers, gripping them until my knuckles ache.

"I know," I bite out.

Linda watches me for a moment before moving to sit on the end of my bed. The sympathy in her dark brown eyes is too much to bear and I look away.

"I get it, you know," she says. "It's the lack of closure. You didn't break up. You didn't really get to say goodbye ..."

I wince and clench my fists tighter. Jaik is lucky he's in another solar system, because if I ever see that smug face again, I'm going to put my fist in it.

"He dragged her away," I grind out, the all too familiar anger bubbling in my blood.

Linda flinches at my tone, but her voice is gentle. "I know."

"Dragged her," I say, forcing myself to look at her. "Literally dragged her off me."

"I know," Linda repeats. "Is that it then? Is that what you're holding on to? Because wherever Jaik is right now, I can guarantee he's not thinking about you and whether you're angry at him."

A chill runs down my spine and I lessen my grip on my bedcovers. She's right, and even if he was still on Earth he wouldn't care. He'd probably still be making moves on her, right in front of me.

"You've got to let her go," Linda says, placing a hand on my leg.

The anger that erupts from me is something that I've been nurturing and cultivating for so long that it slips from my mouth with spiteful ease.

"Don't tell me what I've *got* to do," I snap. "Why do you even care? What difference does it make to you?"

"I care, Dylan," she says, her voice level, even as she leans away from me, "because you're my friend. We all care. We want you to be happy."

I snort. "What does happy look like then? You want me to find someone else? Paste a smile on my face? Will that make it better? Do you realise how selfish you're being?"

Linda's eyebrows disappear beneath her fringe. "Excuse me?"

"You, the others ... you want me to move on because I'm bringing you all down. So what? If I pretend—if I smile and joke and laugh—you can all feel better? Give each other pats on the back and say well done? What good friends you are?"

Linda's on her feet, her eyes wide. "You do hear yourself right now, right?"

"If your happiness depends on mine, then you need to just get used to being sad, because I'm not there yet."

I've run out of steam and my eyes are burning as I drop my head and stare at my hands, my breathing heavy. I wait, tensed, ready for the door to slam. But it doesn't. Instead, the bed dips and Linda sits down beside me, taking my hands in hers. I blink in surprise but can't bring myself to look at her.

"You know," she says, "I told Jaik he was 'super-hot' before he left."

A bark of laughter bursts from my lips. "Seriously? Oh man, I bet he loved that."

"We all get it, you know," she says, squeezing my fingers. "I know none of us felt the way you did with Crystal, but she affected us all. We all fell in love with her a little and we all feel the hole she left behind."

I breathe in a shaky breath, but don't speak—afraid of the hurtful words that might spill from the darkest part of me.

"It's hard to believe it all really happened sometimes," Linda continues. "My head hurts if I think about it for too long."

I still can't bring myself to speak, so I don't.

"We're not giving up on you, Dylan," she says. "Take all the time you need, but know that we're not going anywhere. We're all going out tomorrow night. Eddie says he text you about it, but you didn't reply. I hope you'll come."

My gaze falls to the phone on my desk. I can't remember the last time I replied to a message. Would it be better or worse if there was a way to communicate with Crystal? Possibly worse. To be able to talk to her and know that I'd never actually see her again? There's long distance and then there's just … well …

By the time I draw a breath to speak, I realise Linda's no longer holding my hand. In fact, she's no longer in my room. I blink, trying to remember her leaving, but I can't. With a groan, I go to my desk and pick up my phone. Not bothering with the dozens of other messages, I scroll for Eddie's name.

Sat night. Laughton's Pub. 7pm.

I stare at it for a moment, trying and failing to imagine myself out with my friends, laughing and having fun. I click on the next message.

I'll sign ur name on the card.

Card? I close my messages and open the calendar. October 14th. Jordan's birthday. His eighteenth. Shame and guilt shudder through me and I sink down onto my chair, staring at the message. I'm the crappiest friend that ever existed.

A fresh wave of humiliation washes over me as I recall how I told Linda they were being selfish. I hold my head in my hands. So caught up in my own grief, I didn't think for a second about what was going on in everyone else's lives. No one else lost Crystal. No one else got their heart smashed to pieces. No one else's family was falling apart. I never once stopped to think.

It occurs to me that I don't even know if Sera and Jordan are still together. They were the last time I saw them, but now I think about it, it was weeks ago. What else have I missed while I've been wallowing in self-pity?

Shoving my phone in my pocket I make my way downstairs. Katie's in the lounge watching television.

"Where's Mum?" I ask.

"Shop."

Good. That means she won't need the car. I swipe the keys from the hook near the door and pull on my shoes.

"Where are you going?"

I look up to find Katie frowning at me as she leans against the doorframe.

"Out."

She rolls her eyes. "Where? What should I tell Mum if she asks?"

"I'm just going for a drive," I say. "I won't be back late."

Katie narrows her eyes. "You should drive past a hairdresser. You look like a homeless person."

I open my mouth to reply but she turns her back and returns to the nest of blankets and magazines she's made in front of the television.

Part of me considers looking in a mirror, but I already know what I'll see, so I don't. Self-care hasn't been high on my list of priorities lately. Shrugging on a jacket, I make my way outside to the car.

When I made this decision, I failed to realise that it's Friday rush hour and the roads are packed. It takes me half an hour longer than I anticipated but it's not as if I have any plans, so I turn up the radio and zone out.

318

By the time I park up, the sun is lower in the sky and everything is bathed in that soft orange light that makes everything feel summery and magical. It used to be my favourite time of day, stirring happiness in my chest. Now, it draws a sigh from me as I stare up at Huntingdon Pike.

I came here every day for a week after she left. Every night I came and sat and waited. Hoping. Wishing. No one knows and I don't think I'll ever tell anyone. My cheeks heat at the thought. Shoving my hands in my pockets, I start the steep walk to the top.

It hurts, seeing the summit. Seeing the exact spot I saw her last. It physically hurts. It's also beginning to feel like it didn't really happen.

To anyone else, it's just a patch of tufted grass with a view. No one would know that three aliens appeared here two months ago. The Dyja must have been at least six foot five each, looking like something from Star Wars with their hooded robes. I'd almost expected them to whip out a lightsaber.

My heart pounding not just with the exertion of the climb, I stand on the spot where Crystal was ripped from my arms. Where I fell to my knees and refused to be moved. I don't remember much of the rest of that night.

Taking a shuddering breath, I walk around the small brick tower and slide down against it, leaning my head against the rough surface as I stare out at the view. Perhaps I shouldn't have kissed her that night outside the bowling alley. I knew then that it was going to end this way. Okay, I didn't know it was going to hurt this much. If I'd known, then maybe …

As the sun descends behind the hills, I pull out my phone and read through the dozens of messages I've ignored. With each thread I work my way through, I can feel the tone change from sympathy to annoyance and I wince.

I can't help it. There's no self-help book that tells you what to do when your girlfriend leaves for another planet. I don't know how to get over this.

My phone warm in my hand, I look up at the darkening sky as stars start to appear. Every space app that exists is on my phone. I researched. I tried. I tried to figure out where her solar system might be—whether I could see her sunstar from here. I knew her planet had three moons, that there were at least two other planets—Zarbilian and Ankaria—in her solar system, but it wasn't enough to go on.

Before Crystal, I was never particularly interested in space, so I didn't know much about it. I hadn't realised the sheer size of it all—the vastness. I'd hoped trying to find her solar system would make me feel better, but all it did was make me aware of how completely hopeless it all is. I might as well have been trying to find one particular grain of sand on a beach.

The worst part is the not knowing. Did she make it back okay? What state is Starlatten in? Are they at war? What would that even look like? Is she coping with being queen? Is she scared? So many questions that I'll never have the answers to.

Never.

How do you deal with 'never'? Perhaps that's the problem. Everyone's treating it like some summer fling.

Like she's gone back to her hometown. It's not like that though. Even with a summer fling, there's a chance you might see each other again. Whether it's the next summer or even years later. You can stalk each other on social media and keep in touch if you want.

I don't have any of those options. It's like she died. That's what never means. I'll never see her again. I'll never speak to her again. Never.

Perhaps I'll never get over her. Maybe I'll never be the same. One day, I might be able to let it go, but there'll always be a part of me that loves her. I know that much.

I also know that if Crystal could see me now, she'd tell me to stop moping. Almost able to hear the words, a smile pulls at my lips. I close my eyes and imagine her fingers brushing the hair from my forehead, her expression stern as she tells me to stop being ridiculous and start being a better friend.

Decisiveness settles in my stomach and my shoulders feel the slightest bit lighter. Maybe there's some truth in the hateful words I spat at Linda earlier. If I pretend—if I paste on a smile and carry on—maybe eventually it won't be fake. I'll still grieve. I'll still hurt. But I'm not going to hurt my friends any more than I already have.

Gripping my phone, I swipe to Eddie's last message and reply.

Thanks. I'll be there.

I'd forgotten what it's like to be around people. After weeks of holing myself up in my room, the noise of the crowded pub is sensory overload. Eddie hands me a drink and I smile, trying to fight the urge to run and hide in a dark, quiet corner.

My mum had tears in her eyes when I left the house. My stomach clenches at the thought. After setting up in the bakery this morning, I went to get a haircut. I didn't see her when I got back and the shock on her face when she saw me leaving the house tonight was almost laughable. But then her lip started trembling and the guilt knocked me sick.

I hadn't realised the effect my moping was having on her. The very fact that she was moved to tears by the fact I'd showered and had a haircut was a slap to the face.

"I'm so glad you're here," Jordan says, his grin huge as he pulls me into a one-armed hug. "It's good to see you."

My answering smile is genuine, but it fades quickly. "I'm sorry I've been such a rubbish friend."

"We get it," he says, squeezing my shoulder. "It's okay."

I nod, trying to force my mouth back into a smile.

Jordan watches with a grimace. "Mate, be sad. It's fine. The fact that you turned up is the best birthday present I could have asked for. I missed you."

I know he's trying to make me feel better, but his words stir pits of shame in my gut. "You must have had some pretty rubbish presents then," I say.

He laughs and pulls me in for another hug, his drink splashing on my shoes. I don't care.

"You're going to be okay, Dylan," he says, his dark eyes serious. "You know that, right? It might take a while, but you're going to be okay."

"I know."

Linda and Eddie appear beside us with Sera snaking her way under Jordan's arm.

"Can someone please tell my sister that bulls are colour blind?" Eddie demands.

I blink. "Excuse me?"

He scowls as Linda sticks her tongue out at him. "She made some stupid comment about me being like a bull and seeing red."

Jordan laughs. "And?"

"And, bulls are colour blind," Eddie says, looking at us as though he's the only one making sense. "It's a myth. Bulls seeing red. They can't see any colours."

I frown, even as the corners of my mouth twitch. "I don't think that's true."

Eddie balks. "What?"

"Yeah. They can definitely see red. I watched a documentary on it." Jordan catches my eye and tries not to smile. Of course, we know it's true, but winding Eddie up is the gift that keeps giving.

"You did not see a documentary because it's not true."

I'm expecting steam to pour from Eddie's ears at any moment and I press my lips together to keep the laughter in.

"See?" Linda says, folding her arms. "I told you."

Eddie roars loud enough to make the people around us take a step away. "But it's not true!"

Beside me, Jordan snorts and I can see Sera's shoulders shaking with the effort of keeping a straight face. I can't hold it in anymore and I laugh.

I laugh until my sides hurt and my eyes are streaming. At some point Eddie storms off, muttering something about how we're the worst friends ever and he's going to go and find some new ones.

I'm still chuckling, my cheeks aching, when Linda catches my eye. Before my smile can be pulled away by the apology I know I need to give, she throws herself at me, wrapping herself around my middle.

After a minute, she squeezes me one last time before pulling away and turning to Sera, chatting about some chemistry test they had yesterday.

Jordan calls my name, waving me over to the bar but as I move to join him, I see a flash of curly hair out the corner of my eye. My heart races and I turn to find it, but it's not her. Of course, it's not her. With an apologetic smile at the curly-haired woman I'm staring at, I continue my way to the bar.

They're all there now, still teasing Eddie as he protests that he knew we were winding him up and he was playing along. I smile, my face still sore from laughing, and realise perhaps what Jordan said is true. It's going to take a while, but I'm going to be okay.

I'll be okay.

I can live with okay.

OUT NOW

STARLATTEN BOOK TWO

KEEP READING FOR A SNEAK PEEK
AT THE FIRST CHAPTER

CHAPTER ONE

Crystal

Black flags bearing the silver Starlatten emblem crack and snap in the warm winds on tall pewter poles, as crowds gather around the towering palace gates. Resting my forehead against the thick glass, I stare, transfixed by the symmetry of the three interlocking circles which represent our moons, a star gleaming from the top, as they rise from a half sun. My gaze moves to the assembling masses stretching out below—a rippling sea of faces. Today is a day of mourning. Today marks one orbit since the attack on the *Galastasia*.

Warm air whips in through an open window above and my eyes drift shut as it caresses my face. A soft humming rises from the crowd and as it drifts in through the window on the wind, I open my eyes, watching the flags fight against the pale green sky. It's our funeral song.

We are the dust of stars.
We shine so bright.
We love and are loved,
Bright sparks in the night.
Shine until we burn out,
Returning to dust.
We return to the stars.
Remember; we must.

I let the gentle melody wash over me. It's comforting to see the people still care so deeply about me and my family. Of course, today isn't just for my family. Pain clutches at my chest at the thought of the two thousand men, women and children who also died that day.

A cloud passes across the bright white sunstar and in the shift of shade, I catch my reflection in the glass. My eyes widen at the tear on my cheek. I hadn't realised I was crying. Reaching to wipe it away, I take a shaky breath, my exhale fogging the glass. It's dangerous having so many people congregated at the palace. The rebels might see. They might attack. My eyes scan the crowd as though I might be able to pick out Zarbilian soldiers lurking amongst the mourning citizens.

After the attack on the *Galastasia*, the rebels took control of Starlatten in a barrage of power, fire and death. Stajahl, the capital city, is the only region of Starlatten that remains untouched by the rebels. Not far from the palace is the Starellia cavern. If the Zarbilian rebels discover it, they'll gain access to an unfathomable amount of amulet stones. It would mean the end of everything.

Despite the horrors occurring outside the city, my heart swells at the steadfast faith of the people. Their faith in the royal family. In me. Standing here, looking out at the crowds, I can almost feel my parents standing at my side; tall and proud, their crowns catching the sunlight. My lips curl into a smile at the thought.

It pains me that the people think I'm dead. No one seems to know for sure whether the Zarbilian rebels know I'm alive. It's unlikely Cadicus Kain was able to tell them I survived the attack, and if they don't know, Commander in Chief Risiki and the ambassadors want to keep it that way.

Part of me longs to open the doors and step out onto the balcony to address the people as I've watched my parents do so many times before. Not that I have any idea what I'd say. I just know it would be appreciated. It would give them hope.

"Don't even think about it."

I don't look up. "How could you possibly know what I'm thinking?"

"I know exactly what you're thinking. You're thinking you should go out on that balcony and give the people hope."

I push myself from the glass and turn to face Jaik. "Why would I be thinking that?"

"Because that's the kind of person you are." He walks over and leans against the warm glass beside me, fixing me with his bright green stare.

I smile and shake my head, turning back to the window. My fingers reach for my curls out of habit but fall back to my side when they don't find them.

"Your hair looks good up," Jaik says, his eyes following the movement.

I give a faint nod in response. My mass of curls, worn high, trailing down my back, is a reminder of my daily training. On Earth, I was weak in more ways than one. Cadicus ran circles around us and if it hadn't been for Jaik and the element of surprise with his amulet, we would have all been killed. I won't allow that to happen again. I can't.

Every morning, I meet with my trainer, Master Tomu. He's also a master in amulet arts, so following two hours of combat training, we work on amulet skills. My arms and stature bear the results of my training and I feel strong. On the outside, at least. No one needs to know what a crumbling mess I am on the inside.

"How was your training session this morning?"

"You'd know if you turned up," I scold gently.

"I know. I'm sorry." Jaik holds his hands up in surrender. "I got caught up in a strategy meeting with Risiki."

"Excuse me?" I squint up at him. Since we returned home, Jaik has been following in his father's footsteps, learning the ins and outs of our government with me. "There was a strategy meeting without me?"

Jaik grimaces, running a hand through his wavy sandy brown hair. He's grown it out and it suits him. "I'm not supposed to talk to you about it."

I glare at him. "I am your queen. If you don't tell me, I'll go and find Tarin and make *him* tell me."

"Okay, Okay." Jaik steps toward me, his voice soothing. "The reason you weren't involved is because it's about your grandparents."

My heart stutters.

Before the invasion, my grandparents lived in Dehjawl, a quiet city not far from Stajahl. It was badly damaged in rebel attacks and no one is sure how many people have survived. Teams have been trying to find survivors, but as the city is under Zarbilian control, it's a slow and dangerous process.

"Your grandmother is alive," Jaik says, his eyes sparkling. He reaches up and squeezes my shoulders. "It's not all good news though. I'm afraid your grandfather was killed in the first wave of attacks."

I stare through Jaik, my heart fracturing as I picture my grandfather's cheery round face permanently creased in laughter. My father's father. My mother's parents died before I was born.

"Tarin is leading a team of our best Dyja to get her and bring her here," Jaik continues, his eyes trying to catch mine. "They left last night."

"Oh," I manage.

I've all but written off the idea of family and to find out I might actually get to see my grandmother again is hope I'm not sure I'm strong enough to bear. There's just so much that could go wrong. The Zarbilian are powerful, cold and calculating, with weapons unlike any Starlatten has ever seen. Even if the Dyja are successful in rescuing her, they'll have to make certain they aren't followed back to the capital.

"Are you okay?" Jaik asks, his green eyes dark with concern.

"I think so," I murmur. The feeling of loss is so constant, I'm not sure if I feel any different. Is it possible to feel emptier when you're already hollow inside?

"Come here, Queenie." He pulls me toward him, and I lay my head against his chest, closing my eyes as his strong arms hold me close. His heartbeat strong and steady against my ear, I wrap my arms around him and savour the feeling of safety.

It took a while, but we've forged a new friendship on Starlatten. Jaik is funny, kind and usually knows what I'm thinking, even before I know myself. My gut tightens as I recall the first few lunar cycles after we returned, and I try to push the guilt back to the dark corner I keep it in. I'd been so angry with him.

Turning my head, I exhale and stare at the horizon. Somewhere out there, Tarin is leading a team across enemy lines.

When I arrived back on Starlatten, I was assigned four Dyja to guard me around the clock. It drove me to distraction, so I begged Risiki to allow me some space. It was then that Tarin stepped forward. The youngest of the Dyja, at only twenty-two orbits, I had all but dismissed him as an apprentice. He knelt before me, looked me in the eye and told me his brother had been the Dyja who gave his life to get me to the evacuation deck that fateful day. When he asked if he could have the honour of being my protector, I stared into those determined, dark blue eyes and knew he would keep me safe.

Over the past few lunar cycles, however, Tarin has become more than just my personal guard. He's now one of my closest friends. We talk, train and laugh together. I also adore his husband, Fahr, who is one of the palace medics. I swallow, my heart pounding at the thought of him out there at the mercy of rebel forces. If anything happens to him…

"He'll be fine."

I lift my head, staring up at Jaik in disbelief. "Would you stop doing that?"

"Sorry." He grins. "You're really easy to read."

Smiling at him, I shake my head before leaning back against his warm chest. In the palace courtyard, the crowds are still swaying, their amulets glowing softly, like a thousand rippling rainbows. As if in response, my own amulet warms purple against my skin. If only I could let them know that hope is not lost.

Inspiration hits me like a lightning bolt. "I know what I can do."

"What are you talking about?"

Jaik keeps his arms around me, but I feel him tense. I can't tell him. He'll try to stop me for sure.

Staring out over the swaying, humming throng of people, I pull the power of my amulet through me. Purple light floods through my veins as I use the energy to push a message out towards them all.

Be strong, people of Starlatten. May the stars bless you.

"I can't believe you would do something so reckless!"

Sitting at the long silver table, I try to quell the heat blazing across my chest and clawing at my cheeks. "The people need hope. I didn't think it would be such a big deal."

Commander Risiki paces backwards and forwards in front of me, his face a close match to the purple of my amulet. "If there are any Zarbilian spies in the city, they now know you're alive!"

"How would they know it's me?" I reason. "It's not like everyone would recognise my voice."

Risiki stops and stares at me for a moment before shaking his head and resuming his pacing.

In the seat beside me, Jaik coughs. "She does have a point."

I give him a small smile of thanks. Perhaps it had been the wrong thing to do, but it felt right at the time. Of course, I hadn't been expecting the ripple effect it caused. As soon as I pushed the words from my mind, the crowd fell silent. I'm sure I stopped breathing. Moments later, people started cheering and waving at the gates, the sombre atmosphere of the anniversary replaced with euphoria.

It had taken the best part of the day for the Dyja to calm the crowds and urge people to return to their homes.

"The point is," Risiki continues, sitting down on a large metallic chair that only accentuates his short stature, "we are trying to keep you safe. If everyone knows you're alive, it makes my job a lot harder."

I groan, throwing my hands up in frustration. "What is the point of me being alive, if I can't do *my* job?"

"And what exactly do you think your job is?" Risiki sits forward, lacing his fingers together and fixing me with his sharp brown eyes.

"I'm the queen," I reply, my chin high in an attempt to hide the squirming feeling in my gut that comes from saying the words I still can't quite accept. "My job is to protect the people of Starlatten."

Risiki gives a small smile. "If the Zarbilian find out you are here, they will attack the city. Is that keeping the people safe?"

"The Zarbilian are going to attack the city anyway." I scowl. "It's only a matter of time. The people will be better prepared to fight if they have hope."

Risiki stares at me for a moment, his face unreadable. Then his eyes begin to crease at the corners and a laugh ripples from his lips. His reaction takes me by surprise, and I turn to Jaik in confusion. He shrugs, as puzzled as me.

"Oh, Your Majesty." Risiki smiles, his eyes sparkling with laughter. "You are so like your father."

I raise my eyebrows apprehensively. "What do you mean?"

"King Jeru was also led by such passion," he explains, the laughter fading to sadness. "He always put the people before himself and his personal safety."

My heart clenches. "You miss him, don't you?"

"We all do, Your Majesty," he says. "I can only imagine how painful it must be for you."

I nod, unable to find the words needed to respond.

Risiki seems to sense this and stands. "What's done is done, Your Majesty. The people are indeed 'invigorated' by your message. We'll subtly increase the Dyja presence around the palace and monitor the situation." He bows low and leaves the room.

Jaik blows out a long slow breath. "Well, that was intense."

"You can say that again." Standing up, I stretch before heading for the door. Behind me, Jaik leaps to his feet to follow.

"Where are you going?"

"It's been a long and emotional day." I smile. "I'm going to try to get some sleep. I've got an early training session with Tomu in the morning."

Reaching out, I give his arm a gentle squeeze of gratitude before turning and heading to my quarters.

ABOUT THE AUTHOR

Darby Cupid lives in the desert with her husband, two children and rescue dog. When she's not writing, you'll find her teaching, gardening and attempting to save the planet, one ecobrick at a time.

A lifelong book worm she wrote her first attempt at a novel aged eight and has never looked back.

If you want to find out more about what she's up to, you can find her on Twitter, Instagram or via her website.

www.darbycupid.com

Acknowledgments

This story is over twenty years in the making, with many people involved. Thank you firstly, to those who have been there from the beginning. My sister Lindsay, for being my harshest critic and my biggest cheerleader since day one. Linda, who inspired the character of the same name in the book and has been on this journey from the start.

Thank you to my friends who read early drafts and helped this story become what it is: Lisa, Kitty, Charlene, Sarah and my sister Natalie. You are the best. A special thank you to Abigail – my first 'fan'.

Thank you to my brother-in-law, Michael, for helping me visualize the cover and to Beck and Emily for the incredible cover and artwork. You are all saints for putting up with my indecisiveness.

A huge thank you to my writer friends, who I found through the writing community on Instagram and Twitter, in particular the incredible members of B.R.A. Support Group! Thank you, Claire for your ongoing support and friendship. Thank you, Rebecca for your encouragement, inspiration and helping to make Crystal the best it could be. I would be lost without you both.

Finally, thank you to my husband and children for letting me lock myself away in front of my laptop for hours on end. It means everything to me.

And if you've read this far, thank you to you, the reader. It's all for you.

Thank you for reading

Please add a review on Amazon and Goodreads to let me know what you thought!